THE DUCHESS DE NUIT

A TALE OF LUST AND BLOOD

C. DE MELO

VAMPIRE:

1. A preternatural being commonly believed to be a reanimated corpse that is said to suck the blood of sleeping persons at night.

2. (in Eastern European folklore) A corpse animated by an undeparted soul or demon, that periodically leaves the grave and disturbs the living, until it is exhumed and impaled or burned.

DEDICATION

Thank you, D.

Chapter 1
London, UK
Present Day

"Fear is pain arising from the anticipation of evil."
(Aristotle)

The pounding of steel against stone—barely audible at first—grew so loud that it caused vibrations within my body. The incessant clamor caused the misty line separating reality from dream world to blur and dissipate. I envisioned myself at the bottom of a murky lake, inching slowly toward the surface.

Damn this bloody noise!

Despite the incessant clamor, I sensed the presence of others. As I continued my slow watery ascent, I heard commands spoken with unchallenged authority and obedient replies delivered in hushed tones. A flurry of activity hovered near the surface of my imaginary lake, like a swarm of angry insects.

After being jostled unceremoniously within my confined space, the massive lid above my head hissed open and a rush of warm air caressed my face. My ears prickled; there were whispers in the wind. It wasn't until I tasted the sweet liquid fire that I truly began to rouse from my deep slumber. I felt my brow crease as realization hit me. I wasn't being fed just any blood—the few precious drops being administered were from my sire, Arsham. His potent blood forced memories into my head like an angry wave, flooding every corner of my brain.

Squinting against the soft electric light, I sat up groggily. Rubble and dust were scattered on the floor around the punishment coffin. Two males wielding sledgehammers stared at me with open curiosity. I didn't recognize either one of them.

How much time had passed?

A third male stepped forward, towering over the other two. The perfectly chiseled features of his face stood out dramatically thanks to his clean-shaven head, affording him a cruel beauty. His good looks, paired with his affinity for finely tailored clothing, made him a sex symbol by today's standards. Mortal women didn't stand a chance against his charms—female vampires fared little better.

"Angelique."

I met Arsham's piercing gaze with apprehension before accepting his large proffered hand. I stood on shaky legs and his strong arms were instantly around my waist in order to lift me out of the coffin.

"Leave us," he said to the two males without breaking eye contact with me.

They immediately inclined their heads and walked away. Arsham gripped my upper arm like a vice and marched me into the most lavishly decorated space within our lair.

"I hated doing this to you, but you forced my hand," he said in the same tone a stern father would use with an errant child. Looking down his proud nose at me, he added, "I hope I've given you sufficient time to reflect upon the error of your ways."

When I nodded, he put out his hand. I dropped to one knee and dutifully kissed the giant blood ruby on his finger.

"My lord," I whispered, lowering my head.

Pleased by my submissive genuflection, he allowed a smile to touch his lips. "Rise, my child." I stood, swaying slightly in the process, and he took hold of my elbow to steady me. "It's been a long time since you've last fed."

I caught a glimpse of myself in the gilded mirror over his shoulder. A priceless antique from Versailles, it flaunted golden scrolls and delicate floral motifs. The mirror's reflection was nowhere near as lovely as its magnificent frame. My gaunt, exceedingly pale face hosted dark shadows beneath a pair of sunken eyes.

"How long have I slept?" I asked, tearing my gaze away from the polished glass. My intense thirst caused me considerable pain, and my voice sounded hoarse.

Rather than answer my question, Arsham circled me like a dangerous panther sizing up its prey. His glittering dark eyes ran up and down my body, taking in my hideous countenance. Shifting self-consciously beneath his scrutiny, I touched my disheveled hair while discreetly glancing down at my crumpled dress.

"Even now in your blood-starved state, you hold the power to bewitch me." Reaching out to caress my cheek with surprising gentleness, he added, "Your eyes still manage to sparkle like midnight sapphires."

I focused on my feet to avoid my sire's lustful gaze. The dust from the rubble had soiled my black leather boots. He took a step closer and lifted my chin with his fingertip. I thought he would kiss me, but he didn't. Instead, he uttered the one word that would seduce any vampire.

"Drink."

If I were in possession of a human heart, it would have been beating out of control in that moment.

He then did something so shocking that I faltered. Rather than slit his wrist and allow me to drink—as was customary in our clan whenever our sire offered this rare privilege—he tilted his head to the side. The baring of the throat showed complete trust between two vampires. Such displays of affection were usually reserved for official mates, so I didn't know what to think of this unexpected gesture.

Arsham's full lips curved into an amused smile. "Aren't you thirsty?"

I did not wish to be intimate with the vampire who had bestowed such a harsh punishment upon me, but his magical blood called out to me.

No, it didn't call out—it screamed my name over and over until I wanted to cover my ears.

"Angelique?"

I closed the distance between us in one long stride. Gripping his shoulders, I dug my fingernails into his firm flesh as I pushed myself upward to reach his neck. He hissed in response to my aggression. Being much taller than me, he lifted me up so that I could wrap my legs around his hips.

I licked his neck repeatedly, coaxing the vein before piercing his fragrant skin with my sharp fangs. The ecstatic gasp I heard was my own as his sweet, hot blood filled my mouth. I drank deeply.

"Enough..."

I heard his command clearly, but couldn't bring myself to stop. Drinking the intoxicating elixir evoked euphoria.

Arsham growled. "I said that's enough, Angelique!"

Pain shot through my shoulders as he grabbed them with brutal force and pushed me away from his throat. Without a word, he carried me across the plush Turkish rug and sat me down on the edge of an antique table. His hands moved from my shoulders to the front of my dress. Without warning, he ripped the fabric down to my waist. Cupping my breasts, he lowered his head to kiss and suckle each one in turn.

He stood and met my gaze. "I confess, I missed you."

Grabbing a fistful of my hair, he yanked my head back to expose my throat. The exquisite pain of his teeth cutting through my skin compelled me to cry out in pleasure. I kept telling myself over and over that I didn't want to do this, but my sire's blood was a powerful aphrodisiac; an addictive drug. I was as helpless as a fly caught in a spider's web.

Arsham circled my waist and pulled me toward him. I felt him harden as he pushed himself urgently between my thighs. "I want you."

I closed my eyes and imagined another's face. Without thinking, I whispered the forbidden name.

"Damien."

The blow I received for my folly proved so powerful that it knocked me flat on my back. Wincing, I stared up at the bronze coffered ceiling. Arsham's giant form loomed into my range of vision, his face contorted into a mask of fury. He raised his hand to strike me again, but I sprang to my feet in a flash. Filled with his potent blood, I was now powerful and fast.

My eye caught several historical weapons displayed on the

opposite wall: crossbow, battle axe, mace, three sharp daggers, and—to my astonishment—Damien's katana.

Arsham lunged at me again. "How dare you utter that name in my presence?!"

I managed to elude him. "It was an accident, I swear. My brain is muddled…"

His nostrils flared. "Perhaps I should put you back in that coffin for another ten years to improve your memory!"

I froze in my tracks. "Ten years?"

"Not nearly enough time for you to learn your lesson, apparently."

Ten years for a vampire meant nothing, but for Damien…

Was he still in London? Had he been looking for me the entire time? Then a terrible thought crept into my head: did Arsham kill him? I needed answers to my questions as soon as possible, but first I had to deal with my sire.

Dropping to my knees I said, "Please have patience with me, my lord. Your blood is so powerful—I drank too much, too soon. I beg your forgiveness."

Arsham came to stand before me. He lifted my chin and looked into my eyes to determine my sincerity. "I'll put you back in that coffin if you ever repeat that wretched name in my presence."

"It won't happen again."

His eyes turned cold. "Prove it."

In one fluid motion, he unzipped his pants. I was still on my knees. Up until now Arsham had always treated me with the dignity afforded to one of my station. This was an insult, for he could easily obtain such a favor from a newborn of low rank.

I had two choices. I could either make matters worse between us with a refusal, or I could swallow my pride and play along with his little game. I stole a glance at the weapons on the wall as my fingers touched the sleek buckle of his belt. Arsham moaned in anticipation of the erotic pleasure to come.

No.

My dignity demanded my rebellion. I was out the door with Damien's katana in my hand before he had a chance to zip up his pants. I was half way down the long corridor by the time Arsham's big frame filled the open doorway. The two male vampires who had freed me from my prison earlier took up the chase when they realized that I was fleeing from our sire.

I ducked into one of the many private chambers within the elaborate underground lair. A Gucci bag sat on the top shelf of a female's closet, so I grabbed it, stuffed it with clothing, and fled the room. Convinced that I'd lost my pursuers, I headed toward one of the secret exits, which were known only to Elders. I crept outside under the faint moonlight and darted into the nearest alley. Next, I scaled a building and watched from the roof as the two males exited the lair further up the street. One of them continued forward while the other doubled back.

Hissing in annoyance, I ran to the center of the roof and crouched low, gripping the katana. Every muscle in my body coiled like a tight spring. I heard the young male circling the building below, then he stopped. After a few seconds, I tiptoed to the corner of the roof and looked down—he was gone. A shuffling sound made me look over my shoulder.

Shit. My cover was blown.

"My lady, I command you to return to the lair," he cried from the opposite corner of the rooftop.

"Who are you to command me?" I retorted, arching a brow at him. I had to admit, he was quite attractive. Husky and broad chested with a cute baby face.

He lifted his chin proudly. "I do so under the authority of our sire."

So tough. "You don't want to get involved in this, *boy*."

Frowning at the insult, he bared his fangs. "I'm no boy."

I laughed at his macho stance and he charged me. I could have easily decapitated him with the katana, but I punched him hard in the ribs before jumping across the wide alley to the next rooftop. My movements were so fast that he whipped around and stared after me in surprise. His expression became one of fierce determination as he began to pursue me in earnest.

I smiled at him. *So, that's how you want to play it.*

I jumped from building to building, skimming across several

rooftops. Humans hardly ever looked up from the street below, but if they did, I would appear as little more than a blur in their peripheral vision—a mere trick of light and shadow.

The young male did his best to keep up, but I was older, faster, and stronger. I eventually outmaneuvered him and he gave up the chase when I flew into the night at top speed.

CHAPTER 2

"Men rise from one ambition to another:
first, they seek to secure themselves against attack,
then they attack others."
(Niccolò Machiavelli)

Locating Damien topped my "to do list." Hovering over a small park located down the street from where he lived, I silently landed on my toes. My nose wrinkled in protest as I picked up the familiar scent of cat piss mixed with incense.
Felicia.
I swept the area to make sure no one had followed me. Moving stealthily along the shadows, I eventually came to Damien's apartment building in the trendy neighborhood of Soho. The peculiar odor grew more intense, which was a good sign. Damien and Felicia lived in an old Victorian brownstone full of architectural follies. One of the artsy tenants had placed a stone gargoyle at the entrance of the building. Grinning impishly, the fat winged creature displayed sharp little teeth and a forked tongue. Tilting my head back, I saw that the windows on the last floor were completely devoid of light.

I slipped into the side alley and scaled the outer wall to the top. As I peered through the stained glass panes at the darkened rooms beyond, I noticed that the windows were locked from the inside. I could have easily broken in, but this wasn't your average apartment. More than likely, the whole place was booby-trapped. I had no choice but to check back later. I hid the katana on the window ledge and pondered my options. Down below, a passerby's well-lit mobile phone displayed that it was nearly midnight. The sleek gadgets had become impressively hi-tech in the last decade. As I climbed onto the roof, I took in the scene around me. London at night was simply spectacular.

Groups of young women in stylish party clothes and painted

faces prowled the streets looking for a good time. Trendy young men drenched in cologne scoured the streets for girls—and pretty boys. Fashion had definitely changed, but not people. *Never people*. I inhaled the heady scent of pheromones in the air. The tangible sexuality of human beings was enough to make any vampire's mouth water. Despite having slaked my initial thirst with Arsham's blood, I was ready for more. It had been ten years since my last meal, and I was in the mood for hunting.

First, I had to change out of my torn clothes. Shortly before my imprisonment, I had the good sense to purchase a tiny flat and list it under one of my false aliases. Vampires like me who played with fire and took dangerous risks needed to protect themselves. Nobody knew of the flat's existence, not even Damien. I stole into the old Edwardian building and picked the lock since the key was hidden back at the lair.

The sparsely furnished studio sported a retro Louis XVI red velvet sofa, a black metal bistro table with two matching chairs, and an antique Venetian mirror. The original gray wallpaper flaunted a silver Baroque pattern that had peeled off in certain places.

I extracted a manila envelope from the cabinet above the kitchenette's sink. Inside were several fake passports and thick wads of cash in various currencies. After placing the envelope on the table, I rummaged through the Gucci bag and chose a black mini dress. The label read: Dior. Not too shabby. I discarded my torn clothing, then looked down at myself. I needed to bathe. Dare I indulge in such a luxury while I was on the run?

I went into the white tiled bathroom and turned on the tap. The old pipes hissed and popped, but eventually water poured out of the faucet. I turned on the shower. Grabbing the dried sliver of old soap from the sink, I stepped into the tub. Running my hands along my naked body, I enjoyed the feel of my own firm, smooth skin. Despite being over two centuries old, my body had been frozen at age twenty. What a blessing.

I dried myself off with the only towel in the linen closet. Wiping away the steam from the bathroom mirror, I leaned toward the reflection and glanced at my face. Almond-shaped eyes boasting midnight blue irises fringed with thick lashes stared back at me. Arsham's blood had done wonders for my appearance; the shadows beneath my eyes were gone and my fair skin was now luminous. Even my cheeks and lips were rosy. I turned my head to the side, admiring my restored beauty. Long tawny hair, lustrous with shiny golden highlights, framed my oval face. The heavy locks fell in sumptuous waves over my statuesque shoulders.

I fished through the cosmetic bag. Vampires were so naturally attractive that we didn't require artifice, but we often used cosmetics to blend in better with humans. I applied body lotion, perfume, and lip-gloss before slipping into the dress. After zipping up my snug, black leather boots, I ran the damp towel over each of them to remove all traces of dust. They looked new again.

Now, I was ready to go hunting.

I shoved the manila envelope and cash into the Gucci bag before slipping out the door. Sticking closely to the shadows, I made my way to the world famous Ministry of Music. Boasting three dance floors and four bars, most of the humans would be drunk or high at this hour. Finding prey proved too easy a task for thirsty immortals—like an American all-you-can-eat buffet. Being such an easy hunting ground, most vampires wisely avoided it for fear of being attacked by a slayer.

It was the last place where...

I shook my head, cutting the unpleasant memory short. Given what took place at the Ministry of Music ten years ago, there was no safer place for me to hide.

I heard the rhythmic bass long before the club came into view. Ignoring the long line of people waiting to get inside, I headed straight for the entrance where several strapping bouncers clad in black muscle shirts kept things under control. I sauntered up to a big man wearing mirrored sunglasses and pressed a hundred pound note into his hand.

He flashed me a gold-toothed smile and stepped aside. "Have fun, Gorgeous."

Pulsating strobe lights and strategically placed fog machines created a fantasy world. The DJ spun a wild driving beat, compelling humans to dance with frenzied movements. In ancient times, the scene would rival a Bacchanalia. I could feel the energy in the room as mortal bodies twisted and gyrated in ways that tempted and teased onlookers. I admired the fashionably dressed and the beautiful young faces as I wandered through the massive space in search of Damien.

There were several lounge areas throughout the complex. Plush sofas in shades of crimson and deep violet, electric candles, and black satin drapes were carefully arranged to provide pockets of semi-privacy. I stepped into one of these secluded areas and the scent of semen permeated the air. I turned my head and noticed a woman on her knees performing fellatio. Partially hidden behind a black curtain, her slick mouth caused the man's head to fall back in ecstasy. An overwhelming temptation to feed on them came over me. *Not here.* They were so deeply engrossed in their passionate play that I—an Angel of Death—passed them unnoticed.

I continued weaving through the throng of people like a shadow, my eyes scanning each human face.

Where are you, Damien?

A young blonde woman took hold of my hand, her innocent brown eyes clearly showing interest. Pulling me onto the dance floor, she offered me an inviting smile. She was cute and smelled like candy, so I indulged her request. Despite being slender, her hips swayed provocatively. Slipping her arms around me, she began kissing and licking my neck, which I found rather ironic.

"You're hot," she said.

Her high-pitched voice sounded childlike. In response to her flirtation, I slid my hands down the young woman's back and roughly cupped her buttocks. Her eyes widened in surprise. I had grown up in eighteenth century France where such games among women were not uncommon, especially within the royal court. Even the queen was known to indulge in a bit of harmless flirtation—and sometimes more—with her ladies-in-waiting.

"I like it rough," she whispered in my ear before taking my earlobe between her surprisingly sharp teeth.

I pulled away. "Are you sure about that?"

"Oh, I'm sure," she replied with the confidence so typical of a foolhardy youth.

Without another word I clasped her wrist and yanked her off the dance floor.

"Hey," she protested.

Ignoring her pleas, I led her straight into the ladies room, marching past the women in line to the farthest available stall.

An Indian woman in a hot pink micro mini put her hands on her hips. "No way! You need to wait your turn!"

I turned my head sharply and stared directly at her until she lowered her eyes. Buried deep within each human was the primal fear of the predator. This instinctive awareness was usually set off whenever I confronted a mortal head-on. I stared down the other women, too, in case any of them got any ideas about challenging me. They avoided eye contact and remained silent.

I pulled my pretty blonde into the stall, locked the door, and slammed her back against the wall. She giggled in pleasure and threw her arms around my neck like a silly schoolgirl. Inhaling the scent of her bubble gum flavored lip balm, I noticed the pulsating vein in her neck and knew she was excited. Claiming her mouth with mine, I slid my hand up her short skirt until I reached the lace of her panties. I tore the flimsy fabric, jerking her forward in the process. My fingers entered the warm, wet opening and teased her mercilessly.

Within seconds, she panted deliriously, "Wait…stop."

Being a devil, I lowered my hand at once. "Are you sure you want me to stop?"

"Oh, God, no," she whispered with eyes half-closed.

My fangs were lodged in her throat as my fingers coaxed her to climax with familiar expertise. I drank until she reached the state of unconsciousness, then stopped to spare her life. I pierced one of my fingertips and applied my blood to the mortal's wound, healing it instantly.

"Party's over, blondie," I said softly as I wiped away the traces of my feeding.

Sliding one hand around her back and placing her arm around my shoulders, I led her out of the stall. A few heads turned to look at us.

"Better watch out, girls," I warned. "There's a bad batch tonight."

A chubby girl sporting cobalt blue lipstick asked, "Need some help?"

"I've got it under control. Thanks."

I led my semi-conscious prey out of the ladies room and found a bouncer. "She was on the bathroom floor," I shouted above the music.

"I'll alert security," he said, placing his arm around my victim.

I refrained from killing humans. Of course, in the beginning I drank until they expired—all newborn vampires do so out of uncontrollable instinct. In time, when the bloodlust settles down, we can choose to control these base impulses. The rules of Arsham's coven demanded that we kill our prey. No exceptions. If my sire ever discovered that I was allowing humans to live after I've fed upon them, I would be severely punished. Maybe even executed.

Not drinking to my fill meant that I needed more than one mortal to slake my thirst. I prowled amid the vast sea of gyrating bodies, and caught sight of a man heading toward me. The artificial mist swirled around his head, making his features indiscernible. As he exited the cloud of white vapor and closed the gap between us, I stiffened involuntarily. His ice-blue eyes and false smile chilled me to the bone. Suddenly, I was transported back in time to a lonely chateau in Annecy, when I was a naïve and vulnerable human girl…

I've tried hard to forget…I still refuse to utter his name.

"Hello, hello," the man said, exuding confidence that bordered on cocky. "My name is Barry." He ran his hand through a patch of sparse, transplanted hair so that I could get a better look at his gold Rolex.

17

I gazed upon him with feigned disinterest. His features were plain, but he compensated for them with flashy designer clothing and expensive accessories.

Barry eyed me from head to toe. "What's your name?"

"Does it matter?" I countered saucily, using false bravado to suppress the terrible thoughts running through my head.

The resemblance was uncanny.

His eyes widened in genuine surprise. "You're full of sass, aren't you? Are you not into men?"

I'm not into you, asshole. "It's almost two in the morning in the hottest nightclub in London. I doubt you're looking for love, so what do you care what my name is?"

He raised both eyebrows and chuckled. The sound lacked mirth. "Not many women are bold enough to voice such blatant honesty."

"I'm not like many women."

"I can see that. Let me buy you a drink."

Although his touch repulsed me, I allowed Barry to cup my elbow and lead me to the bar. I entertained the thought of ditching him, but something kept me there...something sinister that lurked within me.

"What would you like?" he asked.

I couldn't tear my gaze from his cold stare. "Whatever you're having."

I watched as he moved around a kissing couple. He handed the bartender some money and said something in his ear. The young man nodded and got busy making the drinks. Within a few minutes the bartender placed two identical cocktails on the counter. Barry peeked over his shoulder and smiled at me, then shuffled closer to the kissing couple and pretended to adjust his shirt before walking over to me with two drinks in his hands. I knew he had drugged one of them.

"Here you go," he said, giving me the contaminated cocktail. "Vodka tonic."

"Thank you," I said before downing the entire contents of the glass all at once.

Barry's mouth dropped open. The eager anticipation on his

face was as transparent as the empty glass in my hand. Neither alcohol nor drugs had any effect on me.

Why would an affluent man like Barry feel the need to drug a woman? He didn't seem like the type who couldn't get laid, unless...

Unless he wanted more than merely scoring some sex.

My inner voice urged me to lead the creep into a dark corner and feed, but I couldn't do that. Not now. I decided to play along with his game, putting my hand up to my head. I even pretended to sway.

Studying me with fake concern, he asked, "Are you okay?"

"I feel a bit strange, actually."

His eyes lit up with excitement. "Hey, you don't look so good. Maybe you need some fresh air." Looking around furtively, he added, "I can call you a cab or—better yet—let me give you a ride home."

"Okay."

His arm tightened around my shoulders as he led me toward the exit. I couldn't help but wonder how many other women had fallen into Barry's trap. It took most of my willpower not to claw his eyes out right then and there. He led me to a flashy yellow Porsche with dark tinted windows and opened the passenger door. I pretended to almost pass out while getting into the seat. As soon as he closed the door, I scanned the backseat and saw a roll of duct tape, a hand-held camera, and a coil of nylon rope. A sharp hunting knife and a white towel were shoved under the seat.

Barry got into the driver's seat and pulled out into traffic. He didn't bother asking me where I lived—a dead giveaway that his intentions were far from honorable. I kept my head turned to the side and my eyes closed while his free hand eased up my leg and massaged my thigh.

He hummed a merry tune as he drove, which I found profoundly disturbing. Eventually, he pulled into a deserted parking lot beside an old warehouse. My eyes were still closed, but I sensed his every move. I heard his heart quicken as he unzipped his pants.

"Oh, baby, I can't wait to do you," he said, breathing heavily as he groped my breast.

He stopped touching me in order to adjust his seat. Then he turned to reach for something behind him. After several seconds, the sound of duct tape being torn filled the silence. My eyes snapped open as he was leaning forward to apply the tape to my mouth.

I grabbed his wrist with lightning speed. "Game over," I said, shoving him away from me.

His face expressed surprise and confusion at my sobriety. "How the hell?"

"Disappointed that your little drugged cocktail didn't work?"

"What are you talking about?"

"Cut the shit, Barry."

Grabbing the knife from under the seat, he frowned at me. "I didn't drive out here for nothing." The sharp blade flashed in the moonlight. "You're going to put out, bitch."

I smiled sweetly. "You're wrong about that."

He placed the knife to my throat so I grabbed his wrist again, only this time I broke it as easily as a child would snap a twig. He yelped in pain, dropping the weapon into my lap. I planted my left hand against his chest and shoved him back against the driver's side window.

"Watch carefully, douche bag." Gripping the knife handle with my hand, I stabbed myself in the stomach.

His face turned completely white. "Jesus Christ!"

"Wrong again, Barry. I'm the Duchess de Nuit," I corrected, pulling out the bloody blade and wiping it on his expensive shirt. "And I'm no savior...least of all yours."

He watched in horrified disbelief as the self-inflicted wound in my belly miraculously healed within seconds.

"What are you?" he whispered, his voice thick with terror.

"I've been called many names..."

He swallowed hard. It gave me pleasure to see the coldness in his eyes replaced by pure fear. Sweat broke out on his forehead and I could smell the adrenaline pumping through his veins. The predator had become the prey.

I pointed to the back seat. "Duct tape, rope, camera…do you like hurting women? Do you film their suffering?" I paused. "I used to know someone who liked hurting women. You remind me a lot of that bastard."

He jutted his chin. "So?"

"So…things ended badly for him. Very badly."

"Yeah?" he asked, his voice trembling.

"Oh, yeah. How many victims have you brought here, you sick pervert?"

His fear was momentarily replaced by arrogant indignation. "That's really none of your business, you stupid bitch."

"You're right, it's not my business." I leaned closer and whispered, "But do you know what is?"

He sneered at me. "What?"

"Preventing you from hurting others in the future."

"How are you going to stop me?"

I grinned as widely as I could, exposing my sharp teeth to their fullest. "I'm going to kill you."

"What the—"

My memories of Annecy—*and of him*—drove me to violence whenever I met people who enjoyed tormenting the innocent. Poor Barry whimpered and moaned as I savagely sucked every last drop of blood in his body.

After taping Barry's mouth with duct tape, I tied his wrists and then used the knife to cut a deep gash in his throat to hide the evidence of my bite. Luckily, he kept a plastic lighter and a pack of cigarettes in the console of his car. I lit one of the cigarettes and inhaled deeply. As I exhaled, I watched the smoke swirl in ghostly patterns before my eyes. The delicate shapes dissipated in the darkness as I breathed a satisfied sigh of relief. I dropped the burning cigarette in Barry's lap. The first flicker of flames prompted me to flee the car.

I glanced over my shoulder. "Bye, asshole."

The lights of London twinkled like stars in the distance, and a streak of pale red glowed across the horizon. The sun would rise in a couple of hours, so I needed to seek shelter from its burning rays.

Barry's car exploded, momentarily lighting up the sky with an orange glow. Soon afterward, the music of police sirens filled the night air.

I returned to Damien's place and the grinning gargoyle. I imagined my lover welcoming me with open arms as I stole to the top floor of the brownstone via the stairs this time. My hand trembled with anticipation as I reached for the brass doorknocker. The scent of cat piss and incense overwhelmed me. Suddenly, I caught another scent and froze. Backing away, I flew down the stairs and stood in the entryway.

A man was inside the apartment with Felicia but it wasn't Damien. My thoughts raced as I debated what to do. I peered up at the dark gray sky with concern. I didn't have much time. Sighing in frustration, I crept up the building wall, retrieved the katana from the ledge, and peeked inside the window. Felicia's slim form and red hair were clearly visible. She had hardly aged at all, which was normal for her species. Fortunately, the man had his back turned toward me. I waved my hand to capture Felicia's attention. Catching sight of me, her face expressed shock. The man glanced over his shoulder but I was too fast for him. A moment later I heard the door slam and male footsteps descending the stairs.

Felicia opened the window. "Angelique!"

"Felicia," I cried in pure relief. "Who's that man?"

"A friend. I sent him down the street for some Chinese food." I slipped into the flat and she continued looking at the open window with expectation. "Is Damien with you?"

My stomach clenched. "Wait—he's not here?"

She shook her head and I ran into his bedroom. Everything seemed so different. Despite my sensitive nose, I couldn't pick up even the faintest trace of him.

Felicia hovered in the doorway. "He's been gone for a long time."

"How long?"

"The last time I saw him was the night you disappeared ten years ago. Damien came home from the Ministry of Music totally upset—and scared. I had never seen him like that. He told me what had happened at the club. Vamps were hunting him down, so he had to lay low for a while and he didn't want to stay here for fear of endangering me. After that, he packed some stuff and took off."

"You haven't heard from him since?" I demanded, trying to suppress my anxiety.

Felicia went to a small desk in the living room and extracted an envelope from the top drawer. "About a month later, this arrived in the mail. No return address. It's postmarked locally, so he was still in London when he mailed it. His note said—you know what, I'll just read it to you. 'Dear Felicia. I can no longer remain in London. I haven't been able to find Angelique anywhere, so I've enclosed a letter for her. It's very important that she gets it, so please deliver it as soon as you can. Sorry I couldn't say goodbye face to face. Take care of yourself— Damien.' "

At this point, Felicia handed me a sealed envelope with my name on it. I tore it open and held up the letter. " 'My dearest Angelique, I have searched every corner of the city. Where are you, my love? I don't believe Arsham has killed you—at least not after what you've told me about your relationship with him. Has he banished you from London? Are you in exile, unable to contact me? I'm going crazy not knowing. Where else would you possibly be except your beloved France? I hope I'm right because that's where I'm going. I can't remain in London, and I've got nowhere else to go. I plan to track you down, and I won't stop until I find you. Yours forever, Damien.' "

Tears prickled my eyelids. Given our lifestyles, vampires and slayers tended to live under the radar. Damien had never owned a mobile phone, nor did he have an email address since computers were traceable, too. Finding each other would not be an easy task.

"I'm so sorry, Angelique. Where have you been, anyway? I carried that letter around for months, hoping to see you at some point."

"I've been right here in London the entire time; I was

imprisoned by Arsham."

Felicia's face paled, which was quite a feat since her Scottish skin was already as translucent as fine porcelain. "What do you mean 'imprisoned?' "

"My sire forced me into a punishment coffin and walled it up within our lair. He finally freed me tonight, so I ran away."

"What a monster!"

I glanced down at the letter in my hand and frowned in confusion. "What did Damien mean when he wrote that he could no longer remain in London?"

"I noticed that, too, when I first read his letter. I don't know what he meant, but I don't like the sound of it."

The sound of footsteps on the stairs drew our gazes. I gave Felicia's hand an appreciative squeeze before jumping out the window and melting into the night.

I raced back to my flat. The shades were already drawn so I pulled the heavy drapes together tightly to block out any rays of morning light. Clutching Damien's letter to my chest, I stretched out on the sofa with the katana at my side. As the first fragile rays of sunlight touched the sky, my eyes closed. My last thought before being claimed by the sleep of the undead was of Arsham. His cruelty caused the dilemma that I now faced. He wasn't always cruel, however.

Once upon a time, my sire was very dear to me...

CHAPTER 3
LYON, FRANCE
18TH CENTURY

*"God is a comedian playing to an audience
that is too afraid to laugh."*
(Voltaire)

My father had always wanted two things in life: a son and a noble title. A distant—rumored bastard—cousin of a certain marquis in Bordeaux, he had no claim whatsoever to an aristocratic title. To make matters worse, my mother died shortly after bearing her first and only child in the spring of 1768. To my father's dismay, I lacked the necessary parts between my legs that would have made him a happy man.

One of Lyon's most successful silk weavers, he provided the finest fabrics in Europe to the royal family and the French court. So popular were my father's silks, satins, and brocades that sometimes a courtier would show up on our doorstep. The minute they spotted the king or queen wearing something woven from my father's looms, they would travel to Lyon to be the first to buy the same color and pattern. This served as the greatest form of flattery to our monarchs. Excellent quality cloth did not come cheap, so my father amassed a fortune. At least he took great pleasure in his immense wealth; his only consolation in life.

Two hills dominated our lovely city—one rose from the banks of the Rhône, where silk weavers plied their trade, and the other rose from the banks of the Saône, where wealthy bourgeoisie and nobility resided. Fine furnishings graced our home, and we had a stunning view of the Saône River from the windows.

I rarely saw my father since the nature of his business

required frequent travel. Not only did he journey to Paris on a regular basis, but his fabrics were in demand in other places, too. It was not uncommon for him to be gone for several weeks at a time at the requests of various nobles and monarchs throughout Europe. Whether it was Switzerland, Germany, Spain or Portugal, my father was only too happy to oblige those with discerning tastes and deep pockets. He would always return to Lyon in a good mood after having collected a coffer full of coins.

Practically an orphan, a kind servant doted on me. Sadly, she died when I was seven years old. Not knowing what to do with me, my father decided to entrust my upbringing to my late mother's older sister, Marguerite. The servants were instructed to pack everything I owned into a trunk, then we set out for my aunt's chateau.

Dressed in my best silk embroidered frock, I peered out the window of my father's carriage as we rolled through Lyon's busy streets. My father sat across from me, impeccably dressed in a coat of gray brocade and matching breeches. Shiny silver buttons graced the front of his cream satin waistcoat. As usual, the lace at his throat was pristine white and perfectly starched. A jeweled ring glimmered on the last finger of his left hand.

Fixing me with a stern gaze, he cleared his throat. "Angelique, you must remember everything that I've told you."

"Yes, Papa."

"You will be obedient, respectful, polite, and always remember to remain virtuous. Your aunt will be sending periodic reports on your progress."

"I know, Papa."

"Good. Well, take your last look at Lyon."

We sat in silence for several minutes before I turned my face to the window. I enjoyed the bucolic landscape while my father slept.

Aunt Marguerite received us with warmth and hospitality. She was the widow of a wealthy banker who had left her "well-off," as my father liked to say. Her only child, Thibaut, became crippled from a high fever he had suffered during infancy.

Unable to speak or walk, he spent most of his time in bed under the constant care of servants. My aunt often gazed at her son with eyes reflecting guilt—she was hearty and hale, whereas his delicate constitution kept him from living life to the fullest. In an attempt to compensate this tragic injustice, she purchased a big chateau in the countryside that afforded Thibaut pretty views and fresh breezes from his bedroom windows.

My father left for Lyon an hour later despite my aunt's numerous invitations to spend the night. When we were alone, Aunt Marguerite placed her hands on her ample hips and regarded me for a long time. "Well, you are definitely your mother's child—she was beautiful, you know. A good soul, too. Something tells me you are a lot like her."

***

Aunt Marguerite was a practical person, but also surprisingly modern. Widowed at a young age, she believed women should be educated to the point of being able to fend for themselves. For this reason, I was subjected to daily lessons of math, history, and science by an old male tutor with little patience for children—much less girls. My aunt also believed in a well-rounded education, and had me schooled in art, music, literature, and poetry. I applied myself to my studies and proved an apt pupil.

I would often visit Thibaut after my lessons to share what I had learned with him. Sometimes, I would read aloud or sing to lift his spirits. Although he could not speak, I knew he understood me because his eyes would light up whenever I said something he found humorous or particularly interesting.

My aunt's expansive property allowed for a few crofter's cottages, and their rents added considerably to the already generous amount she received annually. A large stable with six fine horses stood near the chateau, along with a grazing field big enough to accommodate over a dozen cows, and a barn housing a spattering of goats, rabbits, pigs, and chickens. I liked to spend my free time feeding and petting the smaller animals, and helping the servants tend the herb garden behind the kitchen.

A fairly well-behaved child most of the time, I was insatiably curious. My innate desire to know things usually led to mischief. Stealthy by nature, I trained myself to move as silently as a cat. I took great pleasure in playing tricks on the servants, sneaking up on them whenever they least expected it. Before long, I gained the reputation of being an imp with the face of an angel.

Perhaps my guardian had something to do with my wildness. Robust and tall with a booming voice that was far from feminine, Aunt Marguerite seemed larger than life. She wore her dark mass of unruly curls in an unbecoming manner, and her strong hands were as capable as those of any man. Having little patience for domesticity, she preferred being outdoors. She knew how to wield a sword and shoot an arrow with uncanny precision. In addition to riding astride like a man, she regularly hunted deer and wild boar. Breeches and boots were her attire of choice when enjoying masculine sports.

Unlike other girls of my social status, I never learned to sew or embroider altarpieces for the local church. Since I accompanied my aunt almost wherever she went, I grew up learning how to wield a sword, shoot an arrow, and ride a horse. She commissioned a seamstress to create several shirts and breeches for me so that, like her, I could dress appropriately for any sport. Luckily, my father rarely came out to see me, and therefore had no idea of my masculine achievements. I often wondered what his reaction would be if he knew how my radical aunt was raising his only female child.

I grew to love Aunt Marguerite while appreciating the freedom and knowledge she generously bestowed upon me on a daily basis. Her library contained a great number of secular books, which she often encouraged me to read at my leisure. The only condition she insisted upon was that I complete my lessons before selecting something for my personal pleasure. My tutor once wrinkled his nose at my choice of book, claiming that well-bred ladies shouldn't read such scandalous material. When I informed my aunt of this, she threatened to dismiss him on the spot. The old man never uttered a negative word to me again.

The years went by rapidly, and my childhood was a happy one. Even though my aunt doted on me like a loving mother, I did miss my father at times. His visits were extremely rare, but on the year I turned ten everything changed. He began visiting me on my birthdays, Easter, and Christmas.

Shortly after my twelfth birthday, I became a woman. Aunt Marguerite had kindly explained the process of menstruation to me the previous year, so I was already prepared for the cramps that accompanied the blood.

"It hurts," I confessed to the servant who was helping me dress that morning.

The woman's eyes narrowed as she placed her hand upon my swollen belly. "I'll prepare a draught for the pain and fetch some clean rags."

My aunt came into my bedchamber a little while later and inquired, "How are you feeling?"

I scrunched up my face. "Terrible."

"The first two days are the most painful with the heaviest flow." Her face lit up. "We must celebrate your passage into womanhood when you feel better. I will open a bottle of my best cognac. Would you like that?"

"I've never tasted cognac—or wine, for that matter. Father never permitted it."

"Surely he allowed you a bit of diluted wine with honey?" I shook my head and she continued, "A thimbleful of sweet brandy?"

"Not a drop."

"We'll rectify that folly soon enough." She grinned and winked, adding, "If you're old enough to suffer through menstruation, you're old enough to enjoy inebriation."

A couple of days later, I learned about the joys and dire consequences of drunkenness.

***

My father's visits were usually brief in nature; a stiff embrace, the offering of expensive cloth, an inquiry after my health, and a parting admonition to behave in a manner that

29

would never bring shame upon his good name. He would then pop into Thibaut's room and nod at him before sitting down with my aunt to discuss the news of the day.

In time, I acquired several lengths of plush velvets, patterned brocades, smooth satins, and soft silks. These fabrics were often dyed in regal shades of violet or crimson, sky blue, delicate pink, gold, and emerald green. Many were quite costly, flaunting silver or gold thread designs. Thanks to skillful seamstresses, some of these fabrics were transformed into fine gowns, which were carefully stored in chests. I noticed that my father's visits usually left my aunt in a foul mood.

One day, I asked, "Aunt Marguerite, why do my father's visits make you angry?"

She eyed me steadily for several seconds. "Because I don't want to lose you."

"What do you mean?"

"Your father is preparing you for the marriage market, Angelique. The gowns and the fabrics are worth a fortune, and therefore are part of your dowry."

My dowry? "But I am so young!"

She shook her head. "You are almost fifteen, child. Plenty of girls your age are already married."

I was horrified to learn this. My aunt had never even mentioned the word marriage to me.

Seeing my expression, Aunt Marguerite placed her meaty arm around my shoulder. The weight and warmth of the limb comforted me. "Do not fret, my dear. I won't let him marry you off too soon."

"Do you promise?"

"Yes."

"I don't want to get married, Aunt Marguerite."

She made a face before confessing, "Neither did I."

***

My aunt harbored a secret that I discovered completely by accident. I rudely barged into her bedchamber one evening to share a bit of servant gossip. The thin, pale woman in my aunt's burly arms flushed to the roots of her flaxen hair before hiding her face in shame. They were both naked under the rumpled bed sheets, their bodies entwined in a most intimate manner.

I later learned that my aunt's lover, Lisette, frequently spent the night at the chateau. Since the nature of their relationship required extreme discretion, Lisette was rarely present during the day.

The incident brought us closer together, for I was now my aunt's co-conspirator. Personally, I saw nothing wrong with two people expressing their love for each other, regardless of their sex. Of course, this defiant view went against the Catholic teachings forced upon us by society. Although naïve about many things in life, I knew when to keep my opinions to myself.

A few weeks later, a terrible storm caused the window shutters to bang against the wall in the middle of the night. Startled from sleep, I scrambled out of bed to close them. A noise compelled me to pause in my task and strain my ears in the darkness. I heard it again—a soft moan. My first thought was of Thibaut. Lighting a candle, I decided to go and check on him.

I tiptoed down the hallway to his room, only to find him fast asleep in his bed. I followed the sound to my aunt's bedchamber and noticed the door slightly ajar. The moaning grew louder and I realized that my aunt was not alone. I turned around to leave, but my curiosity got the best of me. Faint candlelight spilled through the crack in the doorway. I knew that I shouldn't invade Aunt Marguerite's privacy, but I couldn't help myself.

Lisette lay languidly upon the bed with her head thrown back. Eyes closed, her face expressed pure rapture. My aunt's dark head, nestled between Lisette's legs, bobbed up and down as she...*as she what?*

Being a virgin, I knew nothing of such matters. I watched in awe as my aunt's big hands played with Lisette's perky breasts, her fingers delicately squeezing the pink nipples. This only brought more moans from Lisette's lips as her hips rolled up and down against the bed. My aunt continued to coax her lover's body with what appeared to be sweet torture. Lisette's hips bucked faster and faster until her body convulsed and she gasped aloud in joyful release. Only then did my aunt's face emerge to grin in satisfaction.

The look they gave each other made my cheeks burn. I felt ashamed for having witnessed such an intimate moment. I made my way back to my chamber, keenly aware of the strange throbbing between my own legs.

***

In 1785 my father came to the chateau. It was neither my birthday nor a holy day, so my aunt and I stood at the window watching his approach with bewilderment.

I confessed quietly, "I should be happy to see him, but I'm not. I'm a wicked girl and a bad daughter."

Aunt Marguerite looked at me. "Well, he hasn't been the most attentive of fathers, has he? You are a wonderful young lady. Any man would be proud to have you as a daughter and want to keep you close. Yet, he sent you away to live with me."

"I'm so happy he did."

She smiled and gave me a hug. "As am I, my dear."

"What do you suppose he wants?"

"We shall soon find out."

My father galloped through the courtyard gates with great haste. "I have come bearing good news!"

We ran outside, shielding our eyes from the sun.

My aunt inquired, "What news?"

My father's toothy smile was almost contagious.

Almost.

"Angelique is to be married!"

My aunt and I were distressed by this unwelcomed proclamation. I had turned seventeen in the spring and she could not keep him from marrying me off. We stood motionless as my father explained that he had secured an excellent match for me.

To me, he added, "You will be a duchess by marriage."

Unlike my father, I didn't care about a stupid title—much less a husband. Reluctant to give up the freedom that I enjoyed in my aunt's home, I said nothing.

My father gripped my arms. "What's the matter with you, girl? You'll be rich beyond your wildest dreams! You should be dancing with joy and gratitude!"

I tried to smile but failed miserably, earning his scorn.

Aunt Marguerite's expression turned suspicious. "How did you convince such a high ranking noble to marry our Angelique?"

My father laughed nervously as he let go of my arms. "What do you mean?" he retorted defensively. "Angelique is young, healthy, beautiful—"

"Who is he?" she interjected, alarmed.

Even I could see the guilt etched upon my father's face. He hesitated before lowering his head and mumbling a reply. I didn't quite catch the man's name, but my aunt did. Her eyes widened in shock and an ugly argument erupted between the two of them.

"My sister would never approve this match," Aunt Marguerite protested. "You've heard the rumors. He..." my aunt trailed off when her worried eyes fell upon me.

I knew she didn't want to say anything in my presence that would upset or frighten me.

My father waved his hand in front of my aunt's face in dismissal. "Mere hearsay, Marguerite! People love to gossip. What if there's no truth to the rumors?"

"What if there *is*?" she shot back. "Would you subject your own daughter to such a risk for a mere title?"

My father became so indignant that spittle came out of his mouth when he shouted, "How dare you question my choice?! I refuse to hear another word about it. Collect your things, Angelique. We are leaving right now!"

My aunt began to cry and begged him to reconsider. "Please don't take her away from me just yet."

Ignoring her pleas, he ordered the servants to pack my travel trunk. The house soon became a flurry of activity with my aunt crying in the background. I stole into my cousin's room and took his hand in mine. He had heard everything, and I could see from his expression that he was distressed.

I kissed his brow. "Goodbye Thibaut."

His eyes watered and he made a guttural sound.

"I know, dear cousin. It's awful, but I cannot disobey my father. I'll think of you often and cherish the memories of my life here. Promise me that you will do the same."

He did his best to nod as tears streamed down his hollow cheeks. I forced a smile then turned my back on him. I walked into the main room as my father threw a pouch full of gold coins on the table.

Aunt Marguerite was appalled. "What is that for?"

"Compensation for hosting Angelique all these years," he replied coolly.

"How dare you?" she fumed, picking up the pouch and throwing it back at him. "You and your money be damned! I love Angelique—she's like my own child."

"But she's not your child, she's *mine*," he retorted icily before storming out the door.

My aunt shook with fury. At least my father had allowed us a few minutes to say goodbye.

"I'm so sorry, Aunt Marguerite," I offered as tears gathered in my eyes.

She opened her arms and I ran into them. "Remember everything I've taught you, my dear." Taking my face into her hands, she held my gaze. "You are the daughter that I never had. I love you, Angelique."

"I love you, too."

"You are far too good for the duke." Looking over my shoulder to make sure my father was out of earshot, she whispered, "Your husband-to-be is not a good man. Be wary of him, do you understand me?"

"Yes."

"Your father is committing a great folly, and there is nothing I can do about it." She paused to wipe away a tear. "Oh God. Please promise me that you'll be very careful."

"Angelique!"

We both turned our heads at the sound of my father's impatient cry.

"I promise," I assured.

"May Fate be kind to you, my sweet girl. Farewell."

"Thank you," I said, the words sticking in my throat due to emotion. "I shall never forget you or the kindness that you have shown me."

I never saw Aunt Marguerite again after that day.

CHAPTER 4

"Marriage is like a cage; one sees birds outside desperate to get in, and those inside equally desperate to get out."
(Michel de Montaigne)

One week later, I married a man almost twenty years my senior. My new husband wasn't too ugly, but I would not have chosen him for myself had I been given the freedom to make such a choice. The Duke of Annecy stood at average height with fair skin and flaxen hair. His eyes were as colorless as the sky after rain, accentuating the blackness of his pupils. This contrast afforded him a piercing gaze akin to that of a carnivorous bird.

My father spared no expense for my wedding feast, inviting many distinguished guests to our home. This lavish display afforded him the chance to show off his wealth in the hope of impressing prominent members of our community.

Despite my pleas, he had refused to invite Aunt Marguerite. This saddened me, for I missed her so much that it hurt at times.

Shortly after sunset, my new husband announced our immediate departure to Annecy. This unexpected news caused a hush over the crowd. The evening's merriment had barely begun, and we had not yet danced as a married couple.

Embarrassed by this sudden change of plans, my father glanced around to see the reactions of his shocked guests. "Your Grace, it is your wedding celebration," he pointed out gently. "Surely, it would be better if you spent the night here in Lyon."

The Duke of Annecy looked down his arrogant nose at my father the same way one regards an insect in the garden. "I must return tonight." Turning his cold eyes to me, he added, "There will be plenty of time for *that* later."

A few drunk wedding guests chuckled at his tawdry insinuation. Mortified, I noticed that my father did not appreciate the comment, either. His worried eyes sought mine, and I wondered in that moment if he was recalling my aunt's dire warning. Just before he lowered his gaze, I thought I caught a flicker of regret in his eyes, but it was too late. I now belonged to someone else.

We took our leave amid a crowd of well-wishers. I barely had time to bid my father farewell before being ushered into a carriage. The duke sat across from me, his bony knees touching mine. He stared at me throughout the entire ride without uttering a single word, which I found extremely unnerving.

It was nearly dawn when we arrived in the small town of Annecy, which almost bordered Switzerland. Located atop a hill overlooking a large placid lake edged by mountains, stood the Chateau of Annecy. The massive stone castle, nestled inside a cobbled courtyard, was well-protected by high stone walls. The imposing structure had been used as a residence for the counts of Geneva throughout the thirteenth and fourteenth centuries before being abandoned over a hundred years ago. My husband had purchased the property recently, adding it to his collection of fine homes.

The sound of the carriage wheels and horse's hooves echoed loudly in the vast stone courtyard, thus announcing our arrival. My husband's bleary-eyed servants welcomed me with curious stares and solemn faces. They had been roused from sleep and were not happy to stand outside in the chilly dampness of the early morning. None of them spoke a single word of greeting to me. I could feel the tension in the air as the duke led me inside the great hall.

The interior of the fortress consisted of various shades of gray stone. What's more, there were crucifixes literally *everywhere*. Gold, silver, wood, copper and brass; some of them were ornately carved and adorned with jewels, while others included the figure of the suffering Christ. Suppressing a shudder, I continued following my husband through the chateau. No warmth or cheeriness graced the inside my new home, but the views from the windows were spectacular.

The duke ascended the stairs with me in tow, then led me down a maze of corridors consisting of family portraits. No one smiled in these paintings, and all the duke's ancestors possessed the same colorless eyes with sharp pupils.

Would my firstborn child have such unsettling eyes, too?

"Your chamber, my lady," the duke said, finally speaking to me for the first time since our departure from Lyon.

We stopped at the end of a hallway and he pushed open a massive door with black iron hinges. Oddly, it was the only door in the fortress painted red—the color reserved for the doors of whorehouses.

I entered the spacious bedchamber, relieved that it was at least decently decorated. Only one silver crucifix hung on the wall, and a canopied bed with red velvet hangings dominated the room. A small writing desk, a stiff-backed chair, and two oil paintings with biblical themes adorned the space. One painting portrayed Daniel in the lion's den, and the other was of Saint Catherine of Siena kneeling before the papal throne. My eye caught a red leather-bound bible on the night table by the bed, and on top of it was a small silver rosary.

I turned around to thank my husband and noticed that he had stepped into the room and locked the door behind him. I assumed he would leave me alone to rest after the long ride, but his expression revealed another intention. Without warning, he walked up to me and roughly kissed my mouth. When I struggled against him, he slapped me hard across the face.

My hand flew up to my stinging cheek. "Your Grace?"

"I am your husband now. The bible commands that wives be in subjection to their husbands and give them their due. You will submit to me whenever I wish, do you understand?"

Stunned, I nodded in response to his words before he kissed me again. This time, I didn't put up a fight. I recoiled inwardly as his tongue forced its way into my mouth. His hands groped my body through the fabric of my gown, then his fingers tore at the laces of my bodice.

Shocked by his lack of gallantry, I said, "Surely, one of the female servants can help me undress…"

The duke eyed me coldly and yanked roughly at the neckline of the gown, jerking me forward in the process. I winced when

38

I heard my father's lovely fabric being ripped apart so carelessly. He continued to undress me in this savage manner until I stood before him naked and terrified.

He circled me the way a cat does before pouncing on a helpless mouse. His eyes took in every detail of my body, but his expression revealed nothing. My aunt had explained the process of copulation to me, and I had seen my fair share of rutting animals, but I found myself unprepared for this moment.

My husband fell to his knees and stuck his nose in my most private part, inhaling deeply. I wanted to run, but dared not move for fear he would resort to violence. His tongue penetrated me and I gasped aloud. Quickly, I covered my mouth with my hand to stifle any sound. He then ran his tongue all the way up my body, past my navel, between my breasts, up my neck and finally, my face. He licked me like a dog and I tried not to cringe in disgust. Something felt wrong and I grew wary.

"Are you a virgin?" he asked.

"Yes, of course, my lord," I replied, my voice quavering.

He traced the curve of my breast with two fingers and slid them down my body, following the slimy trail his tongue had left behind. He then stuck both fingers inside of me and I cried out in surprise and pain. He nodded, satisfied. He removed his fingers, smelled them, and then placed them inside my mouth, urging me to suckle them. When I obliged his perverse demand, his eyes fluttered shut and he sighed in pleasure. He grabbed my hand and placed it upon his cock. It felt as hard as wood.

"I will offer you a single wedding gift," he said, opening his eyes to look at me. "Do you want to know what it is?"

My body trembled with fear. "Y-yes."

"I will be gentle with you now because you are a virgin. This is the only time I will offer you this courtesy."

His words made my blood run cold.

***

True to his promise, the only time my husband had shown consideration toward me in the marriage bed was when he deflowered me. After that, he subjected me to an array of cruel perversions and humiliations.

39

Despite the countless crucifixes displayed throughout the chateau and the collection of bibles in the library, there was nothing Christ-like about my husband. The outer show of religious devotion served as a clever ruse to hide his malignant nature, for he used my body in ways that were quite unbiblical.

I was shocked to learn that the duke had been married three times prior to our marriage. Each of his young wives had died prematurely, and the circumstances surrounding their deaths were mysterious. According to the information I gleaned from the servants, the first wife died from a horse's kick, the second from drowning in the lake, and the third from a sudden fever. Something else made me fear for my own safety—none of the women had provided the duke with a male heir.

Despite his many faults, my husband did possess one virtue: generosity. He provided me with a fine horse and the freedom to ride daily. An accomplished lady's maid with a fair disposition served as my companion. The duke allowed me to travel into town with my maid whenever I wished, and he gave me plenty of coin to buy whatever I desired at the market.

Evidence of my husband's love of luxury lurked everywhere. New dresses were commissioned for me according to his tastes. We dined on excellent food served on the most beautiful gilded porcelain plates, and we used elegant silver cutlery. Fine wines flowed freely into delicate crystal goblets.

Aside from being submissive to his nocturnal desires, my husband forbade me from speaking to any member of the opposite sex. This included his soldiers, male servants, or male vendors at the market. Spies followed me everywhere and at all times to make sure that I obeyed this most sacred rule.

I abided by the duke's commands and took comfort in his library. Most of the books my husband owned were religious in nature, but he liked philosophy, too. Thankfully, Socrates, Plato, and Aristotle were at my disposal. The books were only a small consolation.

I rode my horse every day to get away from the bleakness of my life. Sometimes, I would sit inside my chamber and stare out the window for hours. I liked it when the mist shrouded the tops of the mountains and hid them from view. On these days the water in the lake resembled melted silver. I relished watching the hawks as they hunted for food. They would soar gracefully over the lake and plunge with accurate precision to capture fish in their razor-sharp talons. I often closed my eyes and wished that I, too, could sprout wings and fly. I would go far away...far from the suffocating clutches of my vile husband.

The duke decided to present me at court several weeks after the wedding. This was customary, especially since he had procured the king's permission to marry me in the first place. My father had been to court many times, and had personally met the king and queen on one occasion. He described Marie Antoinette, and I longed to catch a glimpse of one of her notoriously extravagant gowns. My father had described her attire as theatrical, but after seeing his sketches I mentally labeled them as ridiculous. Since we would be arriving the first week of July, most of the court would not be in stifling hot Paris, but rather in the coolness of the countryside at the famed Palace of Versailles.

We left Annecy at dawn. The humid, rainy weather caused muddy potholes in the road. Our carriage wheels got stuck only once, but it still made our travel slow and tedious. When the sun had set, we stopped at an inn. No one in the region traveled at night because of bandits and thieves. According to legend, however, there were worse things to fear than outlaws. I once overheard the servants talking about unholy beings that killed people after the sun went down. Demons that drank blood and would suck a man dry in the blink of an eye. Of course, these were only stories meant to scare naughty children.

We awoke the next morning to sunshine and drier roads. Versailles was located a few miles from the center of Paris, so we arrived in good time. As our carriage made its way to the famous royal residence, I was unprepared for its grandeur. I gawked open-mouthed at the meticulously manicured gardens and endless velvety green lawns. In addition to a wide variety of flowers and neatly clipped hedges, splendid fountains and outdoor sculptures adorned the grounds.

41

"Stop gaping like a common peasant," my husband chastised while pinching my arm.

I lowered my eyes at once. "Forgive me."

"If you shame me in any way, I swear I will beat you within an inch of your life. Do you hear me, girl?"

I nodded while fighting back tears. Clever and cruel, my husband liked to hit me where the bruises would never show. I descended from the carriage with the aid of a footman and dutifully took the duke's proffered arm. His outward show of gallantry sickened me.

A liveried page materialized and led us into an enormous hall decorated with splendid oil paintings and Oriental vases overflowing with delicate summer blossoms. An impressive crystal chandelier hung high above our heads. Each of the faceted crystals captured the sun's rays, creating a thousand tiny rainbows on the walls, ceiling, and floor. The colorful flecks danced and flickered all around us. I wanted to giggle in sheer delight but did my best to appear composed. I beheld the countless treasures, silently marveling at the sheer wealth of our monarchs. Various shades of rich gold sparkled on mirrors, furniture, and frames; it looked as if everything had been touched by the mythical King Midas!

We were shown to our lovely room, which afforded every comfort a guest could possibly require. I stood admiring the rose chintz bed hangings when a page informed us that the king was away on royal business, and would only be back four days from now.

"These extra days in Versailles will cost me a fortune!" the duke bellowed once the page had departed.

Not wishing to say or do anything to fuel his anger, I pretended to look out the window at the formal gardens.

"As for you…"

I turned around to face my husband. "Yes, my lord?"

"If you so much as raise your eyes to another man, you'll be sorry. You are never to leave this room unaccompanied. Do you understand?" I nodded and he added, "A married woman can easily lose her virtue and good reputation at court if she's not careful. Keep in mind that courtiers are extremely witty and often cruel. Since you're little more than a stupid country bumpkin, I doubt that you understand the concept of satire. The nobles here will tear you to shreds and reduce you to tears with their sharp tongues and sarcasm if given the chance. I will not tolerate being the laughing stock at court due to a dull-witted wife, so it's best if you avoid them altogether."

"Am I never to leave this room?"

"Don't be ridiculous, my pretty fool. You'll accompany me to dinner and stand in audience if the queen is present. When the king returns you will be officially presented, and you will curtsy exactly as I have previously instructed. You will only speak when spoken to, and you will not volunteer your opinion on anything. Am I clear?"

"You have been very clear, my lord."

The duke walked to the door. "I'm going out for a breath of fresh air."

"Before you go…"

He sighed impatiently. "What is it?"

"I've heard of the famous Hall of Mirrors. I would like to see it, if possible—with you, of course."

"Perhaps."

The duke left me alone with my maid, who avoided my gaze and quietly proceeded to unpack my clothing and toiletries. I wanted to curse aloud in frustration but wisely refrained, for she reported everything I said and did to the duke. I was always careful never to show any emotion in the presence of others.

How I hated my husband!

Despite the limitations the duke imposed upon me during my brief stay at Versailles, I managed to learn and observe many things. Extramarital affairs were quite rampant at court, and many so-called "noble ladies" behaved little better than common sluts.

After supper, the evening's entertainment led to gambling and raucous behavior—even the queen was rumored to be a notorious gambler. The wine poured freely and people inevitably got drunk, which only led to further debauchery.

Couples would stray into the cover of night, and women gave themselves freely to multiple partners after the last candle had been snuffed out. More shocking still were the courtiers who defecated in dark corners like dogs! I was never present to witness these spectacles firsthand since my husband sent me to my room after supper each night. I learned them from my maid, who repeated the gossip she'd heard from the palace servants.

I spotted the queen misbehaving one sunny afternoon while flaunting a ridiculously wide gown of yellow gauze festooned with pink satin roses. She strolled along the garden path, hand in hand with one of her many noble maids. At one point, she stopped and kissed the girl's lips. Naturally, I wondered if the queen also indulged in forbidden acts with her women as my Aunt Marguerite did with Lisette. Unlike the courtly wives who made cuckolds of their husbands, the queen could never take on a male lover because it was considered an act of outright treason against the crown—a serious crime punishable by death. The king would be more inclined to turn a blind eye to a dalliance with another woman.

I eventually arrived at the conclusion that my husband had cultivated his sexual perversions amongst the members of the aristocracy. Everything short of bestiality was openly practiced in the French court—and I had my doubts about that, too.

I enjoyed a small personal victory during dinner one evening. An elderly man seated beside me insisted on carrying on a conversation. I looked to my husband, who discreetly nodded in consent under the extenuating circumstance. After being given permission to speak with a member of the opposite sex, I eagerly discussed various books and the authors who penned them. We talked of classic literature and philosophy, then exchanged opinions on the contemporary satirist, Voltaire.

The old man eventually turned to my husband and said, "I'm sorry that I've not had the pleasure of meeting your lovely wife sooner, Your Grace. I'm assuming this is her first time at Versailles?"

"Yes," the duke replied, taking my hand and caressing my knuckles. "We were married quite recently."

"Well, I congratulate you both. The duchess is not only intelligent, she is delightful, and we hope to see more of her in the future."

My husband attempted a smile. "Thank you."

The old man lowered his voice and added, "Your wife is a refreshing change from the other ladies who are constantly trying to impress us with their sharp wit." He rolled his eyes and shook his head. Turning to me, he asked, "Tell me, what part of the palace has left you with the greatest impression?"

"The gardens are lovely," I replied hesitantly, for I had seen little of Versailles.

"Lovelier than the Hall of Mirrors?" When I did not reply, the old man narrowed his eyes at me. "Oh, don't tell me you haven't visited the most famous part of the palace."

The duke interjected, "I was planning to give my wife a tour this evening when the candles were lit."

"Ah, very good," the old man said with a nod. "You will enjoy that, my lady. I'll be sure to ask you again which part of Versailles impresses you most the next time we meet."

I looked down at my plate and tried not to smile. A double victory! True to his word, the duke took me to see the incredible Hall of Mirrors later that night. The long room flaunted gleaming parquet floors and painted ceilings from which hung many grandiose crystal chandeliers. Floor to ceiling windows ran along one of the walls, affording a view of the moonlit gardens. The opposite wall had the same floor to ceiling window frames set with mirrors instead of glass panes. The mirrors reflected brilliant sunlight by day, but at night they reflected glittering chandeliers and hundreds of lit candles, creating a magical wonderland.

I sighed, enchanted. "This is incredible." I wanted to dance and twirl under the chandeliers, but I knew better than to indulge in such an act.

"Indeed it is. Now you'll know the correct answer to the old fool's question the next time he asks you," my husband said. His eyes strayed to a group of women chatting gaily in the far corner. "Come along, now."

"Not yet, please."

He frowned impatiently. I wanted to stay a bit longer to admire the gorgeous room, but my husband had other plans for the evening—none that included me, of course. One of the ladies smiled at him, licking her painted upper lip slowly. She quickly fluttered her fan near her face so that only her dark eyes were visible. The duke chuckled softly and nodded at the woman. He hastily escorted me back to my room before continuing his merriment.

I stretched out on the bed and revisited the Hall of Mirrors in my mind, recalling how the candlelight made the gilded mirrors sparkle like liquid gold. What an amazing place! I tried to imagine what life would be like living in Versailles, but it was simply too grand for my imagination.

On the fourth day I was finally presented to my monarch. Louis XVI's face expressed pure boredom as he regarded me from head to toe. I curtsied the way my husband had taught me, then waited to be dismissed by a wave of the royal hand. I remembered to walk backward so as not to show my backside to the king, which was considered disrespectful.

"Well done," the duke whispered as if speaking to a dog.

The Duke of Burgundy invited my husband to go hunting, which meant that he would not return until dinner. Forbidden from wandering the grounds unaccompanied, I had no choice but to wait for him in my room.

No sooner had the duke departed than a note arrived demanding my presence—signed by the king himself! Unsure of what to do, I paced the room for several minutes. Finally, I decided to obey the summons since I really had no choice in the matter. After all, king trumped husband. I sent my maid on an elaborate errand, providing her with a long list of items that would be difficult to find at the local market. Hopefully, it would buy me a few hours.

The page who had delivered the message waited patiently for me, then led me through a secret passageway into a beautiful chamber decked with gilded sofas upholstered in plush red velvet. I was told to sit and wait.

What could the king possibly want with me?

I stood and curtsied low to the ground when he finally graced me with his royal presence. "Your Majesty."

"Rise."

I stood but kept my eyes focused on the carpet.

"Do you know why I have summoned you, my lady?" When I shook my head, he replied matter-of-factly, "I find you attractive. Does that not please you?"

I nodded in response. My husband was going to kill me.

"My old tutor commented on your intelligence and passion for books. Apparently, he enjoyed conversing with you during dinner. It's not often that he's impressed with a courtier. His assessment of you sparked my curiosity."

My head swam. "I am humbled by your flattery, sire."

"Are you a good and obedient wife to your husband?"

I wrung my hands together. "I try to be."

"Have you ever deceived him in any way?"

"Never."

"A loyal wife. What a rare oddity," he said, more to himself than to me. "What if I wanted you to deceive him?"

My head snapped up to look at him. "Your Majesty?"

"What if I asked you to betray your husband?"

I searched my mind for a suitable answer. Finally, I said, "You are my king. I will obey you—even if it's to my ruin."

"Do you honestly believe that obeying me would put you in such danger?"

"I do."

He nodded slowly in understanding. "Ah, that's why I never see you in the evening. The duke keeps you hidden under lock and key."

"Yes."

"Hoarding treasure is selfish, do you not agree?"

"If you say so, sire."

"I do indeed say so. I command you to keep me company this afternoon while your husband is away. He will never be the wiser, I promise. It will be our secret. Agreed?" I stared at him in disbelief, then nodded reluctantly. He continued, "Good. I

47

am willing to bet that you have never been kissed by a member of royalty, much less a king."

"Never," I admitted.

The king bent his head and kissed my lips. The act was neither pleasant nor unpleasant. He must have been drinking only a moment ago, for his mouth tasted of wine.

"Mmm, pleasant. I would have you, my lady." Then, he added out of mere formality, "If it please you."

I had no choice but to nod in consent—to do otherwise would be an affront to my monarch. He proceeded to undress me with nimble fingers that were obviously well-accustomed to removing female garments.

"Your skin resembles smooth, freshly churned butter," he commented, obviously pleased. "Kiss me again."

I obeyed before he led me to the bed and mounted me. I remained silent and submissive as he repeatedly thrust his cock into me, grunting with the effort as he did so.

"That feels good," he moaned, the sweat forming on his brow as he increased his speed.

I felt smothered beneath his considerable weight. The king owed his corpulence to a fondness for sweet treats and pastries. When he bucked against me hastily, I knew the unpleasant ordeal would be over soon. I took care to hide my relief.

"I'm rather disappointed, my lady," he said breathlessly after taking his pleasure. "I had the impression that you'd be a much more willing and passionate participant."

I looked away in mortification. "Forgive me."

He rolled off of me and rose from the bed. "I assume your husband is your first and only lover?"

"Yes."

"What a terrible, terrible waste." He wandered over to a desk, extracted a tiny pouch, and placed it in my hand. "This is for you. Consider it a token of my gratitude and admiration."

To my surprise, he gifted me a pearl. "Thank you."

"I wish you well, my lady," he said over his shoulder before vacating the chamber.

I dressed as hastily and best as I could without the help of a servant. The same page led me back to my room. Thankfully, my maid had not yet returned. Perching on the edge of the bed, I stared at the pearl. Payment for a whore's work. I hurled the precious jewel against the wall as a sob escaped my lips. I decided in that moment that I hated men—and I hated my father most of all for having married me off to a monster.

I feared the guilt could be read on my face when the duke returned later that day. In high spirits after taking down a stag, he barely noticed me. Relief washed over me when he announced our imminent departure.

***

Time passed slowly in Annecy. The duke visited my bed regularly during the first two years of our marriage. When I finally became pregnant, he stopped his nocturnal visits and took on a mistress. Far from jealous, I welcomed the respite and relished having my nights to myself. Fate proved unkind, and I lost the baby during my third month. To make matters worse, it had been male.

A week after my miscarriage, the duke began frequenting my bed. I would often hear lectures on the importance of producing a male heir. Sometimes, his harsh words were accompanied by beatings. He once blamed me for the baby's death, accusing me of harming myself in order to spite him. This hurt me, for I deeply desired a child to love.

Rumors spread quickly and the villagers soon eyed me with suspicion. I heard their spiteful whispers when I passed them on the street. They were unsympathetic toward my plight and offered no comfort. Needless to say, this saddened me and I wore my unhappiness like a heavy cloak around my shoulders.

I thought of Aunt Marguerite often, and wished more than anything to see her again. I begged my husband's permission to pay her a visit, and he promptly denied my request. According to him, married women should not pine for the days of their carefree youth, but should turn to God and become dutiful wives that bear sons. He then beat me as he violated me. I decided to end my life that day, but lacked the courage to do so. Instead, I wept throughout the night.

CHAPTER 5

"Adventure is worthwhile."
(Aesop)

A few months after I turned twenty, we received a royal invitation to the king's birthday celebration. The event was to be held in late August, so the royal court would already be comfortably installed at Versailles.

I had several gowns by now—more than most noble ladies—but the duke's pride and vanity depended on maintaining the appearance of lavish wealth. For this reason, the seamstress was summoned to create a new gown for me.

The better part of my summer days were spent poring over various sketches and fabrics, but still I managed to ride my horse in the woods. Sometimes, I even stripped and dove into the cold water of the lake. This risky new adventure required that I never stay away too long for fear of being caught. I savored those precious refreshing moments, swimming alone and naked under the hot summer sun.

A few days before our departure to Versailles, I rode down to the lake for a quick swim. I have always been cautious in the past but the eerie silence didn't feel right. Suddenly, I smelled it…a noxious odor that reminded me of cat urine blended with church incense. Ever since my pregnancy, my sense of smell had intensified to the point of becoming a nuisance. I picked up the slightest scents from unusual distances.

Quietly dismounting, I sniffed the air around me. Tracking the odor to the water, I stepped gingerly over wildflowers and the thick green undergrowth beneath my feet. The scent grew ever more pungent as I neared the lake. My head spun toward the sound of a twig being snapped underfoot.

A pair of frightened amber eyes met mine. It was a boy, no more than eleven or twelve years old. His hair fell in smooth black locks across a pale forehead. To my astonishment, the odor came from his body.

"Who are you?" I demanded. "And what is that smell?"

The boy's eyes widened in fear. The sound of another twig snapped and he turned to look over his shoulder at a cluster of ancient ivy-covered trees. Something hid in the woods. *Something dangerous*. The boy slowly met my gaze. Neither of us could see nor hear the predator, but we could feel it. The tiny hairs at the nape of my neck prickled as my heart raced.

Keeping his body perfectly still, the boy brought his finger to his lips to silence me. For some reason, this made me feel inexplicably afraid. There were strange markings on his clothes—symbols that I couldn't decipher—and he possessed a feral quality that made me uneasy.

Suddenly, a flock of black birds shot up into the sky. The boy took off in the opposite direction like an arrow being shot from a bow. I had never seen anyone move that fast. Wasting no time, I mounted my horse and urged the animal back to the chateau at full speed. When I heard the boy's blood-curdling scream in the distance, I almost fainted with terror.

I shed tears of relief when my horse exited the forest and galloped onto the open field. If anyone tried to pursue me, my husband's men would fire their muskets and crossbows at the assailant. The gates of the castle opened to receive me, and I swooned upon entering through them. Seeing me slumped over my horse's neck, one of the guards ran forward, totally disregarding the duke's strict rule about interacting with his wife.

The kind man helped me to dismount. "Are you all right, my lady?"

My maid ran out to assist me. Shooing the man away, she put her arm around my shoulders and led me inside. "Your Grace, tell me what ails you?"

"Something in the woods," I replied. "I think…it may be a dangerous animal."

She shook her head in dismay. "There are bears and wolves in these parts. You must be vigilant at all times."

51

I looked over my shoulder. "The duke must not know about this. I don't want him to worry."

She looked at me incredulously. "The men will inform him."

And so will you. I bit my lower lip. "Of course, they will."

She opened the door of my chamber and urged me inside. I went to the window and stared out across the field to the forest beyond. I wondered what could have been hiding in the trees, and what could have made the boy scream. I shuddered at the memory of the sound.

"Wine, my lady?" I nodded and watched as she poured red wine into a chalice. "You look like you've seen a ghost."

"I heard a child screaming in the woods while I was out riding...I can still hear him." I couldn't tell her the whole truth since it would incriminate me.

"A child?" she repeated, handing me the chalice.

"I think he was being attacked by something."

My maid stared at me and said nothing.

Later, the duke questioned me during dinner.

I repeated the watered down version of my story, then added, "My maid said there are wolves and bears in the area."

He snorted derisively. "What does that stupid girl know of wolves and bears? Gypsies are a different story, however. Loathsome, filthy people who will slit your throat in the blink of an eye to steal the gown off your back."

I swallowed hard. "Gypsies?"

He wiped his mouth with a lace-edged napkin. "Are you daft, woman? Yes, gypsies."

He watched me while chewing. I stared down at my plate and pushed the food around with my fork. "I thought it was perhaps an animal..."

"Animals, gypsies—both are dangerous. I forbid you from riding in the woods. You may ride in the open field and the forest's edge, keeping within sight of the castle."

Riding in the woods was one of the few pleasures I still enjoyed in my miserable life. Devastated, I said, "Please—"

"Do not question my authority." He motioned for a servant to refill our goblets. "And if I hear that you have disobeyed me,

I'll beat you as hard as that insolent guard was beaten this afternoon for daring to touch you."

Horrified that a man would be punished for merely expressing concern and helping me dismount, I turned my face to the side. I didn't want the duke to see my reaction. The servant refilling my glass met my eyes for a moment, then lowered his gaze. No one dared speak ill of the duke, but the contempt that many felt toward him was almost palpable.

We left for Versailles a few days later, and I was happy for the distraction. During the long ride, the duke filled my ears with advice and admonitions. I only pretended to pay attention. I couldn't stop thinking about the boy…the sound of his scream would haunt me forever.

"Are you listening?" the duke demanded, breaking into my thoughts.

"Yes," I lied.

I was already prepared for the grandeur of Versailles, and didn't make a spectacle of myself as I had the last time. I accompanied my husband to our guestroom, which was as lovely as the one we stayed in during our prior visit.

The duke announced, "I'm leaving, but you are to remain here." Turning to my maid, he added, "Be sure the duchess looks her very best—her hair and jewelry must be perfect."

She curtsied. "Yes, Your Grace."

To me, he warned, "Everyone will be here tonight."

He turned on his heel and walked out of the room. My maid unpacked my things while I stared out the window. This time we were afforded the view of a magnificent fountain and a row of statues. Dark clouds gathered in the sky above, and the first tentative drops of rain spattered against the glass panes.

My maid held up my new gown and smoothed the folds of fabric. I looked over my shoulder and admired the seamstress's handiwork. Lightweight cream silk with an undulating floral print in the palest shade of periwinkle, the gown was a work of art. The silver thread embroidery along the hem, sleeves, and bodice only added to its elegance.

"Set out my diamond choker," I instructed.

I turned my attention back to the window and noticed a group of four men hurrying along one of the pebbled paths. They must have gone out for a walk in the gardens and were heading back inside to escape the oncoming rainstorm. One of the men stood out in stark contrast to the others. Exceptionally tall and broad shouldered, his honeyed skin and facial features were quite exotic. His lashes and brows were so dark that I could make them out clearly from a distance. Beneath his tricorn hat he wore a formal white wig, and his luxurious black clothing reflected considerable wealth. While his gaze was focused straight ahead, his three companions were staring up at him, floundering like puppies seeking attention from their master.

The moment they passed my window, the mysterious man turned his head and captured my gaze. His smoldering dark eyes burned into mine with intimate familiarity. Modesty demanded that I turn away from his direct stare, but I couldn't move. Something about the man made me wary, yet I found myself being inexplicably drawn to him. The link between us was lost the moment he looked away. Reaching for my fan, I leaned against the wall while panting for breath.

"What's wrong?" my maid asked from across the room.

"Nothing," I replied, fanning myself. "Only the heat."

"Shall I draw you a cool bath, my lady?"

I glanced at the shiny brass clock on the granite mantle above the fireplace. "Yes, please."

The summer storm was intense but brief. The twilight sky promised a lovely evening. My husband arrived at the chamber in order to escort me to the festivities. Looking me up and down, he nodded in approval at my appearance. My hair, piled high with carefully curled locks, cascaded down my left shoulder. Tiny opals were set in the curls to compliment my golden highlights, and the jewels at my throat sparkled like stars.

Rather than dine indoors, the king had opted to take his birthday celebration outside. The storm had washed away the dust and heat, making the air cool and refreshing. Dozens of lanterns were strategically strung from the trees, bathing the garden in golden light. Banquet tables strewn with summer blossoms were set up around a fountain full of sinewy nymphs. Musicians played beside a large area reserved for dancing and socializing, while acrobats in riotous costumes performed daring acts.

I spotted the queen in the distance, and her gown was impossible to ignore. Fashioned from bright gold satin, the paniers were so wide that only an outdoor event could possibly accommodate them. I wondered how many yards of fabric were needed to create such an extravagant gown. The price would no doubt feed a peasant family for a year.

The queen's hair was also a sight to behold. Covered in flour paste and pomade, the powdered coiffure stood over two feet in height. Silk roses, pearls, feathers and even stuffed yellow canaries were nestled within the curls and carefully placed love locks. It must have taken several hours—if not the entire day—to complete such an elaborate creation. Many ladies openly admired the queen's appearance, but I found it rather vulgar.

"Stop staring at the queen, you fool," the duke admonished under his breath while gripping my arm.

"Sorry," I whispered, dropping my gaze. "It's just that her dress...her hair..."

"Our queen is the epitome of good taste and elegance, so I can't blame you for staring." Loosening his grip, he added, "Learn to be more discreet in the future."

"Your Grace."

We both turned around to look at the gentleman who had addressed my husband. I recognized the courtier and smiled slightly when he brought my knuckles to his lips. The only time I was allowed contact with a member of the opposite sex was when etiquette demanded it of me.

"Dear lady," he said. "I hope you can spare your husband for a moment."

I placed my fan up to my chin and lowered my eyes in acquiescence. The duke gave me a warning look before leaving me alone. I watched as they walked toward a group of elegantly dressed noblemen.

A moment later, a page called out, "The queen!"

I curtsied as the queen passed close to me with her ladies in tow. Once again, my uncanny sense of smell picked up various scents as the retinue of silk and satin paraded past my nose: lilac, orange water, lavender, patchouli, and...

My head jerked up as my nose wrinkled in protest. It was the same unusual odor emitted by the boy in the woods. I followed the last woman who sauntered past me, discreetly sniffing the air. The woman turned around and a pair of bewildered amber eyes met mine.

"Good evening, my lady," I said amicably. "If I may say, your perfume is very...unique."

To my surprise, she appeared anxious. "Oh?"

The cloying odor took residence within my nose, constricting my throat in the process. "I detect sweet incense and something else..."

The woman's eyes darted around nervously, then fixed on something over my shoulder. I turned around and noticed the mysterious man that I had spotted outside my window earlier. He stared directly at us, filling me with that strange mixture of fear and excitement.

"Please excuse me," the woman said, obviously upset.

She ran to a side door leading into the palace. Had I offended her with my comment? To my surprise, the mysterious man ran after the odiferous lady. Was he her lover or her husband?

A servant carrying a tray of crystal flutes filled with champagne stopped to offer me one. I drank it too quickly on an empty stomach, and it went straight to my head. Another servant came by to take the empty flute and offer me a full one. I hesitated before accepting it, then took a sip, savoring the way the tiny bubbles tickled my tongue.

I spotted an empty stone bench beside a rose bush and walked toward it. The sound of my feet crunching over the tiny pebbles became louder as I drifted away from the music and revelry. The scent of jasmine filled the warm night air, and I found myself smiling. A delicious warmth spread throughout my body and my head spun slightly from the champagne. A large figure loomed unexpectedly on the path and we collided. I felt the iron grip of a cold, large hand upon my arm.

"Forgive me, my lady," said a deep male voice.

Despite being foreign, he spoke perfect French. The strength and power emanating from his impressive body made my knees weak. His dark eyes glittered like obsidian, and his sensuous mouth drew my gaze. I couldn't help imagining what those full lips would feel like upon my skin. My cheeks burned as I dropped my gaze—for the first time in my life, I entertained a lustful thought.

"No, sir, it is I who should watch where I tread."

The man bowed before me in a gallant gesture. I glimpsed white, sharp teeth as he smiled at me. I chided my overactive imagination and made a mental note to not drink anymore tonight.

"A beautiful woman is never at fault," he said silkily.

Due to my slightly inebriated state, I blurted out, "I'm sorry if I upset your—wife? I asked about her unusual perfume and I think she got offended."

His eyes lit up in approval, and an expression of satisfaction settled upon his features. "Unusual perfume?"

"It smelled of incense and…I cannot put my finger on it," I lied. How could I possibly tell him that she reeked of cat urine?

Be quiet, Angelique, you're drunk.

"I have no wife, my lady," he replied, looking at me in a way that would make a maiden blush.

Flustered, I flicked open my fan. "Oh."

"Rest assured, there was no harm done. Now, if you will excuse me?"

He inclined his head before departing, leaving me in a state of agitation. I admired the outline of his shoulders beneath the finely tailored black coat as he walked away.

I sat down, then noticed my husband watching me steadily through narrowed eyes. My heart sank in that instant. Had he witnessed the entire interaction between me and the handsome stranger? As if reading my mind, the duke slowly inclined his head at me and pursed his lips. Eventually, he broke away from the group and came to claim me in order for us to take our seats at the banquet table. I glanced around discreetly, but *he* was nowhere in sight.

The meal was marvelous. Delicate soups, poached fish, roasted fowl, vegetable soufflé as light as air; dishes that were visually pleasing as well as delicious. The fine wines flowed freely as we enjoyed spectacular entertainment. The desserts were as impressive as the previous courses. Fruit salads soaked in sweet wine, creamy vanilla custards, and towering cakes dripping with decadent icing.

I overheard the courtier beside me make a comment about the exorbitant cost of the king's birthday feast while his subjects starved to death. My husband stiffened beside me as he glared reprovingly at the man. Being a member of the French aristocracy, the Duke of Annecy supported the monarchy. My husband's loathing of the common people and their cause was evident in everything he said and did. I, on the other hand, secretly sympathized with the peasants and their plight.

The celebratory meal ended with a spectacular display of fireworks, then the queen invited everyone to dance and make merry for the king's pleasure. My husband usually escorted me to my room after the meal, but I was allowed to participate. The duke and I danced together for the first time, and I was pleasantly surprised at his skill. People eventually stopped dancing to play cards and silly drinking games, so the duke escorted me to our chamber where I read until I fell asleep.

A chair toppling to the floor startled me from my slumber. I heard the duke cursing into the darkness as he continued stumbling across the room. I held my breath and didn't move, hoping that he would leave me alone.

He lit a few candles. "Wake up, wife."

I continued to feign sleep, but it didn't deter him in the slightest. He grabbed a fistful of my hair and pulled my head off the pillow. I cried out in pain and met his eyes. His face was red and blotchy.

"Time to learn a new game," he said, placing the candelabra on the bedside table.

This usually meant he wanted to try a new perversion.

"You must be tired…it's late, get some sleep."

He took off his shirt as I pleaded a headache, but it was of no use. He removed the remainder of his clothing before yanking up the hem of my flimsy cotton shift and mounting me. Placing both of my hands around his throat, he insisted that I choke him.

"*What?*" I was the one who usually got hurt, not him.

"You heard me, you stupid girl. I want you to squeeze my throat while I fuck you."

Dumbfounded, I tightened my hold around his neck.

He slapped me across the face. "Squeeze harder!"

The duke had grown corpulent in the last year and his neck proved far too thick for my small, slender hands. Incapable of playing the game to his liking, I braced myself for his anger.

Pinning my wrists above my head, he said, "You spoke to a man this evening."

I noticed a thin line of drool sliding down his chin, and tried hard not to cringe away in disgust.

"You smiled at him, too. Is he your lover?" When I shook my head, he added, "I saw you, so don't bother to deny it!"

"I ran into a man accidentally in the garden, but—"

"Whore!" Spittle sprayed into my eyes and his breath was rank with alcohol. "Play my game and I will not beat you again." He chuckled, adding, "At least not tonight."

If I had the power to kill him in that moment, I would have done so. *Gladly*. "You disgust me," I said, surprising us both. It was the first time I had ever stood up to him.

"How dare you?!"

Outraged, he began to strangle me in earnest. My husband was not only perverted, he was insane. Would he dump my dead body into one of the many fountains of Versailles? I tried to claw at his hands, tried to wriggle from beneath his weight, but it was useless. He was much stronger than me.

As my air supply became precariously low, I grew dizzy. I could hear my aunt's warnings '*Be wary…be careful.*'

To my amazement, I began to hallucinate. The mysterious

man I had met in the garden earlier flew in through the open window of the bedchamber. I squeezed my eyes shut and opened them again. No longer wearing a black tricorn hat or a wig, he exposed his smooth bald head. The perfect features I had admired earlier in the evening were now arranged into a mask of fury. He growled like a wild animal, opening his mouth wide enough to reveal frighteningly sharp teeth.

My husband turned around and frowned at the intruder. "What the devil—?"

I noticed a thick stream of blood running down the duke's cheek. Had the man struck the duke? He moved impossibly fast. The intruder then did something so shockingly vile that I gasped aloud in horror. He sunk his teeth into my husband's throat! Terrified, I squeezed my eyes shut and turned my head as I struggled to free myself from beneath the duke's weight. I felt the splatter of hot liquid on my face and arms—*blood*. When I opened my eyes again, I saw the man coming toward me. I glimpsed his sharp fangs just before I fainted.

***

Velvety darkness consumed me. A strange buzzing filled my ears and I was overcome by a total sense of disorientation. My limbs were heavy, as if they were made of lead. I couldn't move or speak...*Was I dead?*

Something found its way into my mouth and pressed against my tongue. I wrinkled my nose against the metallic tang of blood as I suckled something cold. Gradually, I regained my strength and managed to open my eyes. The man smiled slightly as he retracted his finger from my mouth and slowly traced my bottom lip with it. To my surprise, my tongue darted out to greedily lick the last drop of blood from his fingertip.

A tingling warmth spread throughout my body as my mind cleared itself of the cobwebs. I felt relaxed and happy. No—I felt euphoric. Sighing contentedly, I closed my eyes and drowned in pure bliss.

The wonderful feeling dissipated quickly, only to be replaced by a severe rawness in my throat. The pain, tolerable at first, gradually increased to an excruciating throb. My entire body felt like it was engulfed by flames. Was I in Hell? Had my husband's evil perversions landed me this eternal punishment?

My eyes fluttered shut in concentration as I frantically searched my mind for the sweet oblivion that I had enjoyed only moments beforehand. I silently screamed in agony over and over again inside my head. A blinding white light exploded behind my eyes. Everything came to a violent, screeching halt—including the beating of my heart.

The abrupt deafening silence came with great relief. I raised myself on my elbows and looked around the room. The world around me was outlined with unnaturally sharp clarity. My eyes picked out the dust motes floating in the firelight, the individual threads on the coverlet—I could even make out the seams of gold leaf on the gilded frame hanging on the far wall!

My ears prickled at my new capacity for hearing, too. I heard a symphony of crickets, but not the ones below my window. The crickets I heard were deep within the forest, miles away from the palace. I gasped at this realization. Was I a spirit now, no longer made of flesh and bone?

"Angelique."

A deep, melodious voice uttered my name. My sharp eyes turned in the direction of the sound. Divested of his black coat, the man stood at the foot of my bed wearing an open linen shirt and snug black breeches. A heavy gold chain hung from his muscular neck flaunting a round medallion with strange markings. Masculine gold rings with gemstones adorned his long, tapered fingers. He was breathtaking.

Breathless, I inquired, "How do you know my name?"

"I know many things."

"Who are you?"

"I am Arsham of Persia, second son of King Amir."

A prince! "Arsham," I repeated the unusual name in a tone of wonder. "What does it mean?"

"In my native tongue, it means 'very powerful one.' "

I sat up in my bed and noticed that Arsham had covered my nakedness with a bed sheet. Grateful for this small courtesy, I inquired, "What happened to me?"

"You have been reborn." At my puzzled expression, he added, "Do you not feel *alive*—more than you could ever imagine?"

"Yes."

He looked smug. "Consider it a gift."

Our eyes locked, and the lust I had experienced earlier in the garden returned with an intensity that shocked me. I averted my gaze in modesty. "The duke...what happened to him?"

Arsham glanced down at the floor and sneered in disgust. "He is dead."

"Dead?" I repeated, stunned.

"I have done you a great service by slaying this filthy beast. He was unworthy of you, my lady."

I looked down and saw that my husband's throat was violently torn open. The Oriental rug beneath the corpse was saturated with his blood. With the exception of soldiers and surgeons, the majority of people were unprepared for the sight of such horrific carnage. I had never witnessed the slaughter of an animal, let alone a person. The duke lay vulnerable and exposed, which made this the most intimate moment my husband and I had ever shared in our short, detestable marriage. Arsham watched me closely. Despite the gruesomeness of the scene, I was oddly calm. In fact, I felt nothing but relief and found myself suppressing a bout of hysterical laughter.

I was free!

A grin stretched across my face. Out of the corner of my eye I saw Arsham's brow shoot upward. A sobering thought brought me back to the present, and my glee vanished as I met his eyes warily. "Will you now do the same to me?"

He pursed his lips in amusement. "One with a pure heart deserves eternal life, not death."

Eternal life...

Seized by burning thirst, I winced in pain. To my astonishment, the smell of my husband's blood made my mouth water. My arms were splattered with bright red droplets, so I began to lick the duke's blood off of my own skin.

"No," Arsham admonished, taking hold of my chin and

lifting my head upward. "Not like that."

He walked to the pitcher in the corner of the room and poured water onto a linen towel. He came back to the bed and washed the blood from my face, arms, and chest. When he had finished, he moved to pull the rope beside my bed.

"If you summon my maid she will alert the king's guards with her screams," I warned. "We'll both be hanged for the crime of murder."

Arsham chuckled softly, then placed his finger on my lips to silence me. "Hush, child."

A moment later my maid knocked. My gut clenched with apprehension as Arsham opened the door. The girl's eyes widened in surprise at the sight of him. I saw her gaze fall on my husband's corpse on the floor. She was about to scream, but Arsham held up his hand and stared deeply into her eyes. My maid's eyes glazed over. She wandered into the room in a trancelike state and passed the duke's dead body without comment. Arsham led her to the edge of the bed and sat her down between us. Opening his mouth against her soft skin, he revealed a set of sharp fangs. Sinking them into her neck, he began to slowly suck the blood from her vein. There was something sensual and primitive in his actions, and I desired to follow suit.

I put my fingers to my mouth and discovered that I also had a set of sharp fangs. The thought of piercing the girl's skin thrilled me to the core. My new teeth were aching to do it, too. My mind tried to protest against this vile deed, but my body wanted it so badly that I had to restrain myself from literally tearing open my maid's throat. I sunk my teeth into her firm skin, and hot blood shot into my mouth. Drunk with the desire for more, I sucked hard and drank thirstily.

Arsham pulled me back a second before the girl expired. "That's enough for now," he said in a tone of approval.

I liked the fact that he seemed pleased with me. "What are you?" I asked, licking my lips.

I already knew the answer. I had heard the rumors about demonic creatures that lurked in the night. Creatures that feasted on blood.

"I am the same as you are now." He watched me steadily, not moving. I, too, remained still. "Go ahead. Say it."

I whispered, "Vampire."

"You have no fear," he observed.

"No."

Arsham leaned closer, peering into my eyes. "They are the deepest shade of blue, like the midnight sky." He traced the curve of my cheek with his fingertip and commented, "You have the face of an angel." His features lit up with realization. "Do you know what you are?"

I shook my head. "Tell me."

"You are an *Ange de Nuit*—an Angel of Night. Your new surname from this day forth will be *de Nuit* because your eyes reflect the glorious night." He glanced down at the two dead bodies in the room. "Besides, your old surname will only draw unwanted attention."

"Angelique de Nuit," I said, testing my new name aloud.

"It suits you." He surveyed the room with a frown. "The king and queen know I plan to depart early, so they will be expecting my absence in the morning. You must come with me."

Everything was happening so fast! Rather than be frightened, I became giddy—ready to walk away from my old life and step into this strange, new one.

"Where will we go?" I asked.

"To my chateau in Paris. My children will meet me there soon, and they will want to meet you." He glanced down at the two dead bodies again. "We cannot leave things as they are now. Quickly, fetch me the gown you wore earlier this evening. The jewels, too."

Wrapping the sheet around my body, I got off the bed and headed for the armoire. We dressed my maid in my gown and jewels and threw her plain dress into the fire.

When we were done, he said, "You may not be ready to see what I'm about to do, so perhaps it would be best if you closed your eyes."

I went back to the bed and obeyed. I heard many strange

64

sounds as he moved around the room at impossible speed. Finally, I heard the unmistakable thud of something heavy being tossed into the fireplace.

I opened my eyes and gasped aloud. My headless maid lay on the floor beside my husband in a pool of dark red blood. The sickening stench of burning human hair and flesh permeated the room. A knife had been placed into my husband's hand, and the angle of his arm suggested that he had slit his own throat after decapitating his wife. The duke's servants would no doubt talk about their dead master's violent and perverted nature, thus providing a basis for the brutal crime. The Duke and Duchess of Annecy would go down in history as an ill-fated pair.

Brilliant.

"You approve?" he asked.

I nodded in response. "You said earlier that you wanted to introduce me to your children."

"Yes, you are now their sister."

I tilted my head to the side. "You consider me your child, then?"

"Yes, in a manner of speaking. You are my fledgling, my creation," he patiently explained.

"What do I call you? Father?"

He laughed; it was an enchanting and seductive sound. He placed the palm of his hand against my face. I nuzzled my cheek against it, relishing its strength and warmth. I had never been touched tenderly by any male before, and I was totally unprepared for the delicious effect it had on me.

He regarded me with a curious frown. "I am your lord and sire, and you will address me as such." His thumb caressed my cheek and the simple gesture made me sigh. "But something tells me I will be more to you than just that."

Closing the gap between us, he gently kissed my lips while his large hands massaged the nape of my neck. I moaned softly, which only made him deepen the kiss. His lips were coaxing, soft, sensual. My mouth opened to him and his tongue sought mine. When he tried to pull away from me, I clung to him. The gruesome carnage surrounding me should have made me want to flee, but I did not want him to stop.

"Wait here," he said, untangling my arms from his neck.

He got off the bed to listen at the door. When he returned, he removed his linen shirt, revealing his muscled chest and wide shoulders. Leather cuffs encased his thick wrists and he removed one of them. Unsheathing a dagger from his belt, he made a small cut in his flesh. He then held his arm out toward me, offering his blood. The deep red drops glistened against his honeyed skin like garnets.

"Drink," he said.

His eyes narrowed in pleasure as I placed my lips against the inside of his wrist and licked the precious ruby beads with my tongue. Arsham's blood mimicked liquid fire—far more delicious and potent than my maid's blood. When I latched onto his wrist and sucked hard, he gasped aloud. Instantly, every pore of my body radiated ecstasy.

"Only a little bit," he said, retrieving his hand after a few seconds. "My blood is very potent. After all, I am over seven hundred years old."

Astonished, I stared at him. He looked no older than twenty-five! His magic blood warmed my stomach before radiating throughout my limbs. In that moment I became the embodiment of energy, of power, of desire.

I was invincible and I wanted him.

For the first time in my life, I desired a man. Arsham read the expression in my eyes and understood. I watched in fascination as he removed his clothing—he resembled a perfect Greek statue. Lifting the bed sheet from my naked form, he eyed me with appreciation.

"Face of an angel, body of a goddess. You could tempt Satan himself," he said before joining me in bed.

I felt suddenly dwarfed by his close proximity. I trembled with excitement and fear.

"Do not be afraid of me," he whispered.

"I cannot help it, my lord," I admitted. "The duke…"

Arsham placed his finger on my lips to silence me. "There is no need to mention that monster now. I won't hurt you." His eyes swept over my body before meeting my gaze. "Despite being married, I believe you are still very much a virgin."

He lowered his head to kiss my throat and the warmth of his mouth on my skin made me arch against him. Chuckling softly at my naiveté, he took his time touching me. His hands slowly caressed every inch of my body in a way that made me ache inside. He kissed and suckled my breasts, then traced patterns upon my stomach with his hot tongue. I held my breath in anticipation when he heaved himself over me and forced my legs apart with his knee. Despite the immense size of his glistening manhood, it did not hurt me when I took him inside of my body. In fact, I relished the feel of his substantial weight upon me. He was patient with my lack of expertise, teaching me how I could be an active participant in the art of lovemaking. When we had established a rhythm that was pleasurable for both of us, my body came alive. I instinctively met his deep thrusts with eagerness, my hips rising and falling in tune to our own music. Now I understood why Lisette moaned as if in pain when my aunt pleasured her...this was indeed torture; the sweetest I had ever known. My hips moved faster as a new sense of urgency took over my body. Suddenly, I experienced a most delightful release—a climax that ended in an involuntary cry from my lips and a growl from Arsham's. His body convulsed then he collapsed on top of me after filling me with his seed. His breathing was hard and loud. I wrapped my arms around him and put my lips to his ear.

"Thank you," I whispered.

He pushed himself up on his elbows to look down at my face. "My lady, never thank a man for partaking of your sweetness. It is a precious gift."

"No one has ever touched me or spoken to me as you have."

He smiled in response to my words then got out of bed to dress. "We must hurry. The sun will come up in a few hours. Put on some clothes and say goodbye to your old life."

When I began to gather my precious jewels, he stopped me. "There is no need for that."

I let the jewels fall from my hands and quickly donned my

67

best gown. "I am ready."

He moved to jump out of the window, but I hesitated.

"You need not be afraid," he said while offering his hand. "I shall not let you fall."

I accepted his hand and we jumped. To my amazement, we fell to the ground like a pair of weightless feathers. I giggled when I landed on my toes.

"Hush, Angelique," he whispered with a conspiratorial smile. "We must not wake the servants. Come, my angel. We will fly into the night."

We moved with supernatural speed, and I grew heady from the thrill of it. I was now a creature of the night; fodder for fairytales that are meant to scare children.

CHAPTER 6

*"One who deceives will always find those who allow
themselves to be deceived."*
(Niccolò Machiavelli)

Arsham's chateau was a medieval stone fortress complete
with four rounded towers. Two walled courtyards boasted
pleasure gardens and impressive stone fountains. Strategically
located in a fertile valley, it allowed us to easily feed in Paris.
The chateau's interior boasted lavish furnishings along with
every comfort available to man. Unsurprisingly, Arsham had
accumulated great riches during the last seven centuries.
Having been born and raised within a powerful royal family, he
possessed refined taste and the ruthlessness to obtain whatever
he wanted in life.

Several vampires shared the chateau with Arsham, none of
whom had been directly sired by him. These "distant relations"
were the descendants of his progeny. Some lived there on a full-
time basis to maintain the property and care of our sire's needs.
Others, such as messengers, scribes, secretaries, solicitors, and
bankers, came and went with regular frequency. Much like a
beehive, everyone worked for the benefit of the coven.

I was Arsham's seventh child and, despite my youth, this
automatically made me an elder. Elders were the most elite
members within the coven, and we answered to no one except
our sire. The other vampires treated us with the greatest
reverence and respect, and sometimes tried to curry our favor. I
often pondered the wondrous fact that I went from being an
abused human wife to a high ranking-vampire in the blink of an
eye. I owed Arsham a great debt.

None of the vampires—not even elders—were allowed to
create progeny on a whim. Permission to sire must be sought,
and it would be refused or granted depending on the human's

attributes. All vampires were obliged to swear fealty to Arsham in order to join the coven, just as a serf would swear allegiance to his liege.

In addition to learning the ways of our kind, I embraced the night and shunned the day. The elegant Lady Moon became my new mistress as I discovered the solace and serene beauty of the darkness. My old tutor once said that color cannot exist in the absence of light. While that may be true for humans, it was not the case for vampires. I marveled at the array of colors my supernatural eyes perceived in the moonlight. Gilded in silver, these hues were no less vivid and lovely than what my mortal eyes had beheld by day.

Arsham not only made me feel welcome in his home, he provided me with the comforts to which I had grown accustomed in my human life. Lovely gowns, sparkling jewels, and a chamber fit for a queen were all mine to enjoy. While Arsham reveled in my newfound wonder at being a vampire, I reveled in him. My sire had become my lover, and I accepted his embrace each night with the utmost joy. My heart, body, and soul now belonged to him. I was in love for the first time in my life, and I wanted to scream his name from the rooftops of Paris.

***

The day before the annual meeting of the elders prompted a flurry of activity within the chateau. I stood in the corner as Arsham oversaw the preparations. He motioned me over with his hand, so I went to stand before him.

"Sire," I said, inclining my head.

"What's wrong, Angelique? You seem distressed."

"I confess, I'm nervous."

"Why?"

"What if the others don't like me?"

"Nonsense. Everyone will be enchanted by your charm."

A smiled slyly. "As you are?"

He playfully chucked me under the chin, yet his eyes remained hard. We stood in the throne room where the ceremony would take place tomorrow. A large fire burned in the hearth, more for show than for warmth since we never felt cold. I placed my hands on his chest as I stood on tiptoe to kiss his lips. Naturally, this drew the gaze of many.

He pushed me away, his eyes ablaze with indignation. "You dare to assume such familiarity with me in public?"

I staggered in shock as I recalled the intimate sexual acts we had engaged in the night before—acts which were far more familiar than a mere kiss. "I meant no disrespect, sire…"

He looked down his nose at me. "In this coven there are rules. Every member follows a certain protocol, including you. As an elder, you must lead by example."

I lowered my head in shame. "Of course, my lord."

"You are to show me respect and afford me the dignity befitting my status at all times, especially in the presence of others. Do you understand, Angelique?"

"Yes," I mumbled through a haze of tears.

Arsham sighed in frustration, then lifted my chin with his fingertip. "You are young and still learning our ways. Perhaps I have indulged you too much. I will show you mercy *this time*. Go, and return to me when you are worthy of my presence."

I hastily retreated from him. Once inside the privacy of my chamber, I wept and chided myself for being so careless. Of course there were rules to be followed! Arsham was correct; I had much to learn. I certainly didn't wish to make a fool of myself in front of the entire coven.

So why did I feel hurt and offended? Why did my heart hurt, too? After splashing cold water on my face, I applied a bit of rose oil to soften my skin and make it glow. Next, I smoothed my hair and changed into a fresh gown. I went in search of Arsham and found him seated upon his throne. He beckoned me forward with a flick of his wrist.

Hand-carved from rare teakwood and richly embellished with gold, ivory, and copper, the magnificent throne drew my gaze as I stood before him. Arsham leaned forward slightly and put out his hand. I sank to my knees and kissed the blood ruby upon his finger. The large gemstone represented sacred blood, the very essence of our existence. His children would greet him in the same manner tomorrow. *This* was the protocol.

71

"Forgive me for offending you earlier, sire," I said while still on my knees.

"You are forgiven."

After sunset on the following day, Arsham came to my chamber bearing a gift. He held up a midnight blue gown of luxurious satin with gold embroidery gracing the low neckline. "It would please me greatly if you wore this tonight at the ceremony. The blue matches the color of your eyes."

My first impulse was to throw my arms around his neck, but I refrained. "I am honored, my lord. I will wear it with great pleasure, thank you."

Arsham extracted a wooden box from his coat pocket. He flipped open the lid to reveal a stunning sapphire necklace on a bed of gold velvet.

I gasped in surprise. "How beautiful."

He fastened the necklace around my neck, then stepped back to admire it. "No kiss of gratitude?"

When I hesitated, he pulled me against his massive frame and kissed me hungrily, which left me breathless.

"I shall see you downstairs in an hour," he said before walking out of the room.

I donned the gown and admired my reflection. My firm breasts swelled over the plunging neckline and the full folds of the skirt flaunted my slim waist. The large sapphires at my throat glittered within their dark blue depths. I ventured to the main hall where Arsham, seated upon his throne, beckoned me to stand beside him on the dais.

Looking straight ahead, he said, "I want you to observe the ceremony so you can learn how to proceed in the future." He paused. "You look ravishing, Angelique."

"Thank you."

Every torch and candle had been lit to make the chateau glow like a beacon in the night. Window shutters were open to reveal the full moon and the expansive courtyard beyond. Everyone waited with baited breath.

The first vampire to arrive rode in on a mighty chestnut stallion. The horse must have been for show or for her pleasure since our supernatural abilities allowed us to fly. Arrayed in a breastplate of copper with a steel sword gleaming at her side, the fierce Norsewoman dismounted and entered the main hall. Two thick plaits of flaxen hair hung past her shoulders. Even from a distance I could see that her piercing eyes were ice blue.

Stopping several feet from Arsham, she inclined her head. "My lord and sire, how it gladdens my heart to see you again."

Arsham extended his hand. "Welcome, Erika."

Erika walked up to him, dropped to one knee, and kissed the ruby ring on his finger.

"Rise and meet your new sister," he said. "This is Angelique, the Duchess de Nuit."

Firmly grasping my hands, she kissed both of my cheeks. "Welcome to our family."

I smiled. "Thank you."

Erika's eyes held mine in a manner that made me blush.

"Such a pretty thing," she said before tossing me a wink.

Arsham chuckled. "Still sailing the fjords?"

She turned her attention to our sire. "Yes, my lord, and loving every minute of it."

"No official mate, yet? A strong male to guide you?"

"Never!"

"Ah, my wildling."

Erika looked at the other vampires, who inclined their heads respectfully in greeting at their elder. "Greetings from the northern seas, my brethren."

I gathered from the expressions of the others that Erika was well-liked and respected.

Her head whipped around sharply to stare out the window. "Valerio is here."

A swarthy man with a prominent nose and liquid brown eyes flew in through the window, landing gracefully on his elegantly shod feet. Such a dramatic entrance! He walked toward Arsham wearing a suit of pale green brocade with many sheer layers of starched white lace adorning his throat and cuffs. His red-heeled satin shoes were immaculately clean, and his black hair heavily powdered and carefully curled. He bowed with an elaborate wave of his hand, causing the numerous diamonds on his fingers to flash in the candlelight. I could smell his strong cologne from where I stood.

"Most illustrious sire, I am humbled in your presence," Valerio said in French heavily accented with Italian.

Arsham held out his hand. "Come forward, my son."

Valerio knelt and dutifully kissed our sire's ring. "You have added yet another beauty to our coven," he said with a glance in my direction.

"Angelique, this is Valerio."

Valerio bowed gallantly and kissed my hand. "Sorella."

"Fratello" I replied in Italian, liking him instantly.

His vermillion lips curved into a smile as he looked at Erika. "And you..."

They embraced, their mutual fondness apparent to all. I glanced at Arsham, who didn't seem to mind a bit of public affection when it took place between his children. Valerio blew a kiss to the other vampires. They must have been accustomed to his theatrics because no one seemed surprised in the least as they bowed their heads in respect.

Three more elders arrived at the same time: a set of fiery haired twins and a tall, lean man as black as pitch. The twins were Deirdre and Ciara from Ireland. They shared the same sharp, porcelain features and emerald eyes, and wore identical gowns of lavender silk embroidered with white roses. Omar hailed from Africa and wore a long robe the color of blood with onyx beads sewn along the hem. Like Arsham, his clean-shaven head made his noble features stand out. His feet were bare, but his ankles and wrists were wrapped with thick gold bands studded with colorful gemstones.

The three of them greeted Arsham before welcoming me into the coven. While Omar's greeting had been warm, the twins approached me with narrowed eyes and false smiles.

One of the twins whispered, "Is she the new favorite?"

Her sister rolled her eyes. "Don't be ridiculous."

Since I stood within earshot, I thought their exchange rude. Five vampires stood in a large semi-circle facing the throne.

"Is he here?" Erika whispered to Omar, her eyes darting around the enormous space.

"Not yet," he replied.

Suddenly, a hush fell over the crowd as all eyes turned toward the doorway. A tall, broad-shouldered figure wearing the long black robe of a Dominican friar entered through the open door. A hooded cowl hid most of his face. We watched in silence as he slowly approached Arsham.

I craned my neck to get a better look at this vampire who commanded so much attention.

The newcomer pushed back the cowl before kneeling and kissing Arsham's ring. His appearance garnered no reaction from the others, who were prepared, but I had to stifle my gasp.

"Rise, Micah," Arsham said softly.

Micah stood and turned to face his siblings, his expression somber. He inclined his head in greeting without saying a word or meeting anyone's eyes.

Arsham waved his hand in my direction. "Meet your new sister, Angelique."

Micah silently held my gaze for only a moment before joining the semi-circle. He didn't seem much older than me. I marveled at the pure whiteness of his skin and shorn hair. His eyes were pinkish red, like those of a white rabbit. I took in his prominent brow, high cheekbones, strong jaw, and well-shaped nose. Were it not for his abnormal coloring, he would have been attractive—even handsome.

Arsham rose from his throne and motioned for me to stand beside him as he faced his six children. "Angelique, you are now part of an amazing family. Erika is my oldest child, the first progeny that I ever created. A brave warrior princess, she had been left for dead on the battlefield after enemy Vikings raided her village. I came upon her by pure chance while exploring the northern territories."

"What a blessed day," Erika interjected. "Prince Arsham not only saved my life, he bestowed the gift of immortality upon me. I am forever grateful."

They shared a meaningful look before he continued, "I chose

Erika because I had never seen a woman fight with such ferocity and spirit. She is an expert on weaponry and skilled in the art of warfare." He moved on to where Micah stood. "I continued my travels westward until I came to a large island. While enjoying the countryside one balmy evening, I smelled smoke. I followed the scent to a monastery that had recently burned to the ground. It seemed that everyone had either died or fled, but I picked up the scent of fresh blood. Imagine my surprise when I found a semi-conscious albino in a cell barred from the outside. The interior of the cell was lined with precious books, scrolls, and the most remarkable illustrated manuscripts I had ever seen."

My expression must have registered confusion because Micah explained in a quiet, yet surprisingly deep voice, "Christian charity obliged the monks to care for abandoned infants, but they found my appearance offensive. They forced me to live in isolation, locked away from the others."

"You are looking the best manuscript illuminator in Christendom," Arsham interjected. "Micah is fluent in several languages, a respected philosopher, and a scholar. He is one of my most valuable assets."

Micah, obviously not comfortable with praise, kept silent as he stared down at the floor.

Arsham cleared his throat and continued, "I traveled southwest to another island, only smaller and very green. I heard rumors of two great healers in Ireland, so I sought them out. I chose Deirdre and Ciara for their knowledge of the natural world. They know everything there is to know about the forest; which plants are beneficial, which are poisonous, which will heal, and which will kill. We are not affected by such toxins or cures, but I am fascinated by flower lore nonetheless. My own human mother was a natural healer." He paused, savoring a childhood memory. "The twins were accused of witchcraft and sentenced to the gallows. I visited them in their holding cell the night before their sentences were to be carried out."

"The guards who came in to fetch us got the surprise of their lives the following day," said one of the twins—I could not tell them apart.

The other twin batted her eyelashes at Arsham and purred seductively, "We are eternally grateful to our beloved sire."

Arsham tenderly caressed her cheek, making me instantly jealous. "Omar was my fourth creation," he said, indicating the tall African who smiled at me with pearly white teeth. "I eventually bid the lovely twins farewell, and continued my journey south, traversing Spain into northern Africa. What a fascinating continent! I crossed the desert and lost myself in the wonders of the jungle. I happened to come across Omar while he was tracking a lion. Practically naked, he carried nothing but a small spear. I watched in awe as this mortal human stalked such large and dangerous prey without an ounce of fear in his heart. When the lion pounced on him, the spear broke, yet he remained unafraid."

"I was so angry that my spear broke," Omar admitted with a grin. "Prince Arsham could have let the lion tear me to shreds, but instead he took pity upon me."

"Nonsense, Omar. I chose you because of your fearless bravery. I have yet to come across your match."

Omar inclined his head at the compliment. "Thank you."

"Omar became the next chief in his tribe," Arsham explained. "When I tired of the jungle, I headed back north to the European continent, stopping in Sicily to enjoy the sea." He stood beside Valerio and placed a hand on his shoulder. "I came upon a busy square in Palermo where Valerio stood reciting the most inspiring poetry I have ever heard. I stopped to listen, as did countless other people. Valerio eventually began telling stories and jokes. It had been centuries since I'd laughed and enjoyed myself so much. The crowd continued to expand despite the late hour. Not surprisingly, people tossed several coins at his feet. I followed him home and saved him from the blade of a pickpocket. A talented man of such razor-sharp wit and humor did not deserve to die. I chose Valerio for my intellectual stimulation and amusement."

Valerio performed one of his theatrical bows for Arsham. "I am humbled by your words, my lord."

Arsham looked at me. "Valerio was my youngest child until

I created you, Angelique."

I became uncomfortably aware that every one of Arsham's children had been chosen for possessing special gifts. I was neither funny nor witty, I knew nothing of healing or fighting, and I would run away from a dog—let alone a lion.

Arsham came to stand beside me. "I am sure you are all wondering why I have chosen Angelique."

Six sets of gleaming vampire eyes stared at me in expectation.

"I doubt even she knows the reason." Arsham grinned and added, "Do you, child?"

"I do not, my lord," I confessed, slightly embarrassed.

I caught the twins glaring at me as Arsham placed his arm around my shoulders. "Angelique can detect shape-shifters."

This announcement was followed by a collective gasp and wide eyes from not only my siblings, but also from the coven members who had overheard him. I looked askance at Arsham—I had no idea what he was talking about.

He smiled at my confusion. "Do you remember our first meeting in the garden of Versailles?"

"Yes, of course."

"You detected a shape-shifter on that fateful night. She was posing as one of the queen's ladies. You commented on her strange perfume, and thought she was perhaps my wife."

The other vampires chuckled at the last part. "I remember it well, sire."

"You frightened the girl so much that she left the retinue and ran inside." He looked to the other vampires. "I caught up with the lady after she had fled into the palace. Sure enough, she was a feline shape shifter."

My brethren stared at me in awe.

"There was another occasion, too," Arsham said, giving me a knowing look. "A certain boy you encountered while you were out riding in Annecy."

I gasped, putting together the pieces of the puzzle. "The boy in the woods! That was you hiding behind the trees?"

Arsham nodded. "You are the reason I went to Versailles. I

tracked you for days and made my presence known to you when the perfect opportunity arose."

The perfect opportunity being when the duke tried to kill me.

"A mortal who can pick up the scent of shifters? I've never heard of such a thing," Omar said.

Erika smiled at me. "She was destined to be one of us."

Valerio added, "She can help us."

Micah stared at me silently wearing a strange expression.

I looked to Arsham and quietly inquired, "What is a shape shifter, my lord?"

The twins giggled at my ignorance.

Arsham pulled me aside while the others congregated to talk about me. "Shape shifters are enemies to our kind. Thankfully, they are not immortal, but they do age much slower than humans. There are three known varieties of these supernatural beings: feline, canine, and aviary. These creatures look like normal humans but can shift into a cat, a wolf, or a bird. The first two can be found in Europe, but the latter is rare, rumored to inhabit the most remote parts of Asia. Felines originated in Normandy and canines are believed to have originated in Russia."

People who can change into animals? How bizarre! "Why are they considered enemies?"

"Vampires and wolves have a tumultuous history. We have been fighting each other for centuries over a feud that existed long before my birth. We rarely run into them and, fortunately, our coven has never done anything to attract their attention. Unlike the canines, felines do not attack us directly because they are too weak."

"That's a good thing, is it not?"

"They are notorious for aiding slayers." At my confused expression, he added, "*Vampire* slayers. We've lost many vampires to them, especially within the last few decades."

"Can't we defend ourselves against these shape shifters?"

"They are virtually undetectable to us."

I frowned, confused. "Yet they can detect us."

"Correct. This is why you are such an important addition to

our clan. We need your skills, Angelique."

"My skills?" I repeated.

"To protect us. Do you understand?"

"I'll do my best to keep you and our coven safe," I said, suddenly feeling the weight of my new responsibility.

Arsham whispered, "I know you will." He turned around to face the others. "I'm happy to see my seven children gathered together under one roof. Tonight, we will enjoy one another's company and discuss whatever needs to be discussed, but first we hunt. Tomorrow night I shall greet your children."

Valerio held up his hand. "My lord, I have a question. Was Angelique saved from the clutches of death like the rest of us?"

Arsham nodded as his eyes slid to where I stood. "I saved her from being ravaged by a beast."

Valerio grinned knowingly. "Did you kill this beast?"

"I did indeed, with *great* pleasure."

I lowered my head in appreciation for his discretion.

We set off for Paris under the generous light of the full moon. I found hunting as a pack quite exhilarating. We were fast and strong, full of energy and excitement. Arsham insisted we dine on noble blood to celebrate our reunion, so we attacked a group of royal courtiers who had foolishly strayed too far from home on their moonlit stroll.

We returned to the chateau before dawn. I followed Arsham to his chamber as I have done each and every night since my arrival. Despite ridiculous rumors, we didn't sleep in coffins, but rather on beds inside heavily secured rooms impenetrable by light.

"No, my child," he said, barring the entrance to his room with his body. "Tonight you will sleep in your own bed."

Terribly disappointed and hurt, I did not dare question his direct command. Perhaps his mind weighed heavy and he needed time to alone. "Sleep well, sire."

The following night, five vampires arrived. Aside from myself, the only other vampire who had not yet created any progeny was Micah. These five children lived with their makers on a regular basis, and were required to visit Arsham yearly in order to pay their respects. They remained with us for one night then were promptly dismissed. Only Arsham's children remained since they had not yet been given leave to depart.

During the visit of the elders, I noticed their distinct personality traits. I quickly discerned that Micah preferred his own company to that of anyone else. I often spotted him in dimly lit corners, writing in a journal or reading from a book. I couldn't blame him for being antisocial. Being raised by cruel monks who lacked empathy and were incapable of displaying affection must have made for a sad childhood.

Omar and Valerio were quite social and seemed to get along well with each other. They were often engaged in conversation, and the twins would sometimes join them. These talks were generously sprinkled with laughter due to Valerio's wit and humor. Erika wasn't as antisocial as Micah, but she spoke very little. A silent observer, nothing escaped her notice.

Arsham still insisted that I sleep alone in my chamber. After refusing my company for three days in a row, I began to worry. His desire had always matched my own, so I assumed that my feelings were being reciprocated. By the fourth day I harbored doubts, so I crept out of my chamber and wandered down the dark hallways. The chateau blocked out sunlight so it resembled night at any hour of the day.

I missed being in the arms of my sire. I missed his touch, the taste of his mouth...*his blood*. I stopped at Arsham's chamber expecting to hear nothing but silence. Instead I heard the Irish twins giggling from within, and—judging by the erotic moans from Arsham's lips—the three of them were doing anything but sleeping.

Furious, I almost pounded on the door. Luckily, my good sense prevailed over my outrage. I took a step back to ponder my options. The sensuous moans coming from the other side of the door continued to torture me, and my eyes burned with tears. I ran from Arsham's chamber and almost collided with Valerio in the hallway.

"My lady," he said, noticing the tears streaming down my cheeks. "What ails you, dear sister?"

I shook my head, unable to speak. One of the twins sighed loudly in pleasure, which caused more tears to spill.

Valerio nodded as he eyed me knowingly. "Ah."

I sniffed. "I didn't know…"

"Hush, not here. Let's go somewhere more private."

He ushered me into his chamber and handed me a silk handkerchief to wipe my face.

"Thank you," I said.

Going to large armoire in the corner of the room, he extracted a bottle of wine. "Would you join me in a glass?"

"I thought we couldn't partake of food."

Valerio chuckled. "Wine is not food, my lady. It is the elixir of the gods. This particular vintage is mixed with blood in order to please our unique palates." He poured the velvety red liquid into a dainty crystal goblet. "Here, try some."

I accepted the wine and took a sip. It was delicious. "It's wonderful. Thank you, Valerio."

He took a sip from his own glass as he watched me closely. "You're in love with him."

There was no use denying it. "I am."

"Arsham has been entertaining the twins every night since their arrival."

"What?"

He pressed his lips together for a moment. "Obviously, you are not very experienced in the ways of this world."

"Or in the ways of love," I added resentfully.

He plucked at the delicate lace at his throat before adjusting the cuffs of his orange satin coat, which flaunted red flowers. "We all get our hearts broken at some point in life." He looked at me pointedly. "Every single one of us. The young are more susceptible than most, I'm afraid. I know exactly how you feel, for I also fell in love with Arsham when he first created me."

I processed this information as I took in his powdered face and kohl-lined eyes. A tiny black satin patch in the shape of a star adorned the lower corner of his carefully painted mouth. He brushed off a bit of lint from his shoulder and his movements were so calculated, so…feminine.

Of course. How did I not notice it before? "Did he return it?" I asked, accepting Arsham's bisexuality with an ease that surprised even myself.

Valerio smiled sadly at me. "Yes...for a little while. He eventually grew bored with Sicily—and with me. Arsham tires of places and people rather easily."

I took another sip of wine as I processed this sobering tidbit of information. "He obviously has not bored of the twins—and they are older than we are."

"Ah, but he sees them only once a year."

Arsham had been with me every night for several weeks. "But if you love someone, you naturally want to see them every day," I pointed out.

His eyes held mine. "Yes, if you truly love someone."

His words stung me. "He does not love me," I mused aloud.

Valerio pouted and shook his head slowly. "Not the way you love him, *cara*. Arsham loves you in a possessive, yet distant manner. The same way a nobleman loves his prized horses."

I set down my glass and stood. I could not hear anymore. "Thank you, Valerio, for the wine and for..." I could not finish my sentence due to a fresh onslaught of tears.

He smiled slightly and inclined his head at me.

I went into my chamber and locked the door. After my conversation with Valerio, I understood that Arsham could never be loyal to one person—to me. I did manage to finally fall asleep, but my dreams were disturbing. I kept hearing the erotic moans coming from Arsham's chamber in my head, and the graphic images my imagination conjured to go with those sounds were excruciatingly painful.

Erika's eyes were on me from the moment I descended into the main hall the following night. We greeted our sire and each other, then Arsham suggested that we hunt in pairs. Erika immediately chose me as her partner. We walked arm in arm into the night and gazed up at the moon.

When we were well out of earshot of the others, she leaned in close to me. "I saw you last night before you ran into Valerio and went into his room."

83

"So you know about Arsham and the twins," I said, cutting to the chase.

"He likes them, he always has." She paused to gauge my reaction before adding, "It amuses him to have them both at the same time."

"I am a stupid fool," I said, irritated with myself.

"No, Angelique," she countered, placing her arm around me in a sisterly manner. "You are young and inexperienced. Arsham will break your heart, but you'll thank him for it later. Life's lessons are never easy, but they make us strong and resilient. They build character."

"Were you in love with him, too?"

"I love Arsham like I did my human father. I have nothing but contempt for men. Arsham knows it, too, which is why he teases me about finding a mate."

"He never…?"

Erika chuckled softly and shook her head. "I pledged my virginity to the goddess, Freya, when I was twelve years old. Several years later I met someone who made me break that vow."

"A man?"

"A woman. You met her on the second day when the progeny of elders came to the chateau. She is my child, Birsa."

I remembered the quiet, dark haired girl who stood by Erika's side. "She is lovely. My Aunt Marguerite also preferred the company of women."

Erika smiled. "You're beautiful and sensuous, Angelique. It's no wonder our sire has made you his lover."

"I'm no longer in his favor," I admitted sadly.

She laughed. "I may lack sexual experience with men, but I've been observing them for a few centuries now. I know how they think."

"Oh?"

"Arsham is getting his fill of the twins while he can. He will summon you the moment they leave."

"Do you really think so?" I asked hopefully.

"I know so, my dear." She paused, eyeing me steadily.

"Would you like a little piece of advice from your older sister?"

"Yes, please."

Erika's face grew serious and her eyes were hard. "Use this time away from Arsham wisely. Heal your heart and make it strong. Learn to love yourself and your own company. Never again give in to a man so easily."

It was excellent advice—much easier said than done. "I will try to do as you say. Thank you, Erika."

"I expect to see great changes in you the next time we meet."

I thought about her words as we stalked the night for prey.

***

The day before Arsham dismissed the elders, I decided to hunt alone. I heard footsteps in the garden and turned to see a tall hooded figure. It was Micah.

"May I have a word, my lady?" he asked softly.

I hadn't seen him speak to anyone since his arrival, so his request surprised me. We wandered to the far end of the garden and sat upon the edge of a stone fountain. His hood slipped and he quickly pulled it forward to hide his face.

"Forgive me," he whispered.

Filled with compassion, I said, "There's nothing to forgive."

He handed me a small book. "I've been doing some research and I believe you may find this useful."

I read the title aloud. "The Shifters of Europe."

"It's the only book of its kind in existence."

"Thank you, Micah," I said, placing my hand on his arm in a gesture of good will.

When he flinched, I removed my hand. "Sorry."

Micah shook his head slowly, obviously disappointed with himself. "I'm not accustomed to being touched—unless, of course, it's for a beating."

He pulled at his hood again. My hand shot out to grasp his wrist. His body tensed as I slowly brought his hand down and took a step toward him. Tentatively, I reached for the hood and pushed it back to reveal his unusual face.

"There," I said, meeting his eyes. "That's much better."

At first he only stared at me, but eventually the faintest smile touched his lips. "My lady."

I smiled, too. "I'm sure this book will come in handy."

"I have not yet found anything in writing that supports the theory of humans being able to detect shifters from smell alone." He paused, perplexed. "Your talent is unique."

"Surely, I cannot be the only one," I countered.

"If I find anything, I'll let you know."

"Thank you." I was about to go through the courtyard gates and stopped. "Would you care to hunt with me tonight, Micah?"

He pulled up the hood of his cloak to cover his face again. "I always hunt alone."

I watched him walk away.

The elders departed the following night and, as Erika had predicted, Arsham invited me to his chamber. He made love to me as passionately as he had on countless other occasions, but I had taken my sister's advice. I had used the time away from him to harden my heart.

When we finished our passion play, he rolled off of me and leaned on his elbow, frowning slightly. I could see the question in his eyes. He noticed the difference in my demeanor but said nothing. Pulling me into his arms, he kissed the top of my head and fell asleep. I slipped out of his embrace and crept to my own chamber. I had never done that before since he enjoyed sleeping by my side. He confronted me the following night in the garden.

"Look how the moonlight kisses every strand of your silken hair." We were very much alone, so he kissed my lips then demanded, "Why did you leave my bed?"

I shrugged, refusing to meet his eyes. "I thought you would be more comfortable alone."

He stared at me for a long time. His expression revealed nothing. "What saddens you, my angel?"

"Nothing."

"Are you sure about that?"

"Quite sure, my lord."

"Your lips lie to me, but your eyes do not." He took hold of my chin, forcing me to meet his harsh gaze. "Never lie to your sire again."

CHAPTER 7

"The secret of getting things done is to act!"
(Dante Alighieri)

Political turmoil brewed in France. We kept abreast of news reports and paid serious heed to rumors since they were often laced with truth. We also came across various scathing tracts that had been circulating throughout Paris; printed propaganda criticizing the monarchs and their supporters. Often singled out for her frivolity and reckless spending, Marie Antoinette garnered resentment from the French. To make matters worse, their weak king proved ineffective and indecisive. The people resented being highly taxed and forced into starvation in order to support the colonists revolting in the New World. They especially hated maintaining the lavish lifestyles of a useless monarchy. No one exhibited surprise when our messengers arrived with the news of a revolution.

On the fourteenth day of July in the year 1789, a mob of angry peasants stormed the Bastille in Paris. Such a bold act on the part of the people evoked concern in Arsham. The French were so fed up that they soon began murdering supporters of the monarchy, which were mainly the aristocrats. In the early days of the revolution we took advantage of the situation by slipping into prisons undetected and attacking the prisoners who were sentenced to die. Other vampires had no problem killing these innocent people, but I did. They were already being treated horribly simply for being born with a title, and now they would pay for their misfortune with their lives.

The initial bloodlust I had experienced as a newborn vampire had abated, allowing me to think clearly. During this period I learned two things about myself: I still had a human conscience, and I didn't have to kill humans in order to feed.

I wisely refrained from sharing either secret with anyone in our coven. I didn't want to be seen as a deviant or a rebel. Furthermore, Arsham strictly forbade us from sparing the lives of humans. Prompted by spite, I disobeyed his command at every opportunity. In retrospect, perhaps it would have been kinder of me to have bled my victims dry. The deplorable conditions inside the prisons killed many of the people before they even faced trial.

The murderous rage festering amid the French peasants transformed Arsham's concern to fear. As the weeks passed, the situation grew worse. Crowds gathered in the square on a daily basis before one of mankind's most sinister inventions: the guillotine. People watched gleefully as head after head rolled from the bodies of the condemned. Not even children were spared. The infant babes of the nobility were often thrown to the bloodthirsty mob and torn apart with bare hands. Sometimes, they were brutally swung by the feet and slammed against stone walls or simply tossed to ravenous dogs. Blood ran like rivers in the streets of Paris.

Angry mobs destroyed homes and defiled churches. When we received news that the nearest chateau to us had been burned to the ground, Arsham summoned the elders for a special meeting. He announced that he would be leaving on a journey, and commanded the vampires of his coven to disperse and avoid France. It was simply too dangerous for anyone—even the undead—to remain in the country during the current political turmoil.

My sire declared that it would be good for me to see a bit of the world, but he didn't invite me to accompany him on his journey. Deeply offended by his snub, I said nothing.

Thankfully, Erika invited me to stay with her and Birsa. She took me to her homeland in the north where fjords jutted out of the sea, and snow-covered mountains graced the horizon. Their wooden home was fashioned in the style of a bygone Viking era. The large cottage sported a stone hearth and carved furniture depicting whimsical dragon heads. Strange Celtic carvings decorated the window shutters, and woven tapestries depicting mythological battles adorned the walls. A miniature

Viking ship dominated the mantle above the hearth.

Erika found me staring at the ship and said, "My father had a real one just like it."

I met her gaze. "It's beautiful. Do you like sailing?"

"It's my passion."

The cottage stood proudly on the shore of a placid lake that led out to sea. A dense forest full of evergreens and ancient trees encompassed their home. Mountains peeked above the treetops in the distance. I initially assumed that being in such a remote location would make hunting difficult, but I was wrong. The lively port city a few miles to the east provided plenty of blood, thanks to the many foreign sailors and merchants. In order not to give rise to suspicion, Erika and Birsa had trained their bodies to go without blood for long periods of time. They also curbed their cravings by drinking the blood of woodland creatures. I was anxious for them to teach me these tricks, which would make me as resilient as they were.

I found my new surroundings wild and exciting, which pleased Erika greatly. I noticed that Birsa didn't like to stray too far from their home, but Erika and I did. We sailed during the most fearsome storms, riding high on ferocious waves and coming dangerously close to crashing into the fjords. I had never known such thrills! Erika showed me how to navigate the seas and read the starry skies. Her knowledge of astronomy astounded me.

I enjoyed wandering into the wilderness alone, immersing myself in the untamed beauty of nature. I would sit for hours listening to the howling wind or the flapping of insect wings. Sometimes, I would sit and listen to the silence until it became music to my ears. I now understood why Erika and Birsa seldom spoke. There was no need for words in such a magical place.

Each night after hunting, we would sit around the fire and exchange stories. I grew to love and respect my sister. I slept in the room farthest from the one Erika and Birsa shared, but that didn't prevent me from hearing their lovemaking at night. Their erotic moans only made me ache for Arsham, who had not bothered to send word to me since we had parted ways.

***

On the one year anniversary of my arrival, Erika announced that she would teach me the art of war and how to properly wield a sword. My aunt had taught me the basics, but I could never hold my own against an experienced warrior like Erika.

My training began the moment she handed me a finely crafted steel sword. "This belonged to my brother," she said to me one evening after the sun had set. "Birsa does not like to spar, and I have been pining for a worthy partner for years."

I glanced at the timid Birsa—the epitome of submissive femininity, the perfect contrast to the masculine prowess of my sister. I judged myself to be somewhere in between these two extremes.

"Come," Erika said, opening the outside door.

"Now?" I asked, gripping the handle of my new sword.

"Maybe you should change out of your gown." She looked to Birsa and added, "Give her a pair of knickers, will you?"

I stripped out of my skirt and slipped into the snug knickers. After adjusting my bodice, I put on a pair of leather boots and followed Erika outside. Birsa leaned her elbows on the sill of the open window and watched as Erika destroyed my dignity.

After my backside had hit the ground for the tenth time, I announced, "It's useless, Erika. I shall never learn to wield a sword the way you do."

Erika laughed. "Of course you will. You have plenty of time to learn this and much more. An eternity of time."

Her words struck a chord in me. I hadn't been a vampire for very long and sometimes I forgot that we don't die of natural causes or old age like mortals. Perhaps once I have lived through an entire century the concept would finally sink in. I got up and wiped the dust off myself. I looked down at the heavy sword with its carved hilt and held it out, testing its balance within my grip.

"Again," I said, urging her to come at me.

Erika sparred with me every night, and my skills did indeed improve with time. Eventually, I became a decent fighter. Sometimes, I even provided her with a real challenge.

"You're a natural," Erika said to me one day.

I laughed. "A natural what? Disaster?"

"No, my foolish friend. A natural fighter. Your speed and stealth, combined with your ability to detect shifters, makes you a valuable asset to our coven."

I kept my head lowered out of modesty. "Thank you, Erika. That means much coming from you."

***

In January 1793 we received news that King Louis XVI had been unceremoniously beheaded by his own royal subjects. His queen was executed in the same fashion in the autumn of that same year. We expected to hear word from our sire, but nothing came. Surprisingly, this didn't disappoint me. I had no desire to return to France during such dark times. In fact, I was content to remain in the north with Erika and Birsa forever.

"Where do you suppose he is?" I asked of Erika one day as she sat outside polishing her sword.

"Arsham?" I nodded and she continued, "He likes to travel to his homeland and wander through the Middle Eastern territories. The last time he went on such a journey it lasted over fifty years."

"Fifty years?" I repeated incredulously.

She laughed at my expression. "That's nothing for a vampire. You're still very young, but as the decades turn to centuries you'll understand how our concept of time is different than that of humans."

"Will my human emotions fade as time passes?"

"Yes."

I stared at her in confusion. "You're much older than me, yet you foster the emotion of love for Birsa."

"Love, hate, fear, envy—these powerful emotions remain with us forever. Like humans, vampires possess different personalities, which harbor accompanying emotions." She flickered a sly glance at me. "If you're worried about your feelings for Arsham, they'll eventually fade. Give it time."

"I wasn't even thinking of him," I assured primly as I sat down beside her on the wooden bench. Wishing to change the subject, I added, "Tell me more about your people."

She told me tales of Thor and Odin, and how the Christians managed to convert many pagan Vikings to their cult. She described her human family and home life in such great detail that it seemed as if she had only lost them last week. She cried when she spoke of her father, and I envied her for having had such a worthy man in her life.

"You never speak of your family," Erika commented.

"My mother died while giving birth to me."

"What of your father?"

"He's a successful silk merchant. I rarely saw him during my childhood. I don't even know if he's still alive."

"Were you ever married? Did you have children?"

"Yes and no," I replied. "My husband was a powerful nobleman—a duke. A vile man, he hurt me on a regular basis. I did conceive once, but I lost the child."

"I'm sorry…"

"Arsham killed my husband on the night the duke tried to murder me. He saved my life."

"Now I understand why you love him so much."

"My love is unrequited," I countered sadly.

Erika caressed my cheek. "Someday, you'll find joy and happiness in this new life."

I forced a smile. "I already have. I'm here with you."

Chapter 8
France
19TH Century

"Tears are the silent language of grief."
(Voltaire)

Napoleon Bonaparte was crowned Emperor of France in 1804. Erika received a message from Arsham one month after the coronation, commanding the elders to meet in Paris.

"When will we depart?" I asked.

She looked up from the sheet of parchment in her hands. "Tomorrow after sunset. Birsa will meet us a few days later."

"Does he mention me at all?"

"No," she replied before tossing the summons into the flames within the hearth.

I picked up my sword, ready for my nightly sparring match. We didn't speak of Arsham again. I fought well and proved a real challenge to my sister.

"Well done, Angelique," she said, sheathing her weapon. "You can now call yourself a warrior."

I shook my head and smiled. "Let's not exaggerate."

"I never do."

When the palest streak of gold shone from the horizon, we took shelter inside. After securing the windows and doors, we settled in to sleep.

The next night, I donned my finest gown and jewels, then secured my sword to my belt. Throwing my cloak over my shoulders, I bade Birsa goodbye and walked outside. Erika kissed her lover with great passion before meeting me on the path leading away from the cottage.

We walked a few steps in companionable silence before she asked, "How do you feel about seeing him again?"

I shrugged. "It gladdens my heart. He's my sire, and I love him as such."

She stopped and eyed me for a long moment. "Yes, you do. Your eyes no longer reflect pain at the mention of his name. Time has done its job."

With heavy heart, I left the wild north behind me. The old Angelique would remain forever in that wilderness, but a new vampire—a warrior—had emerged.

At one point, Erika declared, "I need to feed."

"We're almost in Paris," I pointed out.

"I know, but I've gone too long without blood. I didn't have time to hunt before our departure." When I looked at her in confusion, she explained, "Birsa's lust is sometimes insatiable and quite time-consuming."

I blushed, if that was even possible for a vampire. "Oh."

Erika laughed heartily at my reaction. A nearby village offered feeding opportunities. We descended upon it silently and stayed in the shadows.

"There," Erika whispered, pointing to a tavern filled with rowdy patrons.

The candlelight pouring from of the mullioned windows made the establishment look somewhat cheerful. Inside, a chorus of male voices sang a bawdy song. We stood across the road under the sprawling branches of an elm tree, blending into the deep shadows. It was only a matter of time and predictability before one of the drunk patrons came out to urinate in the narrow alley that ran alongside the tavern. A young man with a crop of red hair staggered as he undid the buttons at his crotch. Erika was about to attack, but I placed a hand on her shoulder.

"Shape shifter," I whispered, cringing at the offensive mix of cat urine and incense permeating the air.

Erika sniffed the air and frowned, but remained perfectly still at my side. We both watched as the shape shifter did his business and went back inside.

"We should go," I suggested. "It's not safe here."

"Unlike us, shifters have no resistance to alcohol and other potent drugs," Erika pointed out. "Don't worry, he was too drunk to detect us. Besides, he's alone."

"Are you sure about that? What if there's a slayer inside?"

Erika's eyes were focused on the door. "A slayer would have come out by now. We're fine."

"I've never come face to face with one, so I have no idea how they operate."

"Let's hope you never do."

I looked around uneasily. "There's probably another village nearby, perhaps you should hunt there instead."

"Nonsense."

"I don't like this, Erika. Something feels wrong."

"I'll feed on the next man and we'll be on our way."

We stood motionless, waiting. The tavern door opened and a stout man wobbled into the alley. Placing a beefy hand against the brick wall to steady himself, he practically pissed on his own two feet.

Erika left the sanctuary of the shadows and pounced on the drunkard like a giant cat, knocking him to the ground. After she had fed, she looked up at me and grinned, but I didn't return the smile. My eyes were focused on the shadowy figure looming behind her. Following my gaze, she looked over her shoulder and hissed. I heard the unmistakable "swoosh" of metal cutting through air. I clamped my hand over my mouth to keep from screaming as my sister's head fell from her neck and rolled into a filthy puddle. The shocked expression on Erika's face would haunt me for all eternity.

A lithe figure jumped over the two corpses, moving with impressive agility and speed. Horrified, I retreated further into the shadows as a tall man stepped out of the alley. He held a long, slightly curved sword in his hands. Removing a handkerchief from his pocket, he began wiping Erika's blood from the gleaming blade.

My fingers desperately sought the hilt of my sword, and I began to pull it out of its sheath slowly so as not to draw attention to myself.

"My lady," said the vampire slayer as he stared directly at me. "There's no need to hide. You're safe now."

Absurdly handsome, with metallic gray eyes and shiny black hair, he waited for me to emerge from the shadows. I wanted nothing more than to avenge my sister's death.

"Angelique?"

Someone had exited the tavern. I let go of my weapon as the slayer hastily sheathed his sword. The old man who had uttered my name gasped aloud in disbelief. Standing before me was my very own father! Luckily, he could not see the dark alley or Erika's headless body from where he stood. I was overcome by various emotions—anger, love, nostalgia, and pity. He had grown so terribly old and fragile that I smelled death on him. The pent-up anger and hurt I had carried for years simply dissolved in that moment.

Joy eventually eclipsed the unadulterated shock on my father's face. When his brow creased in confusion, I noticed hundreds of wrinkles nestled within his papery skin.

"I thought you were dead," he said in a raspy voice. "I heard that you had been murdered in Versailles."

"I am very much alive, Father."

"God be praised, but...*how*?"

I had to think of something fast. "The duke murdered one of his mistresses..."

"Witnesses said that you were there, too. They had seen you at the king's birthday celebration."

"Yes, but we had separate chambers," I lied. "When the bodies were discovered the next morning, I took the opportunity to flee...I knew people would assume the duke had killed me." When my father continued to stare at me, I confessed, "Oh, Father, he treated me so badly! I had to run away!"

My father wept as he embraced me. He then pulled away and studied my face with a worried frown. "Time hasn't touched you, daughter. How is this possible?"

The red haired shifter exited the tavern and saw me in my father's arms. Despite the lad's inebriated state, he had the presence of mind to stop in his tracks. Turning toward the slayer, he said, "My lord, may I have a word?"

"Not now," the slayer said, his eyes glued to my face.

96

The shifter edged closer. "But..."

The slayer frowned. "Go to the inn. Wait for me there."

"But, she is—"

"Do as I say. *Now*."

The shifter reluctantly obeyed, casting furtive glances at me.

"This is your daughter?" the slayer inquired while studying me intently. "The duchess who was murdered?"

My father's eyes lit up. "The very one, Gilles!"

Gilles inclined his head at me. "Your Grace."

Ignoring him, I said, "Father, you look well." It was a blatant lie, but I didn't know what else to say.

"Not as well as you." Taking hold of my gloved hand, he demanded, "Where have you been all these years?"

"Living quietly outside of France," I replied truthfully.

"Are you heading to Paris?"

"Yes."

"Without stopping in Lyon to see your father even though you've been gone for so long?" Gilles asked archly. "You must have important business to attend to, my lady."

"As a matter of fact, I do," I retorted icily.

"Stop interrogating the girl, Gilles."

"I beg your pardon," Gilles offered in a mocking tone.

"Come inside and have something to drink," my father urged, still holding my hand.

I allowed him to lead me away from the alley. "Who is this man?" I whispered.

"This is Gilles Sauvage of Marseilles, but there is nothing savage about him except his name." My father chuckled at his own joke. "Gilles is my apprentice."

"Your apprentice?" I repeated, eyeing Gilles—who was indeed as savage as his surname implied.

My father beamed. "He's been like a son to me for the last five years. Learning the trade and doing a fine job, too. Best silk dyer in Lyon."

"A silk dyer," I repeated incredulously.

Gilles held my gaze. His eyes were the color of polished silver. "Your father speaks of you often, my lady," he said.

"He's been heartbroken since your death."

My father's expression turned sad. "I was inconsolable when I heard the news. I regretted marrying you off to that man…"

"Stop," I interjected. "That was a long time ago."

His pleading eyes met mine. "Do you forgive me?"

Did I forgive him? I wasn't sure. "Yes," I replied.

His eyes welled up with tears. "Thank you. We'll celebrate this most joyous reunion with some good wine."

"Yes," said Gilles, taking my arm and leading me to the tavern's entrance. "Have some wine with us."

In the wake of my sister's violent murder, the last thing I wanted to do was celebrate. Gilles had already opened the tavern door, bathing me in dim candlelight. The tavern seemed filled to capacity and many faces turned in our direction as we entered the room. I had to keep a cool head in order not to betray my true nature to the humans. I also had to mimic their movements, which meant slowing mine. We walked to a table and my father ordered a bottle of their best wine.

"Here, let me help you with your cloak," Gilles offered gallantly before I sat down.

The moment he removed the cloak from my shoulders, the patrons began to whisper and stare. Fashioned from sumptuous burgundy velvet, my gown boasted gold embroidery. Jewels the size of robins' eggs sparkled at my throat. I looked like a royal courtier.

Even Gilles appeared surprised. "You carry a sword on your person, my lady?"

"A woman must protect herself," I shot back.

"Do you even know how to use it?"

I shrugged. "I manage."

My father took in my rich attire with awe. "You've been living quietly, you say? Who has been providing for you?"

"I have followed in your footsteps," I quickly improvised. "I own several looms and my weavers produce the finest fabrics in Switzerland."

My father stared at me in disbelief, then laughed aloud. He

raised his cup. "To your health, Angelique."

I held the cup to my lips but did not drink. After a moment I placed the wine on the table, untouched. My father drank heartily and spoke of old times. I was deeply saddened to learn that my beloved Aunt Marguerite had died years ago.

Gilles studied me as I struggled with my emotions. I regarded him with contempt, for he had slain my sister, my only true friend in the world. In the morning, Erika's head and body would disintegrate into a pile of ash in the sunlight.

I squeezed my eyes shut and rubbed my temples. *Oh, Erika...*I also mourned for Birsa, who would be devastated when she learned the tragic news. Damn you, slayer.

"Will you, Angelique?"

"What was that?" I asked, jolted from my reverie.

"Will you travel with us to Paris then come home with us to Lyon afterward?" my father repeated.

Gilles grinned, staring at me. "What a splendid idea."

"I cannot," I said.

"Why?" Gilles prompted.

My father said, "Good question, Gilles. Why not? We also have business in Paris. There will be many parties to celebrate the recent coronation of our new emperor. Plenty of fabric will be needed to create the new fashion styles, which means more money in our pockets. I hear the Empress Josephine prefers lightweight silk and extra fine linen. The new styles are much more streamlined and easier to create."

How could I possibly refuse without arousing more suspicion? "Very well," I conceded.

"You've made me very happy." My father drained the remainder of his wine then yawned. "This old man is tired."

"The night is still young," Gilles pointed out.

My father shook his head. "Not for me."

Gilles looked down at my untouched wine. "Did you not enjoy the vintage, my lady?"

"I'm in no mood for it tonight," I replied coolly.

Holding my gaze, the slayer picked up my cup and drained its contents. My father and I stood, and Gilles placed my cloak

99

around my shoulders. I felt his hands on my bare skin and flinched. A knowing smile played upon his lips as the three of us went outside. As we walked to the inn, I couldn't help but cast a furtive glance over my shoulder at the alley.

"You must have a room here, too," my father said, motioning to the large building. I nodded and he added, "I bid you goodnight, Angelique. I'll see you in the morning."

To my surprise, he hugged me.

I held him for the last time. "Goodnight, Father."

"Are you coming, Gilles?"

Gilles shook his head. "In a moment. I would like to have a word with your daughter."

My father chuckled as he shuffled toward the inn's entrance. "I told you she was beautiful."

"That was quite a performance," Gilles said when we were finally alone.

"I have no idea what you're talking about."

"You knew what that creature was in the alley, yet you were not the least bit frightened," he said, grasping the narrow hilt of his strange sword.

I met his steely gaze and said nothing.

He reached out his other hand to touch my face and recoiled. "Ice cold. My shifter is never wrong."

"Are you going to cut off my head, too?"

Gilles stepped back and unsheathed his sword. When I remained perfectly still, he frowned, unsure of how to proceed. I took a step forward and he put the sharp blade to my throat. "One more step and your head will fly, my lady. The affection I have for your father is the only reason I put up with your charade this evening."

The tears I had been holding back throughout the evening prickled my eyelids. "You killed my beloved sister, Erika."

"She was a monster—a killer."

"She was kindhearted and good," I snapped. "She killed to eat, nothing more."

"Just as you will kill me in order to quench your vile thirst for blood!"

100

"I don't kill humans when I feed."

"Liar! I should put an end to your wretched life right now. It would save your father the heartache of knowing what kind of unholy creature you've become."

While his words were angry, his eyes held fascination. I knew that look. "Gilles, I'm not lying," I said, my voice hypnotic. "I'm still the same Angelique my father speaks of, only now I'm immortal." I took a step closer while gazing deeply into his eyes. "I won't hurt you."

Under my spell, he lowered the blade from my throat.

I continued, "You must never reveal my secret to my father for he has little time left. Death is upon him—he won't survive the year. Please let him live the remainder of his days in ignorance. Promise me that you'll do as I ask. Say it."

"I promise."

He was about to sheath his weapon and I stopped him. "What type of sword is that?"

"It's a katana."

"Katana," I repeated.

"It belonged to my father."

"Where did he get such a sword?"

"From his mother. She was Japanese."

So Gilles had a Japanese grandmother. That explained his exotic Eurasian features. "I take it your father was a slayer?"

"Yes, as was his father before him. We are born and bred to kill your kind."

"Then I shall be sure to proceed with caution in the future," I said drily.

"A wise course of action."

"How many of my brethren have you slain?"

"Counting tonight, six." He paused. "I'm sorry about Erika."

"You should be."

Changing the subject, he said, "Your father speaks very highly of you."

"Does he?"

"Every chance he gets. Angelique, I don't want to hurt you."

"You threatened to cut off my head a moment ago."

"That was before...*this*."

"Perhaps you shouldn't kill so precipitously."

"I've never spoken to one of your kind. I had no idea you were capable of—"

"Love? Compassion?" I interjected. "We vampires were once human, you know."

"I assumed you acted solely on instinct."

"We do for the most part, but we never lose our human memories," I explained. "We have the capacity to feel emotion just as you do."

He pondered this information for a moment. "Do you hurt humans when you feed upon them?"

"Our bite is quite pleasurable, unless..."

"Unless what?" he prompted, eyes intense.

"If we're extremely hungry—starved, for example—the bloodlust can be so strong that we simply lose control. At that point, yes, we can cause a tremendous amount of pain to a human as we bleed them dry." Castigating myself for sharing too much information, I began to wander toward the forest. "I really should get going now."

Rather than retreat to the inn, he followed me. "Would I become like you if you fed on me?"

The question took me by surprise. "Only if you consumed vampire blood before the next sunrise."

"I have so many questions."

The hour was late and the village, silent. A crescent moon glowed in a clear night sky while bats and insects flew above our heads. We walked together quietly beneath the humming of their wings.

I could have easily killed him in that moment to avenge Erika's death. So, what prevented me from doing so? Why not rip out his throat and drain him of blood? Was it because he was so attractive? Or did I glimpse genuine remorse in his eyes for killing my sister? After all, he committed the deed in ignorance. Gilles cared for my father, affording the old man a bit of comfort in his last days. Maybe if I taught him about our kind, I could prevent him from killing others.

"Angelique?"

I gazed up at the moon. "Ask your questions and I shall do my best to answer them."

Gilles and I talked for hours. He asked about my former life as a human, and what it was like to be immortal. He wanted to know my thoughts on various issues now that I had limitless time to contemplate life's conundrums. I answered as honestly as I could without betraying my coven or my sire in any way. The slayer listened in silence with wide eyes when I described the rush we feel while drinking human blood. I almost got the impression he wanted to experience the thrill for himself. The night passed quickly and, when I sensed the arrival of dawn, I made to leave.

"Don't go."

I pointed to the delicate flush of crimson hovering low on the horizon. "Daylight will be upon us shortly."

He then did something shocking. Taking a step closer, he bared his throat to me. "Feed, Angelique."

My eyes narrowed. "Is this a trick, Gilles?"

"No."

I closed the gap between us and took him into my arms. Once again, the thought of ending his life entered my mind. Instead, I caressed his cheek as I tenderly kissed his lips. He shivered helplessly in my embrace when my mouth moved from his lips to his throat. Slowly, I coaxed the vein with my tongue before gently biting into the skin. He sighed in pleasure and I could feel him hardening against me. His breathing soon became shallow due to his arousal. I drank only a little bit then pricked my finger so that my blood would heal the fang marks instantly. I licked the blood away, then took a step backward. I could smell his desire from where I stood.

"Come back to the inn with me," he said huskily.

I shook my head. "I must seek shelter."

Saddened and sexually frustrated, he pleaded, "Please..."

"No."

"When will I see you again?"

"Never."

I flew into the night with supernatural speed, leaving Gilles staring after me with palpable regret.

***

Arsham took the news of Erika's death badly. After flying into a rage, he demanded to know the details of the incident. I explained to him that Erika and I had been hunting together in a village when a man wielding a strange sword jumped out of a tree and sliced off my sister's head.

He stared at me incredulously. "A slayer?"

We were alone in the garden and the moonlight made Arsham's eyes gleam like obsidian. "Yes, I believe so."

Grateful that my life had been spared, he remained disappointed that I had failed to avenge Erika's death. I told him the slayer took refuge in a crowded tavern, making it impossible to chase him down without drawing attention to myself and revealing my true nature to humans.

"They're getting better at killing us," Arsham lamented as he paced back and forth upon the pebbles of the garden path. His legs were powerful and his strides long. The tiny stones crunched beneath his weight. He stopped abruptly as realization dawned on him. "I'm willing to bet he was a Sauvage! Damn them all to Hell."

Startled at the mention of the slayer's name, I feigned ignorance. "Sire?"

"The Sauvage family has been sanctioned by the Church to kill our kind. They're the most notorious slayers in Europe. I'm sure it was either the deadly Sylvain or his younger brother, Gilles, who killed our dear Erika."

I was careful to keep my expression neutral. "I've never seen such speed and cleverness in any human before."

"Did you get a good look at him?"

"Young, tall, black hair, fair skin, and extremely agile."

"Probably Gilles." Arsham started to pace again. "You lack experience…if you were older, you would have reacted differently. You would have killed the insolent bastard."

"I wish I had."

"This is a painful lesson for you, Angelique," he said,

stopping to stand before me. In a gentle voice, he added, "I know you were fond of Erika."

"I loved her very much, sire," I admitted as a tear ran down my cheek. It was the only truth I'd spoken thus far.

He wiped it away with his fingertip. "Come here, child."

Arsham enveloped me in his embrace and I took comfort within his strong arms. I felt safe, but I couldn't help wondering if those same arms would crush me to death if he knew what had really happened that night.

He must never know the truth.

When he finally released me, I asked, "How long do you want me to stay here with you in Paris?"

"I want all my children by my side for a while." His head turned sharply and a small smile tugged at his lips. "I think I hear the twins approaching."

***

The elders were pained when told of Erika's death. I noticed the twins regarding me with disgust when Arsham mentioned that I had failed to kill my sister's murderer. I returned their hostility with a hateful stare of my own. Erika had taught me how to think strategically and fight like a warrior, which lent me the confidence I needed to face any adversary; even those within my own coven. If the twins wanted to confront me, I was ready for any challenge.

Birsa arrived two days later. When Arsham informed her of Erika's fate, she fell to her knees and wailed like a wounded animal. "Kill me, sire," she begged through her tears. "Kill me, please, for I cannot live without her."

Arsham stared down at her in outrage. Aware that she was reacting out of grief, he displayed mercy in the face of her insolence. He motioned for me to take Birsa away, so I placed my arm around her and led her to my chamber.

I wiped the tears from Birsa's face. "I'm so sorry."

She cried harder. "Oh, Erika..."

I knew her pain was greater than mine, for she had been with Erika for centuries. Nothing I could say would ease her agony, but I tried anyway. "Erika's death was swift and painless."

Birsa placed her head in her hands and gradually calmed down. Finally, she demanded, "Why didn't you kill him?"

I offered her the same excuse that I had given Arsham.

"Erika taught you how to fight. I've seen the both of you spar. In all the years we've been together, you're the only one who has ever given her a real challenge. Tell me the truth, Angelique. Why did you let the slayer go free?"

I hung my head in shame. "I'm telling you the truth. Everything happened so fast—I tried to chase him…"

I was a liar and hated myself for it.

Birsa stared at me in disbelief. Shaking her head, she stormed out of the chamber. I had never seen this side of her, but it made me feel even guiltier.

I later discovered that Birsa sought Arsham's forgiveness for her outburst, then requested his permission to leave so that she could mourn her loss in privacy. He granted her request. I would have gone with her had she invited me. Maybe she would forgive me someday. In the meantime, I had to figure out where I would live.

Arsham slept alone for three days before summoning the twins to his chamber in order to keep him company. At the end of the week, the elders were dismissed. I had been mulling over my next move and decided to go on a journey. I wanted to explore Spain and Portugal since I've never been to either country. I was curious to see the grandiose architecture and flamboyant art of these once mighty kingdoms. I went into my chamber to pack a few things. A half our later, someone opened my door without knocking. Only one vampire would dare do such a thing to an elder.

"Sire," I said, turning away from my task.

"Where are you going, Angelique?" he demanded, eyeing my travel trunk with a frown.

"Did you not dismiss the elders?"

"I did, but it's my desire that you remain in Paris."

"I don't understand."

"There's no need for you to understand," he stated coolly. "Your duty is to obey my command, and I haven't dismissed

106

you. Am I clear?"

While his words were hard, his expression and tone were not. "As you wish, my lord."

He suddenly pulled me into his arms and brought his mouth down on mine in a passionate kiss. I didn't know what to make of this; he hadn't shown me the slightest bit of affection since my arrival. Could it be that he had had a change of heart? Did our separation make him long for what we once shared?

"I knew you still loved me," he whispered with the irritating satisfaction of a cocky stud.

Arsham didn't love me, but he wanted me to be his lovesick fool. Unfortunately for him, the naïve and vulnerable vampire he once knew had drowned in the fjords. Erika had not only taught me how to fight like a warrior, she taught me the art of strategy in warfare—and this was a war of the heart.

I hid my fury with a sweet smile. "You are my sire. We all love you. It's our duty."

"You've changed, Angelique," he said, studying my face.

"Have I?"

"Perhaps you've spent too much time in the icy North."

He turned and left my chamber, leaving me to unpack. When the twins had departed, I went downstairs to bid Valerio and Omar farewell.

"When are you leaving?" Omar asked of me.

"Arsham has asked me to stay in Paris."

He looked surprised. "Oh?"

Valerio gave me a knowing look. "I wonder what plans he has in store for you."

"I'm sure our sire has his reasons. Stop prying, Valerio," Omar admonished. He embraced me and said, "Take care of yourself, Angelique."

Valerio ignored Omar's comment. "Send word if anything exciting happens."

I embraced my impertinent Sicilian brother with genuine affection, then stood in the courtyard under the moonlight as he and Omar flew into the night.

When Micah appeared in the doorway, I went to him. We

had become friends despite the fact that he seldom spoke to me—or anyone else for that matter. I respected his odd manner, and accepted the friendship on his terms. The hood of his cloak was thrown back to reveal his face.

"Farewell, brother," I said. "I look forward to seeing you again next year."

"Arsham has asked me to stay."

"Me too."

"I know. Our sire has decided that he needs at least two elders to advise him. He chose us because neither of us have children, and we live like nomads."

I stared into his pinkish red eyes while processing this information. "Advise him on what?"

Micah looked over his shoulder before taking hold of my elbow and urging me away from the chateau. We walked to the farthest end of the garden. Lowering his voice, he said, "I believe our sire may be experiencing fear."

"Fear of what?" I whispered, confused.

"The old ways are being quickly replaced by science and progress. Change is inevitable…"

We were experiencing an age of great enlightenment. New discoveries and theories were being launched and debated on a regular basis. To a vampire accustomed to doing things a certain way for over seven centuries, change would be very difficult.

"Arsham is afraid of modernity." I mused aloud.

"Yes," Micah confirmed.

"You're the second oldest vampire in our coven now that Erika is no longer with us. Are you not afraid of modernity?"

"I'm a scholar. Change does not intimidate me in the slightest. On the contrary, I'm intellectually motivated to research and explore. I see every new theory as an exciting possibility."

"That explains why he wants you here, but what does he want with me? I am no scholar."

"You are the youngest vampire in this coven, and that makes you the most adaptable. Your youth enables you to be flexible, to accept new ideas with an open mind. Arsham needs us to ease

108

him into the nineteenth century."

"I see." I smiled at him. "Do you realize this is the most you've ever said to me since the day we met?"

Micah's lips twitched upward—almost a smile. "I should embrace change, too, I suppose."

Emboldened by his good-natured reaction, I placed my hand on Micah's chest. He didn't flinch. "Yes, you should. Especially since I need a friend."

He lifted his hand and it froze in midair for a few seconds. Frowning, he tentatively placed his hand over mine and nodded. "You can count on my friendship."

***

I gradually settled into a routine. Despite the kiss Arsham and I had shared the night he commanded me to stay, we never made love. Perhaps my indifference had put him off, perhaps I had wounded his pride, or perhaps it was the pretty vampires that surrounded him on any given day. Either way, I didn't care. I kept my distance, treating him with the respect he demanded and nothing more.

At first he seemed nonplussed by this, but as the weeks passed I caught him staring at me on many occasions. His eyes often followed me as I crossed a room, and his indiscernible expression made me wary.

I didn't see much of Micah. Whenever our paths did cross, he made an effort to speak with me. Sometimes, we enjoyed brief conversations. Slowly, he was emerging from the shell in which he had been hiding for centuries.

The entire upper story of Arsham's chateau eventually became a training facility. Devoid of walls, the enormous space contained a row of long windows on one side and finely cut mirrors on the other—much like the Hall of Mirrors at Versailles, only less glamorous. Vampires could practice the art of fencing, sword fighting, and hand-to-hand combat.

Determined to maintain the skills that Erika had taught me, I spent most of my time sparring with the best fighters in our coven. I quickly gained the reputation of being a formidable opponent. Before long, a few of the vampires began watching me closely. No accusation or suspicion resided in their gazes, but I avoided their curious eyes nonetheless.

Whenever I picked up a sword, I often recalled to mind Birsa's words: 'Why didn't you kill him?' Her question haunted me. At one point, I almost left the chateau to hunt Gilles down, but my good sense prevailed. It would be better for me if I simply stuck to my original story. *My original lie.* The thought of the slayer inevitably made me think of my father. Was he still alive and weaving his wonderful silks?

While sparring with a male vampire one evening, Arsham sauntered into the training facility wielding a sword. At the unexpected sight of our sire, we stopped and bowed our heads. The onlookers who had been cheering us on grew silent and backed away from the fighting floor.

Arsham had his own elite guards to spar with and a private fighting chamber at his disposal—he rarely showed his face at the training facility. Assuming he wanted a change of scenery, I adjusted my attire and was about to sheath my sword when he raised his hand to stop me. I froze as his eyes ran from the tips of my boots to the top of my head. Never having seen me wearing anything except gowns, the black fitted vest and matching knickers intrigued him.

After allowing his eyes to linger on my hips for a moment, he lifted his sword. "Shall we?"

"You wish to spar, sire? With me?"

His eyes narrowed. "Yes."

My sparring partner inclined his head at me and left, allowing Arsham to take his place. The onlookers retreated to the far wall to allow us plenty of room. They watched in wide-eyed silence as Arsham suddenly lunged forward with a fierce thrust, knocking over a wrought-iron floor candelabra. It hit the terracotta floor with a loud crash, chipping a few tiles in the process. Luckily, I was fast enough to counter the attack. Our swords clashed and I spun around, barely missing the point of his blade as it hissed past my ear. Arsham wasted no time lunging at me again, but I ducked to the side as the blade sliced through nothing but air.

He chuckled. "Swift and clever, Angelique, but let's see how you deal with this!"

My sire's sword flashed in the candlelight. He swung his weapon with such force and velocity that its trailing wind extinguished one of the nearby candles. I parried quickly and my blade nicked the flesh of his bicep. At the sight of our sire's spilled blood, the vampires gasped in horror. Arsham stood still and so did I. He stared at the wound I had inflicted upon him, then raised his eyes to mine before hissing angrily.

"Forgive me, sire," I cried, backing away from him.

He ignored my apology and came at me with raised sword. A terrible battle cry escaped his lips. I immediately ducked, parried, and spun around. Instinctively, I lifted my sword so that the sharp tip rested at the nape of his neck. Arsham stood perfectly still, breathing hard. The room brimmed with tension as everyone stared in anticipation of what would happen next.

"My lord, I do not wish to fight you," I whispered, lowering my weapon.

Arsham turned his head to look over his shoulder. His eyes were ablaze with fury and something else. A slow smile spread across his lips, but it lacked mirth. He straightened, still keeping his broad back to me. "Erika taught you well, my child. Your skills are an asset to this coven."

I took his words as a dismissal and thought we were done sparring. When I sheathed my sword, Arsham spun around and pressed the tip of his blade to the base of my throat.

"Kneel!"

I stared at him in disbelief. His sword followed me as I knelt, its sharp point drawing a bead of blood. One could hear a pin drop in the room in that moment. I spotted Micah hovering anxiously in the doorway, watching me with worried eyes. After a long, tense moment, Arsham lowered his weapon and held out his ring. I hesitated, then leaned forward to kiss the blood ruby. I noticed that my sire's breathing grew shallow and his pupils were dilated as he looked down his nose at me.

"Rise." I obeyed and he put his lips to my ear. "Go to my chamber immediately."

111

I went to Arsham's chamber and waited by the door with my head lowered. What punishment lay in store for me? My sire turned the corner and I braced myself at his approach. Without looking at me, he silently opened the door. I entered his chamber and he locked us within it. When he gripped my shoulders, I prepared myself for a beating. Instead, he pressed up against me and plundered my mouth. His hands cupped my buttocks, pulling me forward against his groin. His mouth eventually moved to my throat and he licked the beads of blood he had drawn with his sword.

Pulling away to look at my face, he whispered, "I would have you now, Angelique."

"Sire?"

He growled. "Do not deny me. It has been far too long."

When his teeth cut into my skin, I cried out with pleasure. He undressed me with the speed and skill that only the greatest of seducers possessed. There would be no tenderness, no sweet kisses or caresses this time. Kneeling before my naked body, he bit the inside of my thigh and smeared the blood on his fingers before gliding them into me. He then stood, slammed my back against the wall, and entered me. Gripping my buttocks roughly, he lifted me up and began ramming into me with such desperate need that it verged on violence. I wrapped my legs around his waist and gripped his shoulders for support. With each deep thrust he growled like an animal. At one point, I thought he would tear me in half.

When he finally gave me permission to drink the blood from his wrist, I did so eagerly. As the potent blood surged through me, my body quickened in response to his and he ravaged me like an insatiable wild beast. I had finally mastered the art of enjoying physical contact without becoming emotionally involved and savored the erotic moment. After he fell asleep, I crept to my own chamber and slept soundly until sunset. I rose when the first star twinkled in the sky and left the chateau to hunt.

Arsham was seated with his guards when I returned. "Ah, there you are, Angelique."

I inclined my head in respect as I sauntered past him.

"Wait. You've been hunting?"

I stopped in my tracks and faced him. "Yes."

There was an awkward pause. "Was it a good hunt?"

How odd. "Very good, sire."

He nodded slowly, studying me. "Carry on."

I inclined my head once more, turned on my heel, and walked away. I could feel the weight of his stare on my back. The sun would not be up for several hours, allowing me plenty of time to sharpen my sword and spar the time away. As I reached the stairwell, someone gripped my arm.

It was Micah. He put his finger to his lips and motioned for me to follow him. We ducked into a narrow corridor that led downstairs. A single torch burned in an iron sconce at the top of the long stairwell, casting a dim light upon the rough stone walls.

"Where are we going?" I whispered.

"The cellar," he replied.

The musty odor of ancient mold accosted us as soon as we descended into the bowels of the chateau. There were no torches here, and I detected the squeaking of mice in the pitch darkness. Micah gripped my hand and led me to a small chamber. A single sputtering candle cast its feeble light upon a long table laden with books.

I wrinkled my nose. "What is this place?"

"One of many hideaways where I'm free to study undisturbed."

"You take drastic measures to be alone."

He raised a brow at me. "Some of the younger ones enjoy spying on me."

"Well, you're an intriguing vampire. As for this place—" I looked around. "A bit macabre, no?"

"I think you mean a bizarre vampire," he countered, ignoring my question.

"No, I mean intriguing. Send these youths with nothing better to do upstairs to the training facility. I'll turn them into competent fighters."

"I wish I could."

I walked to the table and gently placed my hand upon a book. The dry leather was almost brittle. "What are you researching?"

"That's what I wanted to show you. Look," he said, picking up a book from a large pile.

Micah's finger pointed to a detailed illustration of a man. It took me only a second to realize that the meticulously rendered ink drawing was a portrait of Gilles Sauvage.

I regained my composure and tried to appear ignorant. "Who is he?"

"This is Gilles Sauvage," Micah replied, watching me expectantly. "Does he look familiar to you? Is this the man who killed Erika?"

I squinted, swallowing hard. I shook my head nervously and pushed the book away from me. "I'm not sure."

"Look carefully, Angelique. Take your time."

I licked my dry lips and took the book into my own hands. I brought my head down to stare at the drawing. Gilles's eyes stared back at me. Damn him.

"I know this is difficult for you," he said. "I know how much you loved her."

"I did love her...very much."

"Was it him?" When I shook my head, he sighed in disappointment. "This book was written by a bishop who blessed the families working under the authority of the Vatican to kill vampires. He singles out the Sauvage family for their exemplary valor. They are notorious for working with shifters."

"I see."

"There's something else I want to talk to you about." He hesitated, unsure of how to proceed. "It concerns Arsham. He has become...obsessed with you lately."

"Are you referring to yesterday's sparring debacle?"

"Yes." Averting his eyes he added, "I know what he did to you in his chamber afterward."

I assumed everyone in the chateau knew, too. I remained silent, waiting for him to continue.

"I've been watching him for months," Micah said,

straightening a pile of books as he spoke. "He has you followed every time you are out of his sight."

"By whom?" I demanded, shocked by this revelation.

"Usually a guard who reports to him afterward." He paused, looking sheepish. "Even I have been commanded to keep a close eye on you."

I crossed my arms in irritation. "Whatever for?"

"I told you, he's obsessed with you."

"Why are you telling me this?"

"Because you're my friend, Angelique, and you deserve to know the truth. You show me kindness whereas others shun my hideous countenance."

"You are not hideous, brother. I admit your appearance is unusual, but you possess a beauty that is unique."

"Just be careful."

"I will." I placed my hand on his shoulder and he covered it with his own. "Thank you, Micah." I motioned toward the door. "Are you coming?"

"No. I have quite a bit of reading to do."

He turned his back to me and adopted the perfectly still pose I had seen so often. To any human eye, Micah would seem a lifeless statue carved from flawless, white marble. I left him and raced upstairs, feeling immense relief the moment I took hold of my sword. I chose a challenging sparring partner, and let my mind wander as my well-trained body took over.

***

As time passed, my emotional indifference toward Arsham sparked a strange possessiveness in him. Micah was right. His obsession with me, combined with his fear of modernity, made him seem crazed at times. He even went as far as trying to control my hunting preferences.

"I forbid you to feed on beautiful young men," he said to me one night when he spotted me coming in from a hunt.

"Why?" I retorted boldly.

"I loathe the idea of you in the arms of anyone who might entice you."

I laughed aloud at this preposterous statement and he

115

slapped my face.

"Never mock me again," he warned.

I took a step back. "My lord…"

Arsham gripped my shoulders tightly as his eyes bore into mine. "I made you, Angelique. You are mine." He shook me roughly. "Do you understand?"

His mouth came down on mine in a savage kiss. We were alone in the main hall where anyone could walk in on us. Had he not reprimanded me for showing him affection in public?

"Someone will see us," I said when he nuzzled my neck.

Picking me up in his arms, he carried me to his chamber and made love to me with surprising tenderness.

"Tell me you love me." When I refused to speak he gripped a fistful of my hair and yanked my head back. "Say it."

"I love you."

He looked hurt. "Say my name."

"Arsham."

He kissed me again, this time biting my mouth and drinking my blood. He then offered me his wrist, and I drank his magic blood without preamble. I relished the warmth that spread throughout my body and the euphoria that followed. Then I saw something that I had never seen before: Arsham's eyes glistening with unshed tears. The sight of this tugged at my heartstrings, but my heart remained cold and impenetrable.

Never again.

"To whom do you belong, Angelique?"

Myself. "I am yours, sire," I said flatly.

He knew I was lying. "Where is the love you once had for me? Where is that passionate fire? What happened to your heart?" When I did not respond to any of his questions, he lowered his gaze and turned his face away. "Leave me."

I quietly vacated his chamber and sought the comfort of my own. I thought he would dismiss me and allow me to leave Paris, but he didn't. He insisted that I remain at the chateau, but he never summoned me to his bed again while we lived in France.

116

CHAPTER 9
ENGLAND
19TH CENTURY

"Experience is the teacher of all things."
(Julius Caesar)

Despite our shattered love affair, my unwavering loyalty to Arsham and my conduct within the coven were irreproachable. My reputation as an exemplary elder garnered respect, obedience, and even fear from other vampires. As the years passed, my sire gradually piled responsibilities upon my shoulders. Eventually, he appointed me co-counselor with Micah—a most prestigious position.

The human world around us was changing quickly, and Arsham refused to adjust his pace in accordance to it. I, on the other hand, adapted easily to new ideas and inventions. I found these innovations exciting instead of fearsome. For this reason, I had virtually become Arsham's right hand in many matters regarding culture, society, and trends. Micah kept up with the times through constant research. He eventually became an expert in business, finance, and security. Arsham trusted the two of us with private information, and if there was important news to be delivered to the coven, we were the first to know.

We remained in France until the rise of the British Empire. At that point Arsham decided it would be best to move our coven to England. He sold the chateau in Paris and purchased a modest mansion in Chelsea so as not to draw attention to himself or his coven.

Being in one of the nicest neighborhoods in London meant that we were surrounded by humans. Unlike the solitude of the French countryside, the bustling city of London teemed with life. We were now forced to blend in with humans and mimic the living on a regular basis. Arsham administered strict rules regarding our behavior, our dress, and our mannerisms. We practiced human movement and learned new words and cadences of speech. We read all the latest books to unlock the social moirés of these modern times.

We soon discovered that Arsham wanted more than our successful infiltration into the human world. His ultimate goal was to create a vampire army. We had discussed the possibility of expansion on previous occasions, and now he was ready to put his plans into action. In order to become the biggest and most powerful coven on the European continent, we needed space to create more vampires.

Under Micah's supervision, Europe's best engineers and architects were hired to design our underground lair. On the surface, our home seemed as normal as any other in London. Underground, however, a labyrinth of corridors twisted and turned endlessly beneath the city. In addition to being extremely well paid, these workmen were sworn to secrecy and bound by legal contracts to honor their promise. The project was such a major ordeal that the elders and their children were summoned to act as supervisors during the initial stages of construction.

To keep the architects in as much ignorance as possible, most of the "outside laborers" were actually vampires disguised as humans. During the night, a relatively low number of vampires could easily perform the work of several human men due to their strength and speed. Naturally, keeping such an ambitious project a total secret became impossible. Curious people sometimes stopped and listened to the commotion taking place within our high garden walls. Those who were brazen enough to trespass were met with the vicious Doberman Pinchers Arsham had acquired as daytime sentries. The ferocious black dogs were big and muscular. One journalist who tried to sneak onto the property was so badly bitten that his leg suffered terrible infection. Word quickly spread to avoid the mysterious property altogether. I grew to like the intimidating black dogs and showed them affection each night during their feeding time.

The newspaper soon wrote an article about an "eccentric tycoon" who was spending a fortune remodeling his home "in a most secretive manner" in the heart of London. Arsham flew into a rage upon reading the article and ordered me to pay a visit to the editor of the newspaper as soon as possible.

I donned a fashionably tailored coat and long skirt in navy blue, along with a spectacular hat. The black mesh netting covered the upper half of my face and two glossy cock feathers sprouted from silk roses in shades of blue and black. As I admired my reflection in the mirror, I had to admit that I cut a formidable figure. I picked up the wrapped parcel on my bed and went in search of Micah.

I found him bent over a book in the library. He'd given up the monk's robe a few decades earlier in favor of simple trousers, boots, and tailored coats—a marked improvement. The majority of us favored the color black since it allowed us to blend into the night with ease, thus facilitating our hunting expeditions.

"You look quite fetching," he said when he noticed me standing by the door.

"Thank you," I said, placing the package on the desk.

"What's this?"

"A gift. I went shopping last night. Hopefully you like it enough to wear it when you accompany me this evening."

"Arsham instructed you to pay the editor a visit, not me."

"I know. I want you to come with me."

"Angelique…"

"Micah, the world is so different now—it's exciting! You can't experience it through written words alone, you have to get out there and see it for yourself."

"I hunt," he pointed out defensively.

"That's not the same thing. Besides, you always hunt alone and you return immediately afterward. I want you to come with me. Please?"

He sighed resignedly. "I'll go *this* time."

I smiled as Micah unwrapped the parcel. Inside was a beautifully tailored wool coat and matching trousers in burgundy plum with black pinstripes. A black silk shirt, black top hat, and black satin cravat completed the outfit.

He shook his head with a slight smile on his face. "Really, Angelique, this is too much."

"Hurry up and get dressed."

He left the room to change and returned looking like a distinguished English gentleman. I clapped my hands in delight.

"What will we do about my eyes?" he asked.

I reached into the velvet purse that dangled from my wrist and pulled out a pair of round spectacles. The lenses were tinted dark green. "This should do it."

Micah donned the spectacles. "How do I look?"

"Handsome and distinguished." I slipped my hand into the crook of his elbow. "Shall we, sir?"

"Yes, my lady."

We set out as soon as the sun had set. The sidewalks and streets bustled with people, horses, and carriages. Two muscular guards in identical tailored black suits escorted us on our mission. Humans instinctively moved out of our way while staring at us. We parted through crowded London like the ancient Israelites crossing the Red Sea. When we arrived at our destination, a thin woman with lanky hair and crooked teeth greeted us warily from behind a small wooden desk.

"We're here to see the editor," I said politely.

I could smell her fear. "He's busy at the moment."

I let go of Micah's arm and stepped closer to the desk. "I'm sure he'll want to see us immediately," I said, compelling her to do my bidding.

The woman stood. "Please follow me."

She opened the door and we entered a spacious room containing a large desk beneath a series of windows. A burly man of about fifty with curled, white mustachios frowned at the intrusion. He wore a crumpled tweed coat and his shirt collar seemed too tight for his meaty neck.

"I said I was unavailable today!" he bellowed.

His initial outrage subsided when I smiled sweetly at him. He was about to return the smile when he spotted Micah and the two guards in my wake. The woman silently retreated, closing the door.

"Are you the editor?" I asked.

He frowned. "Who wants to know?"

I walked around the desk and placed my lips to his ear. As I spoke to him in hushed tones, he stared nervously at the three silent figures standing unnaturally still on the opposite side of the room. By the time I had finished speaking with him, the terrified man promised never to write another word about us again. My companions threw him contemptuous glances as further warning before following me out the door.

"That was entertaining," Micah commented drily as we exited the building.

I turned to the two guards. "Leave us."

"Arsham commanded—"

"That you accompany me to the newspaper office, and you just did. Mission accomplished. Now, please, go."

They respectfully inclined their heads and took off in the opposite direction, leaving Micah and I alone. I took my brother's arm and leaned against him, mimicking the manner of human women with their male escorts. We slowed our pace and strolled under the evening sky, blending in with dozens of other couples taking advantage of the mild weather. The public gardens were in bloom, and the scents of jasmine, lilacs, and daffodils sweetened the air.

"We should head back," Micah said.

"We should enjoy this lovely evening," I countered, inhaling deeply to drive the point home. "We have done as Arsham commanded and the night is still young."

"But—"

"Shhh," I prompted, placing my finger to his lips.

After a while, he said, "I would prefer to sit and watch."

My eye fell upon a dimly lit café across the street. The posh place offered outdoor tables and cushioned chairs. He led me to one of the tables, then pulled out my chair. We ordered a pot of tea and a plate of biscuits and pretended to consume both as we watched the world.

"Isn't this horrible, Micah?" I inquired sarcastically.

He threw me a rare, toothy smile. "It's actually pleasant."

"See? I told you the world had changed for the better."

Before long, Micah was chatting away about literature, art, and politics. The new trend of intellectual café culture came naturally to him. A nearby couple sipped absinthe and we were secretly amusing ourselves by observing the effect it had on them. Suddenly, I caught a whiff of a familiar scent.

Micah tensed. "What's wrong?"

I gripped his wrist and whispered, "Shifter."

He stood immediately, pulling me up with him. We left money on the table and hastily melted into the shadows. Our steps were silent as we headed for the darkness of a nearby park. The scent became more pungent. We stopped and I turned around in a slow, tight circle until I pinpointed the shifter. It was a dark haired young man seated on a bench. Another man made his way toward us, and he held the long, thin sword I had seen almost a century ago. There was no mistaking the black hair and the slight slant of the eyes. Gilles's gaze had held fascination, but this slayer's eyes were filled with hatred.

Micah hissed. "Sauvage."

Before I could intervene, he attacked the slayer with lightning speed. The shifter tried to flee the scene, but I was too quick for him and broke his neck in one fluid motion. A nearby scream made me look up. A woman leading a child by the hand had stopped to stare at me in horror. I let the dead shifter's body fall to the ground.

"Help! Police!"

Micah dodged the slayer's katana. Ignoring the woman's cry for help, I reached under my long skirt for the dagger I normally kept strapped to my thigh. The slayer rounded on Micah, who hissed and bared his fangs menacingly in return. I remembered all too well what the last Sauvage did to one of my brethren. There was no way I was about to let it happen again. I grasped the blade of my dagger and crept until I had a clear view of the slayer's back. With a flick of my wrist, the dagger flew through the air and lodged itself into the slayer's shoulder. The sword fell from his grip as he yelped in pain. Police whistles filled the air along with the pounding of several heavily shod feet. I grabbed hold of Micah's wrist and pulled him away.

"Let me finish him off," he insisted.

"Police are closing in—I've already been seen!"

Reluctantly, he stopped resisting and we flew into the night. I looked over my shoulder to see the slayer pulling my dagger from his wound. He fell to his knees as the police arrived.

We told Arsham of our encounter and the news spread throughout the coven. There was a Sauvage in London working with a shifter, and he may not be the only one. New security rules and protocols were immediately implemented. Arsham purchased the latest model pistols by the case, and we used the vast grounds within the walled garden as a shooting range. I was both pleased and relieved to learn that my aim was true, and set myself to the task of teaching newborns how to defend themselves and our coven. Things would never be the same again in London.

My visit to the editor had proved successful in preventing the printed word, but that didn't stop the rumors. People loved to gossip, and there was still too much to say about the mysterious new residents of Chelsea. Luckily, this didn't trigger the curiosity of vampire slayers. Perhaps this was due to our strategy of living our lives out in the open rather than cowering in the shadows. They would never think to search for us in such a posh neighborhood. Besides, there were many eccentric, lavishly wealthy families in London.

"Why not put the humans at ease, sire," Micah suggested to Arsham one day. "You could make a public appearance or attend a social event."

Arsham shook his head. "Out of the question."

I decided to intervene. "Micah is right, sire. Presenting yourself publicly would satisfy their insatiable curiosity and allow the people to talk of something—or someone—else."

Our sire heaved a sigh. "The idea is unappealing to me."

"Very well," I conceded. "We can simply continue to be the object of their obsession indefinitely."

That made him relent. "I will do it, but not alone. Both of you shall accompany me wherever I go."

I was familiar with the rules of Victorian society. I could not simply show up on his arm without a pretense. "Whom shall I be, sire? Your sister, your cousin?"

Arsham frowned. "My wife. Micah will be your brother."

Micah and I exchanged glances; he seemed more disturbed than me by this arrangement.

"And our names?" I inquired.

Arsham shrugged. "Smith."

"Mr. and Mrs. Smith?" I asked, refraining from commenting on the suspiciously generic nature of such a surname.

"Yes." Arsham paused in thought then added, "Under no circumstances can we attend a dinner."

Micah nodded in agreement. "A wise choice, my lord. Our lack of appetite for human food would draw too much unwanted attention."

"I agree," I said.

Within a few weeks we had carefully chosen a smattering of social events to attend, but socializing with the humans required a bit more effort than merely blending in with them. We wandered out in the evenings to practice with random people; short conversations about the weather, asking for directions with map in hand, purchasing flowers from a vendor. With each interaction we grew more confident in our abilities.

Arsham had already taken care of our wardrobes, providing us with the latest Victorian fashions. We wore cosmetics to mimic human complexions, and practiced blinking and breathing. Micah wore tinted spectacles in various shades to hide his eyes, and applied rouge to his alabaster skin to make it seem more lifelike. When anyone inquired about his spectacles, he would reply that he had a rare condition which required protection from light. We quickly learned popular dance steps, and soon joined humans on polished parquet floors beneath sparkling crystal chandeliers. The faces surrounding us were usually flushed with delight, while fragile human hearts pumped hard and fast. During these moments it took most of our willpower not to indulge in a feeding frenzy.

We attended charity events, balls, and twilight garden parties. Sometimes I caught Arsham smiling, as if he were actually enjoying himself. One evening at a charity ball, he spun me around on the dance floor and, rather than hand me off to a waiting gentleman, he held me tightly in his arms. I caught Micah staring at us from across the floor, and I could see that he was as shaken as I by our sire's boldness.

Lowering his lips to my ear, Arsham whispered, "Had I met you before I became what I am now, I would have chosen you as my royal bride."

His eyes held a softness that I had never seen before as he passed me off to the waiting gentleman.

Later that night as I danced with Micah, he asked, "What did Arsham say to you?"

Although I trusted Micah, I refrained from telling him the truth. "I could barely hear him above the music."

He narrowed his eyes at me. "Be careful, Angelique."

We made our way home in a hansom cab with Arsham holding my hand as though we were human lovers. I caught Micah's look of disgust before he shifted in his seat to stare out the window. The cobblestoned streets were slick from the rain, reflecting the golden glow of gaslights. The sound of the horse's hooves echoed loudly in the night.

Arsham brought my knuckles to his lips, then inquired, "Did you ever think of children?"

The abrupt question caught me off-guard. "I haven't met anyone that I wish to turn, sire."

"No, I meant mortal children. When you were human—did you ever think of having any?"

Micah gaped at Arsham in disbelief.

I met my sire's eyes. "I came to be with child once, but I lost it." Perhaps the intimacy of the small space and having my hand held like a human girl prompted this confession from me.

Arsham's face grew sad. "I'm sorry to hear it, Angelique. You would have made a wonderful mother."

Micah's expression went from disbelieving to incredulous.

Arsham became pensive and looked out the window for the remainder of the ride home.

The memory of my miscarriage caused me to feel emotions that I had long forgotten. I kept my tears at bay as the driver pulled up in front of our home. With a crack of the whip, he took off into the night once we had alighted from the hansom. A drunkard wobbled on the sidewalk ahead, reeking of gin. Arsham set upon him instantly and urged us to join him. Micah and I declined, then watched as our sire drained the man dry. He left the corpse on the sidewalk. Tomorrow, the police would assume another worthless drunk had met his untimely demise.

I walked through the iron gates and into the house in contemplative silence. Micah and I bade our sire a good rest and turned to go, but Arsham grabbed hold of my wrist. Micah turned around and Arsham waved him away. Micah's eyes met mine before he bowed his head and headed toward his chamber.

My sire caressed my cheek and whispered, "I need you." When I hesitated, he added, "Please."

Please? Arsham never asked for anything. He commanded, he demanded, and he took what he wanted by force, if necessary. I nodded and he took me to his bed for the first time in many decades.

***

Arsham desperately searched for something, and it became painfully obvious that he hoped to find it in me. I shared my sire's bed after that night. Most of the time he desired to be held throughout the day while he slept. When the sun rose, he nestled into my arms like a child seeking comfort from his mother.

My heart remained barricaded toward him—and all other males for that matter. My mind would often race as I watched my sire sleep. Perhaps this new age was finally taking its toll on him. I knew he sometimes mourned for the old ways. Would I behave in the same manner hundreds of years from now? Is this the price we must pay for immortality? Do we eventually dive into a sea of loneliness and madness?

During this strange phase, Arsham declared his desire to go on a journey. The announcement came after our yearly meeting of elders. Deirdre and Ciara were excited by the prospect of possibly accompanying him. When Arsham declared his intention to take only me with him, they became sullen and openly hostile in my presence. Micah, Valerio, and Omar were instructed to stay behind in London and act as coven leaders during our absence. Valerio and Micah would oversee the final phases of the construction project whereas Omar was appointed head of security.

Micah took me aside one evening and led me out into the garden. Under the full moon, he asked, "Are you certain that you want to go with him?"

"Do I really have a choice in the matter?" I countered.

"I suppose not…I was afraid this would happen."

"What?"

"Arsham is grooming you and preparing the coven." When I stared at him in confusion, he added irritably, "Surely, you cannot be so naïve?"

We stopped walking and I placed my hand on his arm. "Do you think he wants me as his official mate?"

"The entire coven thinks that."

Was there a twinge of resentment in his voice? "What do you think, Micah?"

"I think you're going to get hurt. Again."

I laughed softly, taking in his elegant gray suit. "Dearest Micah, I'm touched by your concern—"

"Don't patronize me!"

Taken aback, I said, "I didn't mean—"

"You assume that I'm still a monk. Just because I've never…" He trailed off and pressed his lips together tightly.

When he remained silent, I finished the sentence for him. "Lain with a woman."

Micah glared at me in a manner that confirmed his virginity. Realization hit me—it wasn't resentment that consumed him. He lowered his head in shame.

"Micah, look at me," I urged softly.

He shook his head. "I may not be human, but I'm still male."

"Of course you are. Look at me, please."

Slowly, his eyes met mine and I knew. I had seen that look in my own reflection when I was in love with Arsham: the pain of unrequited love. "Oh, Micah…"

My pity only angered him, and he jerked away from me. "Don't you dare, Angelique."

As he turned to go, I called out, "Wait!"

He stormed off and I returned to my quarters, defeated.

I was too worried about Micah to sleep. It distressed me to be the cause of his pain. Maybe he was awake, too, and we could talk privately about the matter. After all, we were friends.

I crept to Micah's chamber and placed my ear to the door. I heard the sound of ragged breathing, fast and shallow. Standing back, I raised my hand to knock on the door and stopped. Instead, I did something shameful—I crouched and peeked through the keyhole. Micah sat upon the bed masturbating to the light of single candle. His face reflected a combination of anger and frustration.

***

Arsham and I departed a week later. Rather than use our supernatural abilities to travel, my sire wanted to experience a locomotive. His fascination with modern machines meant it would take longer to reach our destination, but we had nothing but time on our hands. By now we could mimic human behavior so well that no one gave us a second glance.

We traveled south, crossed the English Channel into France, and then boarded another train going east. Arsham wanted to show me his birth city. I made it clear to the purser that "my husband" and I were never to be disturbed during the day. I explained that he was a famous foreign author who found inspiration nocturnally, and I followed my strange request with a generous tip. Needless to say, no one bothered us.

Relief washed over me when we finally arrived in Persia. We spent many weeks traveling throughout the region, and I marveled at the sheer magnificence of the ancient art and architecture. He took me to the palace where he was born, and I learned many things about Arsham—things he had never shared with any other vampire. To my dismay, he insisted that

I accompany him on the hunt. I hated killing humans, but I had no choice while in his presence.

Our journey continued to India, China, and Japan, where I saw many katana swords on display at a museum. My experience with Eastern cultures opened my eyes and my mind. How different their ideologies were in comparison to our Western civilization. I reveled in the sumptuous fabrics and fantastic gods being worshipped in these lands. I also found the Eastern philosophies on life and the afterlife intriguing. They held deep wisdom that rang refreshingly true. I hid in the crowds at night and listened with rapt attention to holy men and gurus in the squares. Arsham allowed me to wrap myself in vibrant silks in shades of saffron and fire, and chant with Buddhist monks during a midnight ceremony involving hundreds of candles.

We traveled on foot through wild, vast territories. I sat and listened to the sound of silence in the mountains, and the seductive whisper of the wind as it blew through the lush valleys. I stretched out naked in a grassy field lit by the moon and absorbed the Earth's energy. I pondered the mysteries of the universe, learned local languages, and read everything I could get my hands on.

Arsham spoke of his youth while we were atop the Great Wall of China. We were the only two people for miles, and I was in awe of the sheer magnitude of such an architectural feat. Maybe it was the solitude or the historical significance of the site, but for the first time I saw my sire as a human.

In addition to being the second son of a great Persian king, Arsham had been destined from birth to marry a woman he didn't know or love. Childhood betrothals were common since it forged strong bonds between ruling families. Arsham claimed to have had a privileged upbringing in a luxurious setting. He also admitted to having had many beautiful noble ladies as mistresses, but he never loved any of them. In fact, the only woman he had ever loved was his mother.

"I would watch my mother from afar whenever she sat in her garden. She liked to sing—she had a good voice. All I ever wanted as a boy was for her to love me as much as I loved her," Arsham confessed. His expression turned bitter. "But her heart belonged to my older brother, the future king."

I deduced that my sire's inability to love stemmed from childhood rejection. The Persian king had proved a distant father, praising his sons only when they displayed prowess on the battlefields. Although only one was destined to become king, both brothers were trained to rule and were well versed in the art of weaponry, military strategy, and diplomacy. This precaution was taken in the event that the firstborn died and the other be forced to take his place.

As the second son, Arsham had held a high-ranking position in the royal army. He married his betrothed and soon became father to a fine son. Unfortunately, his wife died two years later while giving birth to a stillborn daughter. Shortly after this tragedy, a merciless plague swept through the land, killing thousands. Arsham lost his only son and his beloved mother on the same night. Mad with grief, he tried to take his own life.

I placed my hand on Arsham's shoulder in a gesture of compassion and understanding as he recounted his story. Beneath the cold arrogant exterior existed a vulnerable being capable of great emotion. My own heart, which up until now harbored resentment, softened in the presence of his pain.

The wind howled above our heads. Since we were so high from the ground, we felt the full brunt of it against our bodies. We faced the east, ever vigilant of the coming dawn.

Focusing on the horizon he said, "I cut open my wrists. I knew it was cowardly. I should have thrown myself onto my sword like a real man, but I just couldn't bring myself to do it. As I lay there covered in my own blood, a vampire interceded."

I whispered, "Someone you knew?"

"A slave." He turned his head toward me. "To this day I can't believe that a lowly slave granted me the gift of immortality. When I awoke, I was a vampire. The slave had vanished, leaving me alone. I knew I couldn't stay in the palace anymore, so I left Persia. The rest is, as they say, history."

"But, sire, you had no one to teach you our ways. How did

130

you manage alone?"

A wry smile touched his lips. "Like you, I was intrigued by my newfound strength and power. Many lessons I learned on my own, a few I learned during my travels after having met others of our kind. I then set out to do what I had been trained to do since childhood—conquer and rule. Once I realized that I could create other vampires, I formed my own kingdom."

A long pause followed his words. I kept my hand on his shoulder and he covered it with his own.

"I have never told this story to anyone," he confessed.

The unspoken understanding that what I had just heard was meant for my ears only hovered in the air between us.

He finally looked down at me and frowned. "We must take cover. Dawn approaches."

***

When we returned to England from our journey several years later, I was a different person; I was enlightened. Valerio and Micah had done a fine job of overseeing the construction in London, and Arsham asked them to stay on permanently. Omar had cared for the coven during our absence and had little to report. We had lost none of our ranks to the slayers and shifters prowling the city.

Our underground lair complete, Arsham took great pleasure in selecting its furnishings. Inspired by our recent journey, he purchased rich Oriental carpets, enormous brass lanterns with intricate cut-outs, and exquisitely carved furniture.

The Victorian mansion in Chelsea existed merely for show. The impeccably furnished ground level served to keep up the pretense, but the second floor served as a training area for weaponry and fighting. Arsham recently commissioned a large training arena underground, but it would take years to complete.

It only took a few days to settle back into a routine after my long journey abroad. To my dismay, Micah avoided me. He had changed drastically, too. Oozing confidence, his cocky swagger drew the attention of young females in our coven.

Sad to have lost my good friend, I spent most of my time practicing my sword fighting and the martial arts I had learned while in the East. One evening while polishing my sword, I noticed Micah hovering in the doorway.

Wearing tight black leather jodhpurs, black leather boots, and a loose black shirt open halfway down the front to reveal his hairless chest, he watched me quietly. The black against the smooth alabaster of his skin was striking.

I smiled and stood. "Micah."

Ignoring me, he strolled into the training area and chose a sword from the vast collection hanging on the wall. He came to before me, thus challenging me to spar with him.

"Do you think you can beat me?" I teased.

Micah attacked me. I staggered back to defend the blow. He lunged at me again with a fierceness that shocked me. I sidestepped and parried, only to turn around and deflect yet another aggressive blow. The point of his sword caught the top of my sleeve and he pulled down hard, tearing the fabric all the way down to the cuff.

"You've been practicing, I see," I said, examining the damage done to my perfectly good shirt.

He wasted no time ripping the other sleeve. Irritated, I fought back in earnest. The tip of my sword scratched his left cheek and drew blood. Hissing in outrage, he plunged his sword into my thigh. I cried out and knelt, but quickly rolled out of the way of his blade. My wound healed quickly and I looked in dismay at the stain of blood on the fabric of my trousers. Ruined! I heard a ripping sound and saw that the front of my already torn shirt opened to reveal my pale pink corset.

"Was that really necessary?" I demanded, annoyed.

Micah's response was to attack again. I ducked, removing the scraps of fabric that were once my shirt. I pounced, ripping the front buttons off his shirt. He removed it and fought me shirtless. I couldn't help but admire his flawless, white muscles.

A whooshing sound near my ear made me stand at attention. Micah was fast—maybe a bit too fast. He could have decapitated me. I wasn't fighting at the level I normally would if faced by a real enemy, but I would hurt him soon if he didn't stop this nonsense.

132

"Stop, Micah," I said.

He lunged at me again.

"I said STOP."

This time, he lowered his sword and glared at me. I stared at him from ten feet away. He dropped his sword and it landed with a loud, clanking sound on the polished tile floor. Gathering the remains of his black silk shirt, he knelt and lowered his head.

I approached him cautiously. "Micah, what's this all about?"

He jumped up and grabbed my shoulders. Anger, hurt, pain—all of these emotions were reflected in his eyes. "I expect to hear the big announcement at the annual elder's meeting."

"What announcement?" Realization dawned on me and I shook my head. "My relationship with Arsham is not what you think. Our journey together was not of *that* nature. He never asked me to be his official mate."

"How unfortunate for you," he retorted petulantly.

"I would have denied the request."

Appeased, he looked down at his sword. "Forgive me. I would never deliberately hurt you. Sorry about your shirt."

I allowed my heart to soften and opened my arms. He entered the circle of my embrace and hugged me tightly.

"I missed you, Angelique," he confessed.

I sighed. "I missed you, too."

He pressed me against him, and I stiffened when he began kissing my neck. When his hands began rubbing my back, I panicked. He brought his mouth to mine and kissed my lips, but I couldn't bring myself to return his kiss.

Disappointment colored his features when he pulled away. "I guess you'll never be my official mate, either."

"No, but I'll be your friend, which is a far better thing."

"I cannot argue that point."

"Besides, I think there would be many brokenhearted girls in this coven if you took on a mate. I've seen how they look at you whenever you strut past them."

If Micah could blush in that moment, I think he would have done so. Instead, he smiled smugly. I placed my arm around his waist and we made our way outside together with a new understanding between us.

Deidre and Ciara arrived a few weeks later for the annual meeting, followed by Birsa and the other children. I tried to speak with Birsa but she remained distant toward me. She presented herself to Arsham and left the next day without saying a word to anyone.

One day, I overheard the twins confronting Arsham as I passed them in the corridor. They wanted to know when they would be taken on a journey. Arsham only chuckled in response as he caught my eye.

CHAPTER 10

"Not until we are lost
do we begin to understand ourselves."
(Henry David Thoreau)

Once again, the world around us changed. Modern man used his scientific knowledge for evil as well as for good. Weapon technology made mass murder a startling and disturbing reality at the onset of the twentieth century. The First World War claimed millions of lives in a relatively short amount of time. Not only were wars bigger, empires had grown to epic proportions. By the 1920's the British Empire covered over thirty three million square miles throughout the globe. It was the largest formal empire the world had ever known; an empire in which the sun never set.

It became obvious to many that Arsham hated this new world. Micah and I tried to keep him engaged by introducing him to new ideas, inventions, and philosophies. It was no use, however. He began to draw into himself, and left the lair only to hunt. He lost interest in society and he lost interest in me. I could no longer offer him the solace he desperately sought, and was again banished from his bed.

As the years passed, our sire's mood grew foul. The elders and their children now resided permanently under one roof, putting an end to the long tradition of annual meetings. I finally confronted Arsham on this issue, only to be told that the world had simultaneously lost its elegance and its innocence.

I could not disagree with his assessment. The world had become an ugly place full of violence and greed. While these vile traits had always existed throughout history, they were given a new definition in the twentieth century. We were shocked by the blood spilled during the Second World War, and when we heard the tales of Hitler's concentration camps, some of the older vampires were reminded of the terrible Burning Times brought on by the Catholic Inquisition. The United States of America bombed two Japanese cities full of innocent civilians, compelling Arsham to declare humans as evil beings. Never before had murder been committed on such a grand scale; the very concept was unnatural and abhorrent even to us—the soulless creatures of the Night.

***

Arsham roused slowly but surely from his self-imposed exile as we paraded the glory of modern technology before his eyes. There were many marvelous inventions to behold—fast automobiles, television sets, space satellites—and when humans stepped on the moon, our sire became insatiably curious. To the coven's delight, he wanted to experience many things firsthand rather than hearing about them.

He outfitted our lair with the latest and the best of everything money could buy. The Victorian mansion in Chelsea was eventually leveled to the ground, and a state-of-the-art weapons training facility was erected in its place. Our ivy-covered, crumbling brick walls were replaced with hi-tech security cameras and metal fences. Our coven resided within an impenetrable compound, the largest of its kind on the European continent. Thanks to Micah's genius, all of this existed under the clever guise of a private company specializing in high-end security systems. We sold our products to corporate entities and increased our fortunes in the process.

Arsham became the overlord to the sires of smaller covens, even absorbing a few of them into our own. These new, less-powerful sires were given almost the same status as elders, and joined us in the decision-making process.

My sire changed. The tenderness I had glimpsed during the Victorian era became a faded memory. Drunk with power, Arsham became exceedingly arrogant and even cruel at times. He showed little or no mercy toward disloyalty, even going as far as publicly executing dissenters.

Deirdre and Ciara were usually on either side of him, reveling in the role that I had once occupied long ago. The smug look on their faces every time I passed them made me sick, but I didn't envy them in the slightest. I didn't like this cold and shallow Arsham who lived like a modern day gangster.

I began spending more time in our weapons training facility, and less time in the underground lair. Arsham approached me one day while I was teaching a group of young vampires how to wield a sword—an outdated method of defense, but still considered an art form. Deirdre and Ciara were with him.

I lowered my sword and inclined my head. "Sire."

"Angelique," he said. He looked to the newborns and motioned with his head for them to leave us alone. He then came forward, leaving the twins a few paces behind. "My coven has grown to the point that I need someone on my security team. If Erika were still here with us, no doubt she would be receiving this honor."

"I appreciate the gesture, but you already have Omar as head of security."

"Yes, but I think it would be good to have an extra person on duty." He chuckled and added, "After all, two heads are better than one."

I cracked a smile at his joke. "Yes."

His eyes narrowed. "You don't' seem very enthused. Do you have a problem with Omar?"

I was taken aback. "Absolutely not. I love Omar."

"It's settled then. Congratulations, Angelique. Erika would be proud."

I inclined my head again to show my gratitude.

Arsham's hand reached out to caress my cheek and I saw longing in his eyes. I must have shown surprise at this because he quickly hid his emotions with a mask of ice. He held out his hand and I kissed the ring without kneeling since we only knelt during official ceremonies, and those were rare nowadays.

CHAPTER 11
LONDON, UK
11 YEARS AGO

"Love is composed of a single soul inhabiting two bodies."
(Aristotle)

The violence and high crime-rate of the modern society we now lived in made hunting easier than ever before. Fashion also aided our nightly endeavors as Punks and Goths hit the streets in faces as frighteningly pale as our own. These rebellious youths frequented dimly lit nightclubs, gazing languidly at one another with heavily kohl-lined eyes. Large groups often gathered in big abandoned warehouses or deserted churches, listening to angry music while they injected themselves with hallucinatory drugs. Many would then pair off in dark corners to engage in wild sexual intercourse. Such risky behavior in the face of danger could only mean that these youths welcomed death with open arms, and we were ready to accept their embrace. Their blood was ours for the taking.

I will never forget the first time I laid eyes on Damien. Arsham and I were hunting, silently tracking our prey through dark London streets. He sometimes requested my company when he wanted a break from the twins. We had witnessed a pair of stoned teenagers robbing a convenience store at gunpoint before running off into the cold moonless night. Their heightened adrenaline was simply too mouth-watering for us to ignore, so we followed them. When the kids ducked into an alley, Arsham grinned. Their fates were sealed.

The thought of slaughtering the young sickened me, but I went in after them and stopped short. "Wait."

I glimpsed the silhouette of a pale ginger woman in a classic Burberry trench coat. She stood watching me from the rain-slicked street at the end of the alley. Suddenly, a familiar whooshing sound that I hadn't heard in over a century made Arsham and I flinch. That's when I saw him—long black hair slicked back from a familiar face.

The wicked blade came toward my sire's head once more, compelling me push him out of the way. "Watch out!"

Arsham hissed as he spun around to face his attacker. The slayer's black eyebrows came together and he glanced at me in disbelief. Something about the mortal's gaze held me captive.

A dirty alley in France, the park in London...

I hadn't run into one of the infamous slayers since the Victorian age. Our security protocol was tight, our ruse solid, we ruled the London nights practically undetected. My eyes narrowed at the pretentious young man who assumed that he could easily kill the great and powerful Arsham.

My sire was about to chase his attacker when a fierce orange tabby cat sprang out of a half opened window and tore at his back. The creature moved with greater speed and agility than any normal cat would, then hid behind the dumpster. The crafty shifter cunningly aided the slayer's escape!

Baring my fangs, I said to Arsham. "Allow me, sire."

Upon hearing my words the slayer slid into a narrow passage between the two buildings, then slipped through a broken basement window. He obviously knew his hunting territory, which impressed me—albeit reluctantly.

Exiting the front door of the building, he then ran into the street where he knew I wouldn't openly attack him. I saw him sheath his katana, which he had strapped across his broad back beneath a long black leather coat. Pulling the hood of my designer navy blue trench over my head, I continued tracking him. He ducked into the metro station and I did the same.

"Shit," he said as the train closed its doors and took off.

We were alone on the platform at that late hour. I pinned him by the throat against one of the concrete pillars before he could unsheathe the katana. My movements were so fast that he gasped in surprise.

My eyes skimmed over his handsome features before

settling on his sensuous mouth. This particular Sauvage appeared more European than Eurasian; only the straight black hair gave his Japanese ancestry away. We stared at each other for several seconds.

You couldn't bring yourself to kill Gilles, either.

My ears perked when I heard my sire's heavy footsteps approaching the metro station. "Cut me with your sword and run as fast as you can."

He looked at me incredulously. "What?"

"Do it or you'll die, slayer."

Bewildered, he reached for his sword and held it above his head, debating my decapitation. Exhaling a deep breath, he brought the blade down and partially severed my arm from my shoulder before disappearing into the night. Blood soaked through my coat, resembling a shiny oil stain on fabric.

Arsham rushed onto the platform thirty seconds later with a scowl on his face. "You let him get away?"

I could almost hear the unspoken: *Again?*

"He's faster than the other slayers," I lied, clutching my arm.

Arsham led me outside before the next train pulled up to the platform. Ushering me into a deserted alley, he yanked back my layers of clothing. "Look at you. What a mess."

He bit his wrist and allowed his blood to drip into the gruesome wound. Fire burned in my veins, making me feel powerful and euphoric as it healed the deep cut. It made me feel other things, too. I had not tasted Arsham's blood in decades, and he knew exactly what it did to me. A wicked smile spread across his face as his hands went from straightening the collars of my coat to caressing my neck.

"I'll have to get you a new coat since this one is ruined. You saved my life, Angelique," he said before nuzzling my throat.

"It's my duty," I whispered, helplessly drowning in the bloodlust. It had been a long time since I had experienced desire and it was not unpleasant.

I felt him hardening against me, and his muscular leg forced my thighs apart. The rain began to fall in torrents, but we were protected by the generous overhang of an eave above our heads.

The streets were devoid of people and cars.

Arsham pushed me against the brick wall, then lifted my skirt in order to tease me with his fingers. As I moaned in pleasure, he said in my ear, "You would die for me."

"Yes..."

A satisfied smile stretched across his face as he unzipped his pants and entered me. He took me furtively against the wall, and I couldn't deny that it felt good. I hadn't been touched by a human or a vampire in a long time. Being finicky, my erotic encounters had been few and far between. The last one had taken place over fifty years ago at a Beatle's concert in Edinburgh.

Arsham and I had not made love since Queen Victoria ruled England. With each hungry thrust, he whispered something in my ear. I heard him say how much he missed me in his bed, how he often craved my touch, how he dreamed of me, and how he missed my presence in his life. With his final thrust, just before he shuddered to a standstill in my arms, he whispered ever so faintly that he loved me.

Later, I told myself that I had imagined those words coming from his lips. Surely, the bloodlust had played a trick on me. Arsham was incapable of loving anyone other than himself.

The next night, I anticipated a summons from my sire. Relief washed over me when it didn't come. I really didn't want to be his lover again, and I think he felt the same way. Besides, there were the twins to consider. When I saw him leave the lair with them, I was glad. They were dressed to the hilt in sexy satin dresses and high, strappy heels. Arsham wore a smashing Armani suit in gunmetal charcoal. It was Saturday and they were probably going to some fancy nightclub in the city. The twins loved living the high-life, and Arsham loved showing off his pair of identical, bleached blonde beauties to the world. No doubt, they were a source of envy to every mortal man who laid eyes on the flirtatious trio.

I was on my way to the weapons training facility and caught Arsham's eye as the three of them passed me. He nodded and smiled coolly, which told me the twins had no idea what had transpired between us last night. I understood by his look that our passionate tryst was to remain a secret.

"Feel like some company?" Micah asked, falling into step with me.

Spray tanning, high quality hair dye, and colored contact lenses made him blend in with everyone else, but I missed his alabaster skin and unique eyes.

"As long as it's you," I replied.

***

I ran into the slayer a few weeks later while hunting at an underground Goth bar. It was just after midnight, and I stood leaning against a wall watching the crowd. Several wannabe vampires in vintage garments danced before my eyes. Most of them were arrayed in black, but shades of midnight blue, plum, and black cherry were also popular. I admired their white faces, dark eyes, and maroon lips with detached pleasure. Their costumes were impressive—lace half gloves from a bygone era, body hugging silk corsets paired with long satin skirts or tight leather pants, vinyl body suits, and even a couple of top hats. They mixed the best of the nineteenth century with shiny metal spikes, whips, and elaborate tattoos. The result was quite fascinating, especially beneath the black lights.

"I see your wound has healed nicely."

I turned my head and a pair of stormy eyes met mine. "You're a brave man, slayer," I drawled. "What makes you think you'll be lucky twice in your short lifetime?"

He angled his tall, muscular body toward me, casually leaning his broad shoulders against a concrete wall covered in graffiti. His eyes took in my blue corset, short black skirt, and high black boots with unabashed approval. "Why didn't you kill me?" he asked.

I raised my brow. "Are you on a suicide mission?"

"Any other vamp would have ripped open my throat."

"Obviously, I'm not any other vamp."

"Answer me."

Once again I saw the intriguing combination of fierceness and vulnerability in his gaze. "Perhaps I was inclined toward

142

kindness that night. Don't push your luck, slayer."

"Damien." At the sight of my surprised expression, he added, "That's my name. And vampires are never kind."

"What the hell do you know about vampires?"

"Only what's been passed down to me by my father, and my father's father, and—"

"You come from a long line of slayers," I interjected, rolling my eyes.

"Yes."

I laughed. "That's what all slayers say. You imagine yourselves to be descendants of the most notorious vampire killers in history; as if you're a bunch of comic book superheroes." To further mock him, I added, "I bet you pick up a lot of women with that line, too."

His expression remained stoic. "You must be the Duchess de Nuit." The grin vanished from my face and, despite my angry glare, he continued, "You fit her description."

"What would you know about her description?"

"Only what I read in the journal that was passed down to me when my father died. One of my ancestors wrote about you in several of his passages."

I already knew the answer, but I wanted to hear it from his lips. "Which ancestor?"

"Gilles Sauvage of Marseilles."

I turned my back on him and made to leave but he grabbed my arm. I could have easily broken his hand.

"You knew him," he insisted.

"Let go of my arm."

"Your kind feared Gilles. According to him, you were devastated when he killed your sister—what was her name? Ah, yes. *Erika*."

My fangs were slowly emerging. "Shut up."

The mention of Erika's name had prompted the expected reaction, for he said, "His words were true. Some vampires really are capable of human emotion."

"We were humans once...Erika was beautiful. Wild and free, she possessed the purest of hearts."

143

"She was a killer."

"We kill to eat, just as you kill to eat."

"But we kill inferior species for food."

I closed the gap between us and put my face very close to his. I could smell the excitement on him, the adrenaline rush of having me so dangerously near. I licked my lips, allowing him to catch a glimpse of my terrifying fangs.

"As do we," I whispered in a sultry voice.

Obviously, the thought had never occurred to him. To see it take effect on his facial expression verged on comical. He leaned back and lowered his eyes. When he met my gaze again, his arrogance had vanished. *Fait accompli.*

"You won't kill me."

"Keep it up and I just might," I retorted drily.

To my surprise, he smiled. He had lovely teeth. Such teeth were rare in past centuries. Not even the richest members of the aristocracy were in possession of such pretty, healthy mouths. I suddenly wanted to taste his lips, to feel those teeth against my tongue…

Angelique, this human is a slayer. "I have to go."

"Wait!" he cried at my retreating form. "There was another incident involving you and one of my ancestors."

"Yes, I know," I said, accelerating my pace. "It happened in England. I killed his shifter."

"Thomas Sauvage. He was my great, great grandfather."

"He was lucky to have escaped," I said pointedly.

Damien followed me as I maneuvered through the dancing humans. I couldn't go as fast as I was capable of because I didn't want to draw attention to myself. I would lose him easily enough under the cover of night.

"Don't go," he said, catching up to me and taking hold of my arm.

I didn't stop.

He tightened his grip and kept pace with me as I exited the club. "Angelique—"

I turned the corner and slammed him against the wall of the building. Unbelievably, he still held my arm. "Do you have a death wish?"

"No…I only wanted to thank you for sparing my life in the metro station."

I sighed. "You're welcome. Now here's a bit of advice: not all vampires are so magnanimous. Any other member of my coven would have sucked you dry. Do you understand? Stay away from my kind if you value your life. Find another profession, okay?"

"Yeah, and simply wait until one of you attacks me and uses me as a juice box? I don't think so."

"There are millions of people in the city—far more humans than vampires. The chances of you being hunted down are quite slim; practically non-existent."

"Oh, that makes me feel better," he said sarcastically.

I frowned. "I'm trying to give you some practical advice."

"Thanks, but no thanks. Being helpless isn't my style. I like having control of my destiny. If I die as a slayer at least I'll go down fighting for a cause I believe in, and not from being a meal."

He had a point. "Suit yourself."

Cat piss and incense filled the air. I pulled away from him and turned my head in the direction of the offensive odor. The ginger shape shifter who had attacked Arsham in the alley stood ten feet away on the sidewalk. Her white skin and light red hair practically glowed in the moonlight.

"Everything's okay, Felicia," he said.

Staring at me in horror, she didn't seem convinced. "What are you doing, Damien? Do you know what she is?"

"Yes," he replied.

"Are you high?"

Smelling her fear, I offered, "He's not high or crazy—well, maybe a little crazy."

"That's my roommate, Felicia," he explained.

"Your helper from the other night," I said.

He nodded. "She's a—"

"I know what she is. I can smell a shifter a mile away."

"You can smell me?" Felicia asked, obviously upset.

145

"I smelled you in the alley, which is why your attack failed."
I paused. "I can't believe I'm having this conversation with the
two of you."

"Vamps aren't supposed to be able to smell us," Felicia said,
her feet shuffling nervously. "She might be dangerous. Where's
your katana?"

"Felicia, it's okay. Angelique is not like the others. She
saved my life, remember? She's the one Gilles wrote about."

At the mention of my identity Felicia's concern evaporated
and she visibly relaxed. "She's the duchess? Are you sure?"

"Yes."

"I'm going back inside for a drink. Yell if you need me."

We watched Felicia walk away.

I crossed my arms, astonished. "You and your friend have
no fear of me."

He shrugged. "Why would we after what Gilles wrote?"

My eyes narrowed. "Gilles could have been lying. Besides,
people change with time and so do vampires."

"If you wanted to kill me, I'd be dead by now. So would
Felicia." I turned to go and he pulled me back. "Wait. When
will I see you again?"

History really did repeat itself.

I laughed without humor and melted into the night. Why
didn't I kill him? I pondered this question all the way home. I
entered our lair feeling guilty, as if I had just consorted with an
enemy. Omar and Valerio were chatting in one of the seating
areas as I made my way to my chamber.

"Don't you look sexy?" Valerio drawled comically as his
eyes swept over me.

Wearing a ridiculously expensive Versace silk shirt and
black slacks, he resembled a GQ model. His black wavy hair
was cropped very short in the latest style. Witty, charming, and
alluring, Valerio was quite popular in all the gay clubs. An
endless array of pretty boys were at his disposal.

Omar, on the other hand, dressed in accordance with his
quiet, reserved nature. He looked more like a conservative
businessman these days than a warrior. He had a taste for finely

made suits, and sometimes employed the same tailors as Arsham. He had an official mate, too. A mocha skinned beauty from Ethiopia. Omar had passed her in the street and it had been love at first sight. Arsham had granted Omar permission after hearing his case and discussing it with the elders. I remember their touching ceremony with fondness. The joyous occasion was the equivalent of a human wedding. Omar had debated for months before taking the risk.

Arsham's law was clear: if we met a human we wanted to change, we had to first seek his approval and prove to him that the human was worthy of immortality. A detailed list of his or her attributes and talents needed to be presented before the elders. Once permission was granted, the human was brought into the lair by the vampire. Then, before the entire coven, the human would be exposed to the truth and our nature would be revealed. After the initial expected shock, the human was offered a choice: accept the gift of immortality or die. The decision had to be made immediately. No exceptions. Unfortunately, throughout the years I had witnessed a few rejections and the tragic executions were extremely unpleasant for everyone involved. For this reason, the majority of vampires sought their mates and lovers from within the confines of our own species.

Even Omar commented on my appearance, which was something he rarely did since his dark eyes seldom strayed from his mate. "You do look particularly lovely this evening. Where have you been?"

Did my excitement at having met Damien show on my face? I hoped not.

Valerio's eyes narrowed at me. "Is there someone special you've been keeping quiet about?"

Damn you, Valerio!

Omar cocked his head to the side, amused. "Who's the lucky vampire?"

I put my hands on my hips. "Omar, you know better than to feed his fire." I looked at Valerio and added, "There is no one special in my life right now. Except for my beloved brothers."

Valerio chuckled. "Brava!"

"Now, if you gentlemen will excuse me, I need my beauty sleep."

They laughed and wished me a pleasant rest. Once inside my chamber, I went straight to the mirror to study my reflection. My heightened color and bright eyes weren't the result of the creepy Goth's blood that I had consumed earlier. I saw excitement reflected in the mirror.

And I saw lust.

***

Arsham's power and right to rule had gone unchallenged for many decades. As sire to the biggest coven in Europe, and overlord to the sires of smaller covens, Arsham was The Law. He created rules and expected them to be followed without question. Each vampire knew his or her place within the hierarchy and because of this, harmony ensued.

A few nights after my encounter with Damien, the elders were summoned for an emergency meeting. We sat inside a private circular room deep within our lair. Arsham's throne was against the opposite wall, facing the entrance. He stood from his seat and held up an old sheet of vellum containing strange script. The elders looked to one another, confused.

Valerio said, "I don't recognize the writing."

"That's because it's written in Old Persian," Arsham explained. "Someone pushed it under the outside gate of our compound."

"What does it say?" Micah asked.

Arsham replied, " 'No lamp burns until morning.' It's an ancient proverb."

The room fell silent as we pondered the implication.

Omar frowned. "This should be taken as a serious threat."

Micah added, "A threat obviously meant for you, sire, since you're the only one here who can read Old Persian."

Omar said, "I suggest we increase our security and reinforce our current alarm system. We should begin a mandatory weapons training program for everyone."

Arsham held up his hand. "I know you take my personal

safety very seriously, Omar—"

Deirdre interjected, "We all do, sire."

Ciara nodded and added, "We'll find this impertinent fool and destroy him!"

"Death to the usurper!" Valerio said dramatically with a raised fist.

Micah and I watched our sire in silence as the others began speaking at the same time. Arsham sat on his throne, gazing at the letter while rubbing his chin. Something about his expression made me wary.

"Leave me, all of you," Arsham said. "I need to think."

I lagged behind as everyone vacated the room. When I was alone with Arsham, I approached his throne and whispered, "You can count on me, sire."

"I know," he said, not looking at me.

Before stepping out into the hallway, I saw Arsham place his head in his hands.

"I'm going to need you to put in extra hours, Angelique."

My head spun toward Omar's voice. "Of course."

"Many newborns need proper training in order to fight well. If any of them are good enough for the security team, let me know."

"I'm on it." He moved to leave but I stopped him. "I think there's more to that proverb, don't you?"

"I know there is," he replied in a low voice. Taking my arm, he led me toward a sitting area. "Arsham obviously doesn't want to tell us the whole story, at least not yet."

"But it may compromise his safety—ours, too."

Omar's mouth twisted into a grimace. It was something he did whenever he was upset about something. "He must have his reasons. It's our duty to respect his authority and be patient. Keep me posted if you hear anything on the streets."

"I will, and I expect the same courtesy."

"You got it."

We parted in different directions. I spent the next few days recruiting potential fighters to join our security team. Their training would commence immediately.

Arsham kept close to his chambers and avoided going out. When he did venture away from the lair, security surrounded him. The ancient proverb had troubled him deeply and I was determined to find out why. Then a thought struck me: the slayer and his sidekick shifter seemed to know the streets well enough. It was worth a try.

I donned black tights, black boots, and a black trench coat in order to seamlessly blend into the night. I tied my hair back into a sleek ponytail, applied kohl to my eyes, and finished the look with red lipstick. I needed to look the part of a woman out on the town.

I set out in search of Damien the moment the sun had set. I'd been tracking him for several weeks, watching him from the shadows while he went about his nightly business. Even though I told myself that my interest in him was purely out of concern for my brethren, I knew it wasn't true. As much as I hated admitting it, the incredibly sexy slayer had captured my interest.

My search began at the top, in the swanky bars and plush lounges of London. I "descended" to the trendy bars, then lower still to the grungy dives of the city. I was about to head over to a dodgy underground club when I caught a whiff of Felicia. I wrinkled my nose in distaste and tracked the scent. I caught her exiting an Indian restaurant with a group of friends. The combination of strong curry and her peculiar odor made me cringe. She caught my eye and froze on the spot.

I slipped my arm through hers in a seemingly friendly gesture. "Hello Felicia."

"Oh, hey," she replied nervously.

"I need to talk to you alone."

"I'll catch up with you guys at the pub," she called out to her companions.

"Sorry to interrupt your plans, but I need your help. Have you and your partner noticed anything weird in the city? Like a new vampire in town?"

Her eyes widened. "You already know?"

"Already know what?"

"This big vampire attacked Damien last night."

150

"Is he hurt?"

Shit, Shit, shit.

Felicia's mouth opened in shock at my obvious concern. "A few bruises. He'll live."

"Glad he's okay," I said, trying to sound nonchalant.

She wasn't fooled, however. "Some vamp we've never seen before jumped him on the street. Looked like a Viking."

A Viking? The mention of the word brought memories of Erika and the fjords of the North. "Where's Damien now?"

"Why?" she asked pointedly.

"I need to get his version of the story."

She hesitated, determining whether or not to trust me. Finally, she extracted a matchbook from her pocket and wrote on it. "This is the address. Top floor, door on the right. If you so much as harm a hair on his head..."

I could have easily killed the shifter, but her brave front was impressive nonetheless. I decided to play her game. "I need to talk with him, that's all."

"I guess you've had plenty of chances to kill him, huh?"

"More than you know."

Felicia nodded before jetting off to meet her companions at the pub. I crept along the shadows until it was safe to fly at high speed into the night. When I reached Soho, I walked to a historical building full of Victorian embellishments. Smiling nostalgically, I recalled the days of its construction. I went inside and ascended the stairs to the top floor. At the sound of footsteps within, I lifted my hand to take hold of the knocker.

A tense moment of silence passed as someone peered through the peephole. Damien's disbelief mingled with pleasure as he opened the door. Noticing the bruise on the left side of his jaw, my first impulse was to touch his cheek. Thankfully, I was old and experienced enough not to act so precipitously. He stood aside and swept his arm toward the interior of his home.

I crossed the threshold. "Forgive my intrusion."

"I'm at a loss for words."

"I need to ask you a few questions about your attacker."

"What?"

"I spoke with Felicia earlier, she gave me your address and told me you were attacked by a vampire."

"Whoa, hold on—she gave you our address?"

I held out the matchbook. "See?"

"Have a seat," he said, indicating a pea green velvet sofa.

I didn't move. "I don't intend to stay long. I need information on this vampire. Is he new in the city?"

Damien's brow creased. "Why do you want to know?"

"Felicia made him sound like a threat."

"Every vampire is a threat," he retorted evenly.

"Obviously I'm wasting my time. Sorry to have bothered you, Damien."

He grabbed my arm as I turned to go. "I was jumped from behind. He's really strong. Luckily, Felicia was with me. She attacked him while I unsheathed my katana. We managed to fight him off, but it was a close call."

"Do you think he's a loner or part of a group?"

"I don't know." He regarded me thoughtfully. "Does Arsham know you're here?"

"You know my sire?"

"Of course. I can't get anywhere near him because he rarely ventures out, and when he does, he's surrounded by guards. No one knows where he lives, so we assume he changes addresses frequently."

I was relieved that he didn't know about our underground lair. "You realize this is my sire you're speaking of."

"You realize he's a killer, right?"

"No more than the politicians who wage war for profit and kill millions in the process, yet you don't hunt them."

"Point taken." He shook his head and smiled wryly. "Your loyalty to Arsham must be pretty solid if you'll knock on an enemy's door."

"I'm a member of the security team, and this new threat has come to our attention. I'm only doing my job." I paused. "Felicia described him as a Viking."

"Yeah, that's pretty accurate. Big white guy, blond ponytail, prominent features, light eyes."

"Is there anything else you can tell me?"

He shrugged. "I've told you everything I know."

I believed him. We stood facing each other in the middle of his living room and I could feel the heat emanating from his body. I could hear the acceleration of his heartbeat, too.

"How badly did he hurt you?" I asked in order to distract myself. "I see he got your jaw."

"That's nothing," Damien retorted, lifting his shirt. His magnificent torso came complete with washboard abs. A nasty bruise marred most of the left side.

"You should get that checked out," I suggested. "You may have a broken rib."

He lowered his shirt. "I've been hurt worse."

Damien's eyes held mine before tracing the contours of my face and stopping at my mouth. In that moment, my lust fought against my good sense. Thankfully, the latter prevailed.

"I have to go," I said, stepping away from him.

"But—"

"Watch your back."

I opened the door and flew down the stairs. I heard him call my name a few times, but I ignored him. I returned to the lair and reported my findings to Omar. Naturally, I concocted a story on how I obtained the information.

"So, let me get this straight," Omar said, eyeing me closely. "You heard a pair of female shifters talking about a vampire who looked like a Viking."

I nodded. "Their stench was unmistakable. They sat a few stools away from me at the bar."

"They could have been referring to someone else."

"Sure, that's a possibility."

"How did they not detect you?"

"I sniffed them out way before they noticed me, and took off after hearing their exchange."

"You're definitely the stealthiest vampire in our coven."

I tapped my nose in response. "Thanks to this baby. I'll try to glean more information tomorrow."

"Good work, Angelique."

I entered my chamber and closed the door. I hated lying to Omar, but I didn't have a choice.

I continued tracking Damien without his knowledge. The slayer prowled the night with the stealth of a panther. I wondered how many years of training he'd received, and if the techniques were passed down from one Sauvage to the other. His movements were both powerful and fluid, exuding precision and elegance. I couldn't help picturing that magnificent body in the act of lovemaking. The erotic images my mind conjured would make mortal women—and perhaps even some men—blush to the roots of their hair.

One night, while tracking Damien, I had to make my presence known in order to prevent a newborn vampire from being killed. I emerged from the shadows and stepped between the stalker and the prey.

The young vampire, stunned at suddenly finding himself in the presence of an elder, began to stutter. "M-my lady?"

Glancing over my shoulder, I met the slayer's eyes and barely shook my head. The hand that held the katana twitched slightly, but he held his ground.

"I saw you from across the street," I explained to the vampire. "You shouldn't hunt in these parts alone."

Noticing Damien's katana for the first time, the newbie hissed. "Slayer!"

I pushed the newbie toward an alley. "Go!"

The terrified vampire took off like an arrow.

Damien hesitated before sheathing the katana. "You shouldn't interfere in my work."

My eyebrow shot upward. "You shouldn't hunt down my people. You were about to slaughter a kid."

"A vampire," he corrected. "Why are you following me, anyway? You don't want to kill me, so…?"

"Who said I was following you?"

"Oh, so you just happened to be in the neighborhood at exactly the right moment to prevent that vamp's death?"

"Actually, yes."

Damien looked around dubiously at the dilapidated and deserted area. "Really? What are you doing here?"

"That's none of your business."

I turned on my heel and began walking away.

"Wait," he said, catching up to me.

I turned around. "Why don't you leave me alone?"

Damien laughed without humor. "Oh, that's good! You're the one being sneaky and following me around the city, yet you tell me to leave you alone?"

"I wasn't being sneaky, nor was I following you all over the city," I countered defensively.

He stopped. "You know what? Fine. Whatever."

"Fine," I agreed before walking away.

He chased after me and grabbed my arm again, this time urging me to face him. Without hesitation, he closed the gap between us by pulling me into his arms. As he stared into my eyes, his expression revealed curiosity, wonderment, awe, apprehension, and...desire. Upon seeing the latter, my knees went weak, which is quite a feat for a powerful vampire such as myself. His eyes were twin pools of quicksilver and I was drowning helplessly in them. He smelled divine, too—a combination of rain and musk. Suddenly, our lips met, our mouths opened, and the moment our tongues coiled together, my instinct took over.

I pushed him away with considerable force. "No!"

I retreated too quickly for him to possibly catch up to me. When I was at a safe distance, I stopped to look at him. There he stood, a black silhouette in the pale lit circle of a lamppost.

In the days that followed, I resisted the temptation to follow Damien. I needed some distance to gather my thoughts and dampen my desire. Omar kept me busy on the trail of the vampire everyone referred to as the *Viking*. I hadn't told anyone what my sire had confessed to me on the Great Wall of China long ago, but for some inexplicable reason I believed it was relevant. Could the mysterious message Arsham recently received have anything to do with his past? Was the Viking's presence in London tied to that message? As I tried put the

155

pieces of the puzzle together, the Viking disappeared as mysteriously as he had appeared, leaving us perplexed.

No longer on high alert, everyone in the coven relaxed a bit. Arsham, in a rare good mood, threw a party to celebrate. Blood wine flowed freely and music filled the air as we paraded around in our finest clothes.

I couldn't help admiring Arsham in his sleek Gucci suit. He left enough of the top buttons of his black shirt open to reveal his clavicle and the hollow of his throat. To my chagrin, he caught me staring and his lips curled into a sensuous smile that bespoke volumes. Averting my gaze, I made a beeline toward my brothers, Omar and Micah.

Micah held out a goblet. "Fine wine for a fine lady."

I accepted the vessel and smiled. "Thanks."

"You look ravishing in that dress."

The short black dress hugged every one of my curves. "I'm glad you like it."

Omar took a step toward me and lowered his voice. "What do you think of all this?"

I sighed. "I'm trying not to think too much."

Valerio, who walked up to us and overheard my words, said, "A good plan."

The cool music pouring from strategically placed speakers abruptly stopped. Everyone looked around, puzzled. Then, the delicate strings of a violin filled the room. I turned my head toward the sound. Two vampires, dressed in eighteenth century costumes wandered into our midst. I knew the tune well. It was the last melody my human ears had heard on the night of Luis XVI's birthday. The night I became a vampire.

"Angelique."

I turned to find Arsham's face inches from mine. Extending his hand, he inquired, "Would you do me the honor, my lady?"

I allowed him to lead me to the center of the large space. I surprised myself by remembering the steps of the old tune. As I bobbed and swayed in accordance to the music, I became aware of young vampires whispering. Many had never heard Bach's Minuet no. 3. The violins tapered into silence, and

Arsham gallantly bowed to kiss my hand. The speakers blasted modern music once again and several couples joined us. Arsham pulled me into his arms and led me in a contemporary slow dance.

"What was that all about?" I inquired.

"Today is the anniversary of you becoming a vampire and I felt like celebrating. You should be flattered."

Admittedly, I was touched by his gesture. "I am, sire. Thank you. I'm surprised that I remembered the steps."

"I had no doubt that you would."

"That night is forever embedded in my memory," I admitted, allowing my hand to rest comfortably on his shoulder.

"Mine too. You outshone the queen in that fine gown."

"Not a difficult feat since she dressed like a fool."

He chuckled. "I miss the elegance of those times. The luxurious fabrics, the rules of etiquette, the jewels."

"You wouldn't miss it if you'd worn corsets."

He laughed heartily. "Ah, Angelique, you're still my favorite." He studied me closely before changing the subject. "There's something different about you."

"Oh?"

Putting his lips to my ear, he whispered, "I think you fancy someone."

I forced a laugh. "I'm too busy for trivial romances."

"That's what I told myself at first, too, but then I caught you staring into the distance the other day. Something about your expression triggered my memory. You wore that same face when we first became lovers."

I shook my head in denial while avoiding his penetrating stare. "There's no one, sire."

He pulled me closer. "Since you're unattached, why not visit my bedroom later?" He took my earlobe between his sharp teeth and purred, "It was good the last time."

I caught the twins glaring at me from across the room. "And risk being killed in my sleep?"

Arsham followed my gaze and chuckled. "Those two are quite jealous of you."

157

"From the moment they met me, they despised me."

"Consider it a compliment."

The song came to its conclusion, and I was grateful when Micah appeared at my side to claim the next dance. "May I cut in, sire?"

Arsham handed me to my brother and beckoned the twins. They immediately nestled themselves under each of his strong arms while grinning smugly at me. I rolled my eyes.

"They are so bitchy," Micah observed.

"You think?"

"I wonder what he sees in them." When I stared at him, he added, "Right. I meant besides the obvious physical attributes."

I shrugged. "Who cares?"

Micah grinned and said nothing more as we danced the night away.

***

Against my better judgement, I decided to take a stroll in Damien's neighborhood. I rounded the corner of his street and noticed his dark apartment. Nobody home.

Damien turned the corner and froze. "Angelique?"

"Hey," I said, feeling rather foolish.

Shifting the brown paper grocery bag in his arms, he demanded, "What are you doing here?"

Good question.

When I didn't reply, he inquired, "Did that Viking show his face again? Something going on that I should know about?"

"Oh, no...nothing like that." He stared quizzically, so I added, "I came by to see how you were doing."

"Oh. I'm fine. How are you?"

"Fine."

An awkward silence passed before he suggested, "Why don't you come upstairs?"

"I really shouldn't."

"I think you should."

The air between us became sexually charged. I definitely shouldn't be feeling this way about a slayer. Damien began walking toward the front steps then paused for me to follow him. We ascended the stairs and went inside the apartment. I sat on the green velvet sofa and watched him put away his groceries. When he had finished, he pulled a bottle of water from the fridge and drank thirstily.

I looked around at his apartment in order to gather my wits. A typical Victorian apartment, it came complete with built-in shelves, oak floors, and white wainscoting. The tops of the living room windows boasted the original stained glass, too.

"I like your place," I said.

"Authentic Victorian. Come on, I'll give you a tour."

I tracked him through the living room, then past the kitchen and bath. I stopped to admire the original claw foot tub and tiny white hexagon floor tiles. An image of Damien naked in the tub came to mind and I quickly averted my gaze.

"That's Felicia's room," he said, pointing to a darkened bedroom that reeked of her obnoxious scent. He stopped at another door. "And this my room."

I peeked inside. Located in one of the building's turrets, it boasted a rounded wall. The tops of the windows boasted the same original stained glass as the living room. His delicious scent was everywhere, especially on the big wrought iron bed dominating the center of the room. The white rumpled sheets looked inviting. I was overcome with bittersweet nostalgia. It had been a long time since I'd entered a human home.

"This place is so...human," I said as I headed back into the living room. I sat down on the sofa again and admired the pattern of the large Oriental rug on the floor. "Nice rug."

"Everything you see was picked out by Felicia."

I crossed my legs. "Ah."

"Would you like something to drink?" he offered.

A slow, wicked grin stretched across my face in response to his question.

He laughed nervously and shook his head. "Forgive me...force of habit."

"That's all right," I purred, humored by his slip of the tongue. "Are you and Felicia...?" He looked at me blankly and I finished the sentence. "Lovers?"

He shook his head vigorously. "No way. We're more like siblings. May I confess something?"

"Sure."

"I *know* you, Angelique."

"What do you mean by that?"

"I told you, Gilles wrote about you in his journal."

"You told me he wrote about the night he killed my sister."

"He wrote way more than that. There are several entries spanning many years." His face lit up with realization. "Oh, wait. You have no idea, do you?"

"What are you talking about?"

"Gilles was in love with you."

"That's preposterous! I met Gilles only once and never saw him again."

"Well, you left quite an indelible impression on him. In fact, he was so obsessed that he kept track of you. He stalked you for years!"

I sniffed. "Impossible…I would have detected him."

"Not if he blended in with others, which is how he often tracked you—in crowds."

"He did no such thing."

"He worshipped you," he countered. "Now I understand why. I became suspicious of your identity when I first saw you in the alley. You match his description so perfectly. When you spared my life in the subway station, I knew you were the duchess. I came home that night and reread Gilles's entries. I must confess…I've had a secret crush on you for years. I believe we were destined to meet, Angelique."

"I don't believe in destiny."

His face turned serious. "Gilles also knew your secret."

Shit. "I don't know what you're talking about," I bluffed.

"You hate killing humans; you allow them to live after you feed on them."

My heart began to race. "That's ridiculous."

"It's all in the journal."

I sighed loudly in defeat. "You may as well kill me now because if Arsham finds out—"

"Your secret is safe," he assured, his face serious.

"What Gilles wrote is true," I admitted. "I hate killing humans and abstain from doing so whenever possible."

"How noble of you."

"You mock me."

"I'm actually serious! Most vamps are assholes. According to Gilles you have a kind heart."

"My 'kind heart' has afforded you the power to destroy me. Arsham doesn't know I spared Gilles's life. If he knew I had the chance to avenge Erika's death and didn't take it, he'd be furious. My coven would probably demand my execution."

"Stop worrying, will you? I would never betray you. I only wish that all vampires were like you." His brow creased. "If there's no need to kill a human, why do it?"

"To protect the coven," I explained. "Arsham fears the humans would seek revenge on us for feeding on them if we allowed them to live."

"But you don't believe that."

"No. Do chickens try to kill humans for consuming their eggs? Or cows their milk?"

Damien laughed aloud at my comparison. "I never thought of myself as a chicken or a cow." He stared at me, debating whether or not to tell me something. "Would you like to see Gilles's journal?"

"I would. Very much."

I watched as he got up from the chair and crossed the room. His shoulder-length hair was slicked into a ponytail and his black athletic shirt clung to his biceps. My eyes lingered on his broad, muscled back. He went into his bedroom and came out a moment later holding an old leather bound book.

"It's fragile," he warned, placing the book in my lap.

I stole a glance at his throat and saw a pulsating vein. My mouth watered. I wanted him so badly it hurt. "I'll be careful, I promise," I said, gently opening the journal.

Inscribed in sable ink on the inside cover were the words: *This is the private journal of the Sauvage family, sworn to protect the loyal followers of Christ from the evil machinations*

161

of Satan. May the good Lord protect our family and give us the strength to do His sacred work. —Gilles Sauvage of Marseilles, born in the year of our lord, 1780.

Below were the inscriptions of other slayers, including Thomas. With trembling fingers, I turned the pages until I came to the date of Erika's death:

...The creature was in the middle of a feeding frenzy when I caught sight of the most enchanting woman I had ever seen in my life. She stood across the road, and I feared the vampire would slay her next so I cut off its head. To my surprise, the woman was Angelique, the long lost daughter of my employer— the duchess who had mysteriously disappeared many years beforehand. Despite the passage of time, she looked unnaturally, impossibly young. I soon discovered the disturbing truth: Angelique was also a creature of the Night, an unholy being imprisoned by the dark forces of vampirism.

To my eternal chagrin, I did not kill her. I admit, I was instantly besotted by her charms. I could not bring myself to deprive the world of such an exquisite being. Blame my moment of weakness on human imperfection. Angelique made no move to harm me and her words were tempered with sweetness. We spoke until dawn and I learned how different she was from the others of her kind; she possessed a pure spirit and a good heart. I am reluctant to write what followed, but swear on my soul it is true: I let her feed upon me. As her teeth pierced my skin I felt pleasure instead of pain. It was utterly divine; unlike anything I had ever experienced...

I skimmed through the passage until I reached the end:

...She disappeared into the darkness after touching my soul. A dark angel, she had changed me forever.

I flipped through the journal and discovered that Gilles had moved to Paris after my father died. A few entries described scenes that I remember vividly. This proved that he had indeed stalked me throughout his life. Unfortunately, there were also entries describing vampire slayings. Apparently the lesson I had taught him on that fateful night was short-lived. I suppose the need to kill vampires was embedded in a slayer's blood. As

Gilles himself had said, they were born and bred for the task.

I found the passage about my encounter in the park with Thomas. He described the incident accurately, adding his regret for having lost the most skillful shifter in London. Although he had expressed repugnance for Micah, he described me as "a demon with an angel's face."

"Well," I said, closing the journal.

"You don't deny any of it?"

"No."

"So you really did feed on Gilles."

"I did."

He stared at me. "Wow. According to his entry, the experience proved life-changing for him."

"Gilles was exaggerating."

Damien said nothing as he took the journal and walked away to put it back in his room. He came back and stood with his arms at his sides looking at me with longing.

That was my cue, so I stood. "I should go. Thank you for letting me see the journal."

We faced each other and his hand reached out to touch my cheek. I smiled slightly, enjoying the warmth of his touch. Seeing my reaction, he came closer and cupped my face in his hands. I didn't move when he claimed my mouth with his own. This time, when his hot tongue coiled with mine, I didn't push him away. Damien tasted sweet—like summer rain—and I wanted to bite him so badly, it hurt. Slowly, his hands caressed my arms and slid down my sides to my waist. My arms snaked around his neck. When he finally pulled away, the look on his face was a combination of rapture and disbelief. I imagine that my own face mirrored the same emotions. We were both breathing heavily. Neither one of us knew what to say. After all, we were natural enemies.

"What now?" he asked.

I shook my head. "I don't know, but you're missing a perfectly good opportunity to rid London of one more vampire—an elder, no less."

"A powerful vampire."

"And deadly."

He shook his head. "I would never hurt you…I can't."

"And why is that?"

Cocking his head to the side, he pulled me back into his embrace. "Isn't it obvious? After that kiss, how could I?"

"I should go…"

"Don't."

"It's really late."

"You can stay here tonight. You'll be safe, I promise."

The unmade bed was clearly visible over his shoulder, the implication was clear.

"I don't think that's a good idea, Damien."

"Why?"

"Too dangerous."

"Dangerous for you or for me?"

"Both."

"I want you to feed on me. Like you did with Gilles."

I took a step back in surprise. "Do you know what you're asking? Humans become obsessed with vampires after having experienced their kiss. Such an act would bind you to me. Do you want to end up like Gilles? Following me around like a lovesick puppy?" When he continued to look at me unperturbed, I added, "Obviously, his words don't scare you."

"On the contrary, Angelique, they inspire me. I envy Gilles for being capable of such love."

I shook my head. "It wasn't love, it was an obsession. There's a difference."

"Your father talked about you throughout the five years Gilles worked as an apprentice. Gilles fell in love with you long before he met you face to face. Long before you bit him."

Damien had a point, but I maintained my skepticism. "Then he's a hopeless romantic and so are you."

"Is that so bad?"

I shrugged. "It's foolish."

"Maybe it is. So far my life has consisted of stalking vampires and killing them. Trained from birth. I was born a Sauvage by chance, not by choice. Is it wrong to want more?"

"No, but…"

He pulled me close and just before his lips sought mine he said, "Is it wrong to want this?"

He kissed me urgently. I pulled away. "Damien, no."

"You can't tell me you don't feel anything."

I did feel something…too much, in fact. And it scared me. "Perhaps this is more about rebelling against your destiny than it is about me."

His look silenced me. He kissed my throat and put his lips to my ear, making me shiver. "Bite me, Angelique. Bite me the way you bit Gilles; I want to know the same exquisite pleasure."

I pushed him away from me. "No…and don't ask me again. I don't want an obsessed vampire stalking me through the city. That would get you killed in a heartbeat."

"I'm too good at what I do to get caught."

He came toward me again and I lifted my hand, halting him in his steps. "Stop. Just stop."

"Will you at least stay?"

I eyed him wistfully. I wanted to stay. I wanted to taste every single inch of skin on that magnificent body and drown in his stormy eyes, but I couldn't. I had the benefit of age and experience on my side, and I knew that any kind of relationship with a slayer—aside from killing him—would only lead to trouble. Big trouble. Besides, my heart had been barricaded against the emotion of love for so long, I wasn't sure it could function anymore. It was broken.

I was broken.

"I can't," I whispered before slipping out the front door and getting as far from him as I could at top speed.

I only slowed when I was near the lair. I blended into the shadows and gradually stepped into the street. I closed my eyes and remembered the sweetness of Damien's mouth and the fragrance of his skin.

"Hey babe."

I glanced over my shoulder and saw three male skinheads behind me. They were high on something. Hard stuff. One wore an audacious grubby shirt with a swastika.

165

"Don't walk away. Come play with us."

They began making vulgar gestures, but I ignored them.

"Come over here so I can hit that fine ass."

I continued walking. The biggest of the three placed a rough hand on my shoulder.

"Hey, I'm talking to you," he sneered.

I spun around. "Get your hand off me."

He laughed and squeezed my shoulder with considerable force. A human woman would have fallen to her knees in pain. When I didn't flinch, he looked puzzled. I smiled, placed my hand over his, and broke it. The other two skinheads took a step back and stared at each other in confusion.

"You stupid cunt!" the big man cried as he clasped his broken hand to his chest.

One of his friends pulled out a knife. "I say we teach this bitch a lesson."

The knife-bearer lunged at me and within a second he was on the floor bleeding. I spit out his ear and it landed at the feet of the other two morons. My attacker yelped in pain as blood oozed from his wound. I licked my bloodied lips.

"Holy fuck," one of them said under his breath.

I smelled their fear. Despite being high, their primordial instincts were on red alert against a dangerous predator.

"Easy there, honey. We want no trouble, do we boys?" the big one said, still babying his broken hand.

He helped the one-eared man to his feet and the three of them retreated into a nearby alley. By morning, when the drugs had gone through their systems, they would recall the entire episode as a bad trip.

166

CHAPTER 12

*"Sex is as important as eating or drinking
and we ought to allow the one appetite to be satisfied
with as little restraint or false modesty as the other."*
(Marquis de Sade)

I told myself over and over to forget about Damien, and avoided him at all costs. For days, I obsessed over the raven-haired, gray-eyed, katana-wielding slayer. My moodiness eventually attracted the attention of my brethren.

At one point Deirdre approached me. "What the hell is wrong with you?"

I eyed her as one would a cockroach. "Nothing."

She crossed her arms. "You've been moping for days."

"Why do you care?"

"I don't, I'm only curious."

"Piss off, Deirdre," I said before stomping off.

I rounded the corner and ran into Arsham. "What's going on, Angelique?"

"Sire, forgive me. I'm feeling restless, that's all."

"I know you're worried about me."

Ah, saved by Arsham's arrogance.

"What you need is to go hunting," he added, cutting into my thoughts. "Stalk some challenging prey. When was the last time you fed?"

I pretended to agree with him. "You're right."

"I usually am," he agreed as he sauntered past me.

I heard Deirdre whisper to him and tried to control my rising anger at her meddling. I left the lair and wandered aimlessly through the dark streets. The waning moon offered little light. I made my way to a fetish club and tried to distract myself with the outlandish garb being flaunted by rowdy humans. Try as I might, I couldn't stop thinking of Damien. No amount of

167

tempting, skin-tight vinyl, or smooth young flesh could eliminate the memory of his unmade bed and the delicious scent emanating from it.

Mmm, his scent...

I didn't understand why Damien evoked such strong feelings in me. No human had ever piqued my interest—or my arousal—as the slayer did.

I left the fetish club without feeding and continued prowling the streets, aimlessly taking turns, cutting through the park, and slipping into dark alleys. Before I knew it, I was in Soho. *Shit.* I headed toward the façade of the Victorian building where Damien lived. Ignoring the grinning gargoyle someone must have placed there since my last visit, I stared up at the dark windows. He wasn't home. I paced back and forth on the sidewalk, unsure of what to do. My heart told me to stay and wait for him, but my brain urged me to go.

"I knew you'd be back."

I turned my head sharply. Damien and I stared at each other. After a few seconds he held out his hand. I hesitated, but my legs betrayed me as they moved forward. I accepted his hand.

My heart had won.

Neither of us spoke as he led me upstairs to his apartment. The moment he locked the door, Damien pulled me into his arms. We devoured each other with our mouths and hands. I couldn't shake the feeling that this was meant to be, that he was no stranger, but rather someone I had known and loved forever. He led me into his bedroom and closed the door.

"I've never been with a vampire," he confessed.

"How old are you, Damien?"

"Twenty-five. And you?"

"I became a vampire at age twenty." When he continued to look at me expectantly, I added, "I was born in the year 1768."

I watched as he did the math in his head. "Your skin is so perfect," he commented as his hand delicately stroked my cheek. He then placed the palm of his hand against my icy chest. "There's no heartbeat."

"Many humans are incapable of emotion despite their

beating hearts," I pointed out.

"You feel emotion."

"Too much sometimes."

"Now?"

I nodded and he stepped closer to me. The heady scent of his skin sparked my desire. He slipped his arms around me and we shared a sensuous kiss. No rushing, no urgency—only pure pleasure. He eventually led me to his bed and urged me down beside him. After gathering me close, he started talking and asking me questions. We didn't make love. In fact, we talked all night long. Our conversation was punctuated with soft kisses and caresses.

Despite the heightened sexual tension between us, our desire for closeness went beyond the physical. This was something totally new for me, and from what I could ascertain, it was totally new for Damien, too. I reluctantly took my leave of him just before dawn with a promise to return the next evening.

I did my best to avoid Arsham and the others once I was back at the lair. I was afraid the glow of happiness I was surely emitting would be noticed and questioned by those who knew me so well. In the privacy of my chamber, I went to sleep with a smile on my face.

The next night I went to Damien's place. He met me at the door with a look that made me melt on the spot. He led me into his bedroom, closed the door, and his mouth plundered mine. I responded to his kiss with equal passion. We stepped away from each other and he began to undress me. His hands were slightly shaking, and I knew he was nervous. I remained still as his palms ran down the length of my body.

"So smooth…and cold," he whispered.

"I haven't fed in a while," I said, self-consciously, suddenly envying the warmth of human females.

His steely eyes met mine. "You become warm when you drink blood?"

"As warm as you are now."

"Then take some of my blood."

His offer made my pupils dilate with excitement. "Don't

ever ask a vampire to do that."

"Why not?"

"Does my body temperature displease you?"

"No. I only want you to be okay."

"I'm okay."

My fingers worked the buttons of his shirt. I was pleased to see his perfect torso when I pushed the fabric back from his shoulders. My fingertips traced the elegant line of his clavicle and I kissed the skin encasing the long bones. He heaved a shuddering breath as I inhaled the scent of his skin on his throat. Instinctively, my extracted fangs dripped with longing. It took all my willpower not to sink my teeth into his flesh and drink deeply. Running my tongue slowly up the side of his neck, I pressed myself against the hardness of his body.

We stretched out on the bed and his mouth traveled from my lips to my throat, then down to my stomach. I gasped and waited in anticipation of where his mouth would go next. Damien stopped and raised his eyes to meet mine. His gaze revealed pure hunger, which I thought was ironic. He then did something that—unbelievably—no one else had ever done: he kissed me between my legs.

"Oh!" I exclaimed.

Damien's head came up again, his expression one of pure surprise. Seeing the shock and pleasure on my face, he smiled knowingly and lowered his head again. For the next several minutes, I was in heaven. Coaxing me to the brink of ecstasy, he retreated then did it again. I finally understood why Lisette's face expressed pure rapture when I had caught my aunt performing the same act on her so long ago. Such sweet torture! Arsham, the ancient noble prince, had always been too selfish to offer such altruistic pleasure.

When Damien's tongue penetrated deep inside of me and slowly pulled out, I thought I would die. Consumed by desire, I whimpered for mercy. Without another word, he stopped and mounted me. It felt glorious to be filled by him. I lifted my hips to meet each of his passionate thrusts. I couldn't help scratching one of his shoulders in my delirium, and the scent of his blood

170

pushed me over the edge. We climaxed together in an orgasm akin to a small explosion. Behind my closed eyelids I saw white heat. I laid back against the pillows feeling completely languid. After a moment, he leaned on his elbows to look down at me.

As his eyes searched my face, he whispered, "I honestly hope that was as incredibly amazing for you as it was for me."

I wrapped my arms around him in response. My action evoked kisses from him, which I greedily consumed. In the pleasant afterglow of my mind-blowing orgasm, I happened to catch the time displayed on his alarm clock.

"I have to go," I announced wistfully.

"Stay," he said.

"I'm expected back at the lair."

"Please stay," he said, moving to get off the bed. "No one will bother you here."

I sat up, drawing the sheets around my chest. "I can't."

"Don't cover your perfect breasts," he said with a cheeky wink.

I dropped the sheet. Damien walked to the only window in the room. He pulled down the shade and closed the curtains. Next, he went into the closet and removed a quilt. He placed the quilt over the window to ensure total blackout.

"There," he said. "The sun won't harm you. Stay."

Sometimes vampires went hunting outside the city and took refuge in abandoned warehouses or in dark nightclubs after lock up. We weren't exactly micromanaged, and Arsham did tell me to stalk challenging prey to cure my restlessness.

I nodded. "I'll stay."

Damien smiled, locked the bedroom door, and came back to bed in order to make love to me again.

Felicia entered the apartment at around noon, filling the place with her scent. Knocking on Damien's bedroom door, she said, "Hey, are you up? I'm making coffee."

Damien stirred sleepily. "Mmm."

"It's your roommate," I whispered.

He sighed. "No thanks, Felicia."

Felicia tried the doorknob and banged on the door. "Are you

okay, Damien?"

He opened his eyes and stared at the ceiling. "I'm fine."

"I know she's in there."

Damien tossed me an apologetic glance before he scrambled out of bed and unlocked the bedroom door. He opened it a crack and I took cover in the shadows when I saw the living room bathed in sunlight.

Sticking his face in the space between the door and the doorjamb, he said, "Yes, Felicia, I have a guest in here. Now if you don't mind…"

"I know Angelique is in there," she said, trying to peek over his shoulder into the tell-tale dark room.

He tensed. "And?"

"I'm worried about you. She might be harmless, but the other vamps won't be if they find out about you two." She added loudly, "She should know better than to put you at risk."

"Felicia, stop. I don't have to remind you to mind your own business, do I?"

"Nope," she retorted, heading back to the kitchen.

Damien bolted the door. "I definitely need to get my own place. Sorry about that. She means well, really."

"I know she does," I agreed, emerging from the corner of the room. "It's obvious she cares about you. And she's right, I should know better than to put you at risk."

"Please don't ruin the most perfect night of my life by telling me you regret what just happened."

"I don't regret what we did," I admitted, placing my hand against his cheek. "I regret putting you in danger, which is exactly what I'll be doing if we keep seeing each other."

"Felicia can sniff out vamps. I'll be fine."

"I'm glad she looks after you. I can't watch over you during the day so it's nice to know someone else will."

He raised a brow at me. "Does this mean you'll be watching over me during the night?"

"Yes."

He chuckled and sexy sound made me want him again, but I refrained. He was human, after all.

172

"Why don't you get some coffee? Go put her at ease."

"Are you sure?"

"Yes. Besides, I need to go to sleep now."

"Of course. You can lock the door from the inside if that makes you feel more secure."

"Thank you."

He kissed my lips and left the room. I instinctively locked the door as a precaution. I got into bed and closed my eyes, welcoming the sleep of the dead. When the last ray of sun vanished, my eyes opened. I went to the window and admired the thin sliver of moon rising in the twilight sky. I went out into the living room and found Damien on the sofa reading a book.

"Good evening," he said cheerfully.

"Hello."

He closed the book and walked over to me. We kissed. "I was serious about what I said the other night. I really want to know what's it's like to be bitten."

"And I was serious when I told you not to ask me again."

He took off his black shirt and exposed his impressive chest. Turning his neck to the side, he said with a grin, "Oh, come on…you know you want to."

"Of course, I do," I admitted as my mouth watered. "That's not the point. Do you understand the repercussions of such an act? When a vampire bites a human, the most probable outcome is death. The second outcome is the creation of progeny. The third is obsession."

He shrugged. "I'm hoping for the latter."

"I want you to want me of your own accord."

"I already do. Come on, you want it, I want it…"

"I'm not arguing that, Damien."

"Then what's stop—"

My fangs were in his neck before he could finish his sentence. I was not gentle as I had been with Gilles. I wanted him to see another side of me, my true nature. I was a killer, a predator, and all he had seen thus far were my residual bits of humanity; the bits I worked hard to maintain.

When he cried out for me to stop, I placed my hand over his

173

mouth and sucked harder. I forced him into the bedroom and pushed him onto the bed, straddling him. I didn't bother to heal the wound. As he lay on the bed stunned and staring at me in pain and confusion, I went over to the mirror on the wall and took it off its hook. Bringing the mirror to the bed, I held it over him so that he could see his reflection.

"Are you satisfied with my handiwork, slayer?"

Bewildered, he touched the wound on his throat and stared at his bloodstained fingertips. He swallowed hard and frowned before swinging his legs over the side of the bed. Staggering into the bathroom, he reached for a towel. The sight of him struggling made me feel terribly guilty, but I had done it for his own good. I couldn't risk having a lovesick slayer tailing after me in London.

"Would you like me to bite you again?" I asked softly.

"Enough!" he cried, gripping the sides of the bathroom sink with sagging shoulders. "That's enough," he repeated in a hoarse whisper. "I know what you're doing and it's not working. It won't change anything. It won't change how I feel about you."

A rush of regret and pity washed over me, so I healed his wound. "I'm sorry," I whispered, taking him into my arms.

Damien's arms made their way around me and we slid down the wall to the floor. We remained like that for quite some time. He fell asleep and I carried him to his bed, which, despite my supernatural strength, proved no small feat. I watched over him for as long as I could, and was back in the lair before the first fragile rays of dawn broke forth from the horizon.

"Where were you, Angelique?" Arsham demanded from the inside of his private chamber.

I stopped in my tracks and turned around. "Hunting, sire, as you suggested. I went far from the city."

His frame filled the doorway. "The sun is almost up. You know better than to be out so late. You should have sought shelter instead of taking such a risk."

"It won't happen again."

"Come and keep your sire company. I'm in no mood to sleep

174

alone today."

"Where are the twins?"

"I sent them to their chambers."

I hesitated for a fraction of a second. I took him into my arms, but I pretended to be holding the slayer instead of Arsham.

The next night, I went to Damien's apartment and found it empty. I checked all the usual vampire hang-outs: bars, dance clubs, fetish clubs, and he wasn't in any of them. I searched his neighborhood and the surrounding areas. No sign of Damien. I went back to his apartment and waited inside the main entrance of his building. He finally showed up well past midnight.

"Where have you been?" I demanded.

He jumped back in surprise. "Damn it!"

"I didn't mean to startle you."

He gathered me into his arms and held me before climbing the stairs.

"I'm truly sorry for my behavior last night," I said contritely once we were inside his apartment. "I wanted to show you that I'm not the romantic supernatural being Gilles described, but something far more sinister."

"I'm well aware of what you are. I kill your kind, remember? I agree with Gilles, however. I believe you're different. I would have never brought you into my bed if I suspected otherwise." He lifted my chin with his finger.

"Don't," I warned.

"Or what? You'll drain me dry this time? Beat me up while you're at it?"

"I'll never hurt you again."

"Why did you say 'don't' then?" he asked, looking deeply into my eyes.

"Because I'm frightened."

He laughed aloud. "Of what?" When I didn't answer, he asked, "Of me?"

"Yes."

"Bit ironic, don't you think?"

"It's not my physical well-being I'm worried about…"

175

My words sobered him. "I'm risking my heart, too, you know." I nodded and he kissed me softly on the lips.

"I will grant your request. It's the least I can do after last night. I will even gift you immortality, if you wish it."

"Your sire would never agree to that," he pointed out.

"I would do it secretly, without his permission."

Damien shook his head. "I don't want immortality. The thought of living forever while everyone around me dies is unappealing. I would get lonely. The gift you offer is more like a curse."

"When you put it like that…"

"Are you going to deny it?"

I couldn't deny it. I never allowed myself to get close to—much less fall in love with—humans for the very reason he mentioned. The consequence of my emotional isolation was acute loneliness. The immortality I had embraced so eagerly in the eighteenth century had indeed become a curse.

I inquired, "Does that mean you no longer want me to bite you the way I bit Gilles?"

"Oh, no, I definitely still want that. I want it badly."

"Then, so be it."

I used my vampire charm to the fullest as I took him into my arms. His eyes glazed over while drowning in the depths of my midnight gaze. I placed my lips on his neck—the opposite side from where I had bitten him last night. I caressed his nape as my tongue gently licked and coaxed the vein of his throat. His breathing became shallow as he hardened against my thigh.

"Bite me," he whispered, pulling me closer.

I heard him gasp in pleasure as my teeth slowly pierced through the skin. I sipped very slowly in order to prolong his pleasure.

"Oh, God," he breathed, grinding against me.

I pulled away and healed the wound. He picked me up and took me to his bed in a state of pure euphoria. We made love again, only this time it was tender and slow.

"That was incredible," he said breathlessly.

"Yes," I agreed.

176

He placed his large hand on my breast and I marveled at its perfection. "I'm bonded to you now…I'm yours," he whispered faintly before falling asleep.

I got out of bed and dressed quickly. Before I left, I leaned over and kissed his forehead. As my affection for him grew, so did the fear of getting hurt—and getting caught.

***

Damien and I continued to see each other even though the odds were stacked against us. The forbidden nature of our relationship only added another dimension of excitement. We'd meet at the Ministry of Music, since none of my brethren hunted there, then go to his place where we filled our nights with long talks and passionate love play. I insisted on meeting him at the mega club for safety reasons. Ever since Arsham's implementation of strict security protocols and extra vigilance, I didn't want to risk being followed by any of my brethren.

I found it easy to pour my heart out to Damien and tell him things I had never shared with anyone else. Two centuries ago, I told Erika that I had been married to a man who treated me badly, but I didn't divulge any details. Arsham also knew about the duke's perverted nature since it was he who had saved me from that evil man's clutches—but I never volunteered any additional information. I confessed to Damien the heavy burden that I had been carrying for so long. With the greatest empathy he quietly listened as I told him of the abuse I had suffered at the hands of that sick and twisted sadist. The secrets I had held inside for so long flowed from my lips in a torrent—like water gushing through a broken dam. Gently, he wiped away my tears and kissed my cheeks. Without a word he took me into his arms and held me for hours. We made love afterward, and the act was so filled with tenderness that I wept from joy.

After releasing the demons that had haunted me for two centuries, I felt nothing but the greatest relief. The dark recesses of my mind had been cleared, thus allowing room for light. Damien was not only my lover, he was my emotional savior. How could I not fall helplessly in love with him? Despite my fear, I allowed my heart to open like a budding rose in early

177

summer. Was it so bad to break my own promise to myself? I had never been so happy, and my joy literally overflowed into all other aspects of my life. I found myself in a good mood for no other reason than the sheer pleasure of being alive.

Keeping my newfound state of bliss a secret proved difficult. I knew Micah suspected something; I could see it in his eyes whenever we exchanged pleasantries. After all, he and I had spent so many years together. He knew me better than any other vampire. Besides, how long can two forbidden lovers carry on before being discovered?

The Viking resurfaced in London—as if I didn't have enough to worry about. At least it diverted Micah's attention from me. Omar declared it our duty to find this mysterious vampire and interrogate him. By now, I wasn't the only one who suspected him of having something to do with the cryptic proverb sent to Arsham.

With the coven's attention focused on finding the menace, I made the mistake of being lax in my relationship with Damien. We ventured out in public on occasion, hand in hand like human lovers. Although I should have known better, I continued leading my double life, assured that the golden glow of love would protect me like an invisible cloak. Even Micah stopped eyeing me with suspicion.

All was well—or so I assumed.

Arsham approached me one night and insisted that I accompany him on the hunt. I had planned on meeting Damien at the Ministry of Music that night, but my beloved already knew that a "no-show" on my part meant that I couldn't sneak away without drawing suspicion. As Arsham and I exited the lair, two big males fell into step with us.

I demanded, "Where do you two think you're going?"

"They're coming with us, Angelique," Arsham said.

"Why?" I asked warily.

He cocked a brow at me. "Why not?"

I found this quite odd. "Where do you wish to hunt, sire?"

"It's been ages since I've visited the Ministry of Music."

My blood turned to ice, which was no small feat given that

I am a cold-blooded creature. "That place is off limits, isn't it?"

"Our sire can hunt wherever he pleases," one of the guards retorted.

I glared at the insolent guard. "How dare you address me in such a manner?!"

Arsham looked at the vampire and, rather than administer a blow, admonished lightly, "Respect your elders," To me, he added, "I'm in the mood for an easy night, my dear."

I caught the smug look on the face of the vampire who had disrespected me. My thoughts raced as I kept pace with my sire.

"You're unusually quiet, Angelique," Arsham observed.

"Forgive me."

"You spend many nights away from the lair. Where have you been hunting?"

"The Moors," I lied.

Arsham nodded pensively, his eyes distant. "I see."

The driving bass of electronic music reached our ears as we approached the Ministry of Music. Neither Damien nor I possessed mobile phones, so there was no way to warn him. Hopefully, my lover would spot us before we spotted him. My eyes swept the crowd in a desperate search for Damien.

The two males stuck close to my side as Arsham sauntered into the large mass of gyrating human bodies. A pretty brunette caught sight of him and melted. My sire could seduce a female from a distance of fifty paces. I saw his hand snake across her back as she giggled and danced provocatively to the music. Arsham pulled her against his groin and the woman moved in accordance to his slow and sensuous swaying. I could sense her arousal from where I stood. My sire bent his head and whispered in her ear. The brunette nodded and followed him off the dance floor like a calf to the slaughter. She would die in his arms within the next five minutes.

I turned around to face the two males. "Aren't you hungry?"

"We can't let you out of our sight," the insolent one replied.

His companion shot him a seething look. "Shut up."

I walked away and they were at my heels again. I whipped around and said through clenched teeth, "Back off."

Startled, they took a step back and lowered their heads in respect. *That's better*. They kept a mindful distance from me as I searched frantically for Damien. For once, I was grateful of his absence. I approached the bar and leaned on it. I caught Damien's scent and, before I realized it, his lips were at the nape of my neck.

"Hey gorgeous."

I spun around to face him. "You need to go."

It was too late. The two males had witnessed the intimate interaction between the slayer and I, and one of them went in search of Arsham.

"What's up?" Damien asked.

"Arsham knows. Get out of here, now!"

Damien slipped through the side exit with the remaining vampire at his heels. I scanned the room for Arsham before running after them. I opened the door to see Damien holding a bloody katana. The headless body of the male vampire stood upright for one second before crumpling onto the asphalt. Luckily, there was no one outside to witness the gory spectacle.

"Shit, shit, shit!" I muttered as I raced to hide the vampire's body behind a row of dumpsters. It would turn to ash in the morning.

"Come with me, I'll keep you safe," Damien urged.

"No," I said, going back to the exit door. "Arsham will kill you if he catches us together. Go, now!"

He frowned. "Not without you."

I opened the door and Damien moved to follow me.

"Angelique!"

I froze at the sound of Arsham's voice. The other vampire stood beside him. I shoved Damien with all my might.

"RUN!" I screamed before slipping inside and slamming the door shut behind me.

Arsham grabbed my arm, spun me around, and slapped me so hard that my lip split open and bled. The other vampire pushed me aside to open the exit door but Damien was already long gone.

"Shall I chase him down, sire?" he asked.

"No," Arsham replied, eyeing the decapitated head on the asphalt. "Take care of that before anyone sees it."

"Yes, my lord."

Arsham turned his cold eyes to me. "How dare you?"

"Please, let me explain."

"Explain?" he repeated in a deceptively soft voice heavily laced with disgust. "What excuse can you possibly come up with to justify fornicating with an enemy?"

"Damien is not our enemy."

"Sauvage!" Arsham bellowed one inch from my face with his fangs fully extended.

I cringed in the presence of his fearsome rage. "Arsham…"

He snarled at me; a vicious warning that evoked my own primal fear. Without another word he gripped my upper arm and we flew to the lair. Upon arrival, Arsham locked me inside of my chamber. Omar eventually came to fetch me, his expression a mixture of disapproval and worry.

"Omar, you have to help me—"

He held up his hand to silence me. "You know I love you, but the law is the law."

"Please…you fell in love with a human, too," I reasoned. "You know what I'm going through."

"My wife was never a slayer."

"But—"

"Angelique, I'm too shocked for words right now. How could you betray us like this?"

"I'm sorry. I never meant to hurt anyone, I swear. Damien is different."

Omar fixed me a cold stare. "That's enough, my lady."

Defeated, I lowered my head as he led me to the center of the circular meeting room where those who would decide my fate were already congregated. I felt terribly lonely, standing in the middle of that great space with no one to defend me. I watched as Omar took his seat among the elders. Finally, Arsham came in and sat upon his throne. He regarded me with a mixture of anger, disappointment, and incredulity. I looked at Micah, Valerio, and Omar, but they avoided my eyes.

181

"Consorting with a vampire slayer is a serious offense," Arsham proclaimed.

I spread my hands. "My lord—"

"Silence!" Turning to the surviving male vampire who had accompanied us that evening, he said, "Tell the court what you witnessed tonight at the Ministry of Music."

The young male stood proudly before the elders and happily obliged our sire. "I saw Damien Sauvage, the London slayer, kissing the Duchess de Nuit."

His testimony brought forth a wave of hisses and gasps.

Arsham raised his hand to silence the court. "And what else did you witness?"

"The duchess aided the slayer's escape."

Everyone regarded me with unadulterated shock and disgust except for Micah. His eyes reflected hurt and disillusionment.

Arsham said, "As you all know, the penalty for consorting with slayers is death."

"Death to the duchess!" Deirdre and Ciara cried out.

My betrayal proved a glorious victory for the twins. How I hated them in that moment.

Others took up their chant. *"Death to the duchess!"*

Micah stood. "Enough!"

Arsham held up his hand and the room fell silent.

Micah said, "I wish to speak in defense of the accused."

Hearing this, the twins hissed at him.

"Go on, Micah," Arsham prompted.

"The duchess has been a faithful and loyal vampire—an elder—for over two centuries," Micah said, looking at each of his peers in turn. "She has protected this coven from shifters and has even saved your life, sire." He paused, allowing Arsham to nod in acknowledgement. "She has also taught countless young ones how to fight, and many of her students have gone on to become formidable warriors under Omar's command. In short, Angelique has served this coven well."

Arsham rubbed his chin pensively. "That is true, but her crime cannot go unpunished."

"I agree," Micah conceded. "But this is her first serious

offense. Her record has been immaculate and her conduct has been exemplary."

"*Until now*," Arsham reminded him. "As my advisor, do you suggest an alternative to execution?"

Micah met my gaze with eyes as cold as snow. I knew I was about to pay the price for rejecting his affection and accepting the love of a slayer.

"I do, sire," Micah quietly replied. "The punishment coffin."

The room erupted with noise as I sank to the floor in despair.

Arsham stood and a hush settled over the crowd. "How many are in favor?"

The majority of elders raised their hands.

Two huge males came forth to restrain me. "No!"

My sire met my eyes. "Angelique de Nuit you are hereby sentenced to the punishment coffin."

"For how long?" I demanded.

"The period of time will be determined by this tribunal at a later date."

My heart shattered into a thousand shards. The possibility of never seeing Damien again—not even to say goodbye—filled me with grief.

"Please, sire. I beg you to grant me mercy."

"I am showing you mercy by not killing you."

Tears streamed down my cheeks. "Don't do this…"

Arsham averted his gaze and everyone in the room turned their faces from me, including Micah. The two males led me away, kicking and screaming.

"The only true wisdom is in knowing you know nothing."
(Socrates)

I awoke from my slumber in the silent flat with Damien's katana tucked beside me. I needed to get to Lyon as soon as possible in order to find my lover. I kept a few changes of clothing in the closet along with some accessories. Finding an old leather belt, I used it to strap the katana to my back. Next, I slipped on a long leather jacket that I had purchased at a cool vintage store a while back.

My brethren would be out in full force tonight, so I couldn't risk being predictable. Rather than use my supernatural powers to escape, I opted to leave London in the most mundane manner possible: the bus. Sticking to the shadows, I made my way to the nearest stop. The bus arrived and I shuffled into the bluish light of the vehicle's air conditioned interior. A woman with a baby sat down beside me. I couldn't help gazing at the infant's soft, pink face. When the baby opened its eyes and smiled at me, I melted. There were some vampires who feasted on tender morsels like these, but Arsham forbade it. Having been a human father, he found the practice abhorrent.

The baby's mother smiled at me. "He likes you."

I returned the gesture but said nothing. I rode the bus until the end of the line, then sought the darkest alley. When all the other passengers had dispersed, I flew into the night.

I ventured into my birth city filled with hopeful anticipation. The memory of my wedding day inevitably came to mind, for I had not been to Lyon since then. I was struck by the city's cleanliness and beauty. The Lyonnaise government had spent a fortune renovating the Renaissance palaces and other historical edifices. Even the city's traboules were well maintained. These secret medieval passageways connected palaces and streets. I remembered playing hide and seek in the traboules with the neighborhood children before being sent to live with Aunt Marguerite. Recalling the carefree laughter from my young human lips evoked nostalgia.

So long ago...

I wandered through Vieux Lyon, where I once lived. I felt proud and relieved that the city had retained its elegance. I stopped in front of the building that was once my father's house. The ground level now boasted a quaint bouchon with apartments above. The aroma of roasted potatoes mingled with fragrant sausages wafted from the kitchen to the cobbled street. There were several people inside the establishment, dining on hearty fare and washing everything down with red wine.

"Bonsoir, mademoiselle," said a well-dressed hostess while indicating an empty table by the door.

Shaking my head, I veered from my old neighborhood toward the Saône to admire the cruise boats adorned with merry lights. People were dancing to music on one of the boats, and their laughter sounded like tinkling bells in the night. I crossed a bridge and passed several elegant squares as I made my way toward the Rhône. I noticed an advertisement for a furnished flat on the second floor window of an old palace situated on the riverbank. I ran to the main door on the ground floor and hit the buzzer. The door opened and a sour-faced old woman peered at me. I did my best not to cringe from the smell of burned onions and beef coming from her kitchen.

Holding up a wad of cash, I said, "I'll take the flat. Now."

Half an hour later, I was afforded a key and some much needed privacy. The tiny studio offered a magnificent water view. I hid the katana under a thick futon cushion and left the flat to search for Damien. Unfortunately, I had no luck that night and vowed to try harder tomorrow.

When the next day proved fruitless, I purchased a map and strategized a new search routine. Every night I would steal onto the rooftops of Vieux Lyon and look for Damien until dawn. I then searched the Croix Rousse. For safe measure, I also checked the neighborhoods surrounding the famous Tête d'Or Park. My nightly neighborhood searches yielded nothing, so I started hanging out in the city's many bars and nightclubs. I kept watch and eavesdropped on countless people in the hope that one would drop Damien's name. My persistence paid off one night at a cheesy karaoke bar located on one of the quays off the Saône. A group of drunken Danish girls mentioned something about an after-work cocktail party at the Angelique.

"Excuse me," I said to them with a smile. "Did you just mention a bar named Angelique?"

"Not a bar, a boat," one of them slurred before being pulled onstage by her friends.

Another girl giggled and pushed her friend aside. "It's called a barge, not a boat."

"Thanks," I said before heading for the exit.

I walked briskly along the Saône. The city lights reflected and on the water's black surface resembled shimmering stars. I quickened my pace, scanning the big houseboats and barges moored along the river, but found nothing with my namesake. The night was still young so I crossed the presquile and continued onward toward the Rhône. I prowled along the quays, making a point to stick to the shadows. Since I hadn't fed in days, the last thing I needed was to draw attention to my unusually pale skin and preternaturally sharp eyes. Right now, I looked every bit the dangerous predator.

I passed several barges boasting bars and restaurants, but none of them were named Angelique. Then I remembered the Confluence where the two rivers met. Resisting the temptation to fly and possibly attracting unwanted attention, I hopped the last ferry. Running past the mega shopping center, I found what I was looking for: a row of barges. Sure enough, the *Angelique* floated among them. I noticed a spattering of people on deck sipping wine as Buddha Bar tunes spilled from the speakers.

I made my way up the metal walkway and entered the lounge. It was tastefully decorated with ultra-modern white

186

Lucite furniture and chrome light fixtures. A young blonde woman stood behind the bar.

She eyed me up and down as she wiped a glass with a dry cloth. "Bonsoir."

"Bonsoir," I replied. "I'm looking for a man named Damien Sauvage."

"Damien Sauvage," she repeated thoughtfully. "I do not know that name."

"Are you sure? It's important."

She shook her head. "Ah, no. Sorry."

A wiry middle-aged man in stylish clothing approached the bar. "Elodie, what do you know, you stupid girl? You were hired two weeks ago!" He turned to me and said, "I apologize, mademoiselle. Who did you say you were looking for?"

"Damien Sauvage."

He nodded slowly, knowingly. "And you are?"

"Do you know where Damien is or don't you?"

"We should speak in my office where it's more private."

I followed him downstairs to a neat office containing a sleek glass desk and a white leather chair.

"Please, sit," the man said.

I sat down and watched as he reached for a bottle of red wine and poured out a glass. He set the glass in front of me before pouring one out for himself.

"This is one of my finest vintages," he said. "What do you think?"

I decided to play along with his game and pretended to take a small sip. "Delicious. About Damien—"

"You are Angelique."

I tensed. "Who are you?"

"My name is Maurice. I used to work for Damien. When he decided to retire six months ago, I purchased the Angelique from him."

"Do you know where he is now?"

Maurice shook his head. "I'm sorry, no."

I stood. "Well, thank you anyway."

"You know, I've managed this bar for years. I've never met

a business owner as dedicated as Damien. We were open seven days a week and he was here every single night—no exceptions, no vacations. He would spend hours staring out at the water."

The thought of Damien depressed and drowning his sorrows in alcohol pained me.

Maurice snapped his fingers. "Come to think of it, he once mentioned something about moving to Marseilles."

Realization hit me full force. Of course! The Sauvage family originated from Marseilles. Why didn't I think of that?

He continued, "We've been out of touch since he left Lyon, so I don't know for certain. He spoke of you often, you know."

"He did?"

"He referred to you as 'the love of his life.' " Maurice paused. "It's none of my business, but where have you been?"

I bit back tears. "It's a long story, Maurice."

"Isn't that always the case with love?"

"Thank you for the information."

"Good luck, Angelique. Damien is a good man."

I made my way back to the flat, calculating the distance of Marseilles. I could easily cover three hundred kilometers before dawn. Back at the studio, I strapped the katana to my back, shrugged into the long coat, gathered my things, and climbed onto the roof. I took off into the night with renewed hope.

Inhaling the salty scent of the Mediterranean Sea, I landed quietly in the historical seaport of Marseilles. The Panier neighborhood seemed like a good place to begin my search since it was among the oldest areas in the city. I crept along the cobbled streets, blending seamlessly with the shadows. A spattering of people loitered; lovers strolling hand in hand, tourists snapping photos. The charming old architecture of this neighborhood, combined with eclectic graffiti, attracted a mélange of visitors. I continued up a flight of narrow steps that led to a maze of crooked alleys. Vintage stores, trendy shops, and small eateries were tucked within ancient, crumbling walls.

I caught sight of a tall, broad-shouldered figure across the square. Clad in a faded brown leather coat and jeans, the tall blond man strode with purpose—like someone on a mission. He ducked under the shadow of an eave with unnatural speed. Sensing my presence, he stopped and turned in my direction, but I had already taken refuge behind a dumpster. I caught a glimpse of his preternatural eyes and shuddered. The vampire eventually entered a medieval building that appeared to be deserted except for the top floor.

I debated continuing my search for Damien, but something compelled me to follow the vampire. I crept to the back of the medieval edifice and scaled the outer wall to the top. Next, I positioned myself in such a way that I could peek through the window without being noticed. The walls of the spacious apartment consisted of faded brick, and the ceiling flaunted ancient wood beams. Terracotta tiles covered the floors, and a chipped travertine mantel was all that remained of the fireplace that had once graced the room long ago.

A muscular man with a military haircut sauntered into the living room wearing nothing but a pair of jeans. I couldn't see his face, but his magnificently toned body garnered my admiration. A sinewy Japanese dragon tattoo, meticulously rendered in black ink, snaked its way down his spine. The Japanese symbols for "Life," "Death," and "Justice" were tattooed in black on the inside of his right forearm.

Footsteps could be heard coming from the stairwell, causing the man's head to swivel toward the door. He reached into a cabinet and extracted a gun. After tucking the weapon into the waistband of his jeans, he went to stand by the door. I finally saw his profile and my heart skipped a beat.

Damien!

To my horror, the blond vampire stood in the entryway. Then, a chilling thought occurred to me. Could this be the same vampire who had attacked Damien a decade ago—the so-called Viking suspected of sending Arsham the ancient Persian proverb? I wanted to break the window and protect my lover from harm, but something about Damien's calm demeanor prevented me from doing so. I watched in stunned silence as he waved the vampire inside and closed the door.

"Well?"

"We're not ready yet," the Viking replied.

"I've been waiting a long time," Damien said, visibly upset.

"Not nearly as long as my sire."

"What about the twins?"

I stiffened. What the hell was going on?

"We tracked them down in Brussels, but they were surrounded by security."

"You didn't—"

The Viking cut him off. "No."

"What about the other three?"

"Still in London. One heads security, the other two aid in decision-making. They never venture far enough from the lair. When they do, it's always in the company of guards."

At this point my stomach lurched. They were talking about my brethren! I didn't care about the twins, but I loved Micah, Valerio, and Omar. The vampire turned to go.

"Wait, Severin," Damien said.

Severin? Could he actually be a Viking?

Severin stopped.

Damien hesitated. "What about...*her*?"

Severin shook his head and took his leave. Damien paced the apartment like a caged tiger, his face a mask of anger and disappointment. I shifted on the ledge and he must have caught sight of the movement. The glass exploded as searing pain went through my left shoulder.

Only then did I see the barrel of the smoking gun in Damien's hand. The momentum of the bullet made me lose my footing, but I managed to hook my right arm over the window ledge. A fierce burning sensation radiated from the wound.

Silver bullets!

Damien's eyes were cold and jaded, the eyes of a total stranger. His expression softened when he finally recognized me. "Angelique?"

Dropping the gun, he reached down and pulled me up with only one hand; an impressive feat for a mortal. Confusion and worry clouded his face as he knelt beside me. The pure silver seeping into my veins sapped my vitality. I closed my eyes. He left my side and returned in a flash with a pair of stainless steel surgical tweezers.

"Fuck," he said, pushing my clothing aside to reveal my shoulder.

Damien removed the bullet with impressive expertise and squeezed out the excess silver. Breathing a sigh of relief, I watched as my body began to slowly heal over the smoldering hole. He leaned in close to examine the wound. Oddly, he smelled differently than I remembered. Perhaps it was the toxic effect of the silver. He helped me to stand on shaky legs. When I reached out to embrace him, he stepped out of my reach.

"Don't," he said with a pained expression.

Shocked by his rejection, I remained rooted to the spot. "Damien?"

This was definitely not the sweet reunion I had envisioned. We faced each other like two strangers instead of two lovers. The softness I had seen in his face only a few seconds ago was promptly replaced by impenetrable steel.

"What are you doing here?" he demanded.

"Looking for you," I blurted out, stunned by his demeanor.

"You're looking for me?"

Offended by his incredulity, I replied, "Yes, of course."

He laughed without humor, then grew serious. "After three years of searching high and low for you, I assumed you were dead. I mourned a long time. When I found out that you were alive, I waited. *And waited.*" His eyes shone with unshed tears of bitterness. "You never showed, never came looking for me. You suddenly appear out of the blue and expect what...? A hello kiss? A joyful reunion?"

Tears stung my eyes. "Damien, I—"

"You're lucky I didn't kill you just now. What were you doing spying on me outside my—" Damien froze when he noticed the hilt of his katana poking out from beneath the collar of my leather jacket. He removed the weapon from my person with lightning speed. "Why do you have my sword?"

I took a step closer to him. "I can explain..."

He recoiled from me as one would a venomous serpent.

"Arsham took my sword. I saw him do it with my own eyes!"

"Arsham took your sword?" I repeated. "When?"

"The day he told me you were alive and well, that's when."

I shook my head in confusion. "What?"

"Making one of the most famous vampire slayers in London fall in love with you must have felt like a great conquest." He sneered in disgust. "God, I was such a fool."

"Is that what you believe?" I demanded, unable to mask the raw pain in my voice. "I love you, Damien—like I've never loved anyone. I still love you."

My honest proclamation caught him off guard. We stared at each other until despair replaced his fury. "You disappeared. I thought Arsham had exiled you, so I wrote you a letter and left it with Felicia before taking off to France to find you."

"That's why I'm here! Felicia gave me your letter. I've been searching for you non-stop ever since."

He looked at me in disbelief. "You've been in France for the last ten years?"

"No, I arrived several days ago. I departed from London the night after Arsham set me free from my prison."

"What prison?" he demanded, eyeing me warily.

"The punishment coffin…After you escaped from the Ministry of Music I was taken to the lair and put on trial. Some of my brethren demanded my execution for the sin of treason, but Arsham granted me mercy."

"He put you in a coffin?"

"An industrial steel coffin covered with many layers of pure silver. I couldn't escape." I paused. "I've been in London the entire time, walled up within our lair."

Upon hearing this, Damien ran his hands through his buzzed hair. "Oh, no…"

"I only found out how much time had passed when I got out. There's no way to keep track of time when we sleep the sleep of the undead." I took a step forward. "I would never leave you like that, Damien. How could you even think such evil things of me after what we've shared?"

He threw the katana on the sofa and began pacing back and

forth, tossing a look at me every few seconds. Once again I noticed that his movements were off. They were too precise, too fast. Human men didn't move like that. A cold chill crawled up my spine.

He stopped pacing. "How did you find me?"

"I met Maurice," I replied, my voice shaking with suspicion. "He said you moved to Marseilles after selling him the barge. I remembered that your ancestors were from here, so I figured I'd start looking in the oldest neighborhood. I noticed the blonde vampire—Severin. I followed him here." I paused. "Was he the vampire who attacked you in London all those years ago?"

Damien's eyes narrowed as he debated whether or not to answer my question. "Yes."

"I overheard your conversation with him. You were talking about my brethren. What's going on?"

He shook his head. "Not now." His face softened. "God, I've missed you."

"I've missed you, too."

Damien closed the distance between us with one step and crushed me to his chest. I expected human warmth and pliability, but experienced the opposite.

"Angelique," he whispered, smothering me.

I tried to struggle out of his grasp but couldn't. He was far too strong. I gasped when he confirmed my suspicion by baring his fangs.

He explained, "Arsham thought it a fitting punishment once he'd tracked me down in Lyon. Took him years. Rather than kill me, he turned me into the very thing that I hunted." He looked away and added, "That's when he told me that you were doing well and had already moved on with your life. I didn't believe him at first. Every night I held on to the hope that you would find me and we'd pick up where we had left off. One day, I just gave up, sold the barge and moved here."

I stared at him with mouth agape.

He let out a long breath. "I had no idea what happened to you after that night at the Ministry of Music. I stayed in London for a while, but it was too dangerous for me to remain there with

193

Arsham and his coven hunting me down. It was only a matter of time before the other slayers began hunting me, too. Arsham had placed a bullseye on my back. I went to your birth city so I could feel closer to you. I eventually made a life for myself after purchasing the Angelique—it's not like I could get a day job."

"I'm so sorry," I whispered.

"I can't believe Arsham kept you imprisoned. I can't believe he made me doubt you."

I touched his cheek. "Let's not talk of that now. I'm here and that's all that matters."

"I've thought about you every day, even against my own will," he confessed. When he saw the hurt his words caused me, he added, "Put yourself in my shoes."

"I know."

He looked at me levelly. "What now?"

I replied to his question by kissing him. He returned my kiss with a hard insistent passion resulting from male maturity and vampirism. The sweet, human Damien existed no more.

"You've changed," I whispered in his ear.

"A decade's worth of change," he replied huskily.

I traced the features of my lover's face with my fingertips. His gaze was confident, sexy. I continued running my fingers down his jaw, over the trimmed beard, and paused at the deep hollow of his throat.

"Do you like me like this? As a vampire?" he asked, his pupils dilating with sexual excitement at my touch.

"Oh, yes," I whispered, leaning forward to kiss his neck. I ran my tongue along his clavicle, up his throat, and finally devoured his mouth.

His hands were everywhere—cupping my breasts, stroking my back, caressing my shoulders. We undressed quickly, the way starved lovers do, and he carried me to his bed. Our mouths and hands caressed and explored, tasted and teased. I was smothered by the sheer size and weight of him when he mounted me, but feeling his power only heightened my excitement. I cried out when he entered me, and met each of his hungry thrusts with my own. It didn't take long for us to reach a powerful climax together.

"Angelique," he whispered as his entire body shuddered with the last of his orgasm.

As we lay together, satiated, he kissed my cheek. "I've dreamt of holding you in my arms again so many times, only to wake up alone and frustrated."

"That will never happen again. I'm not going anywhere."

"Your sire expects your loyalty," he reminded me.

"The day he hurt you was the day my loyalty died."

"You fell in love with a vampire slayer, Angelique," he pointed out. "There was no way Arsham would have allowed our relationship to continue; no matter how many years you had served him. You broke one of the most sacred laws."

"I'm so sorry for what he did to you. I really am."

"I'm not," Damien said icily. "Well, at least not anymore. I was devastated at first, but now…"

I thought he was going to say it was because we now had an eternity together, but he didn't. What he said next chilled me to the very core.

"It only makes slaying vampires easier for me."

"What did you say?" I demanded, leaning on my elbow.

"You heard me."

"It goes against our instinct to kill our own kind. Damien, you mustn't do this."

"Oh, but I must," he countered with a wild gleam in his eye. "I will repay Arsham for the pain he's caused us. Severin's sire has been wanting to overtake London for decades."

"Severin's sire wouldn't happen to be Persian, would he?"

Damien's eyes narrowed suspiciously. "How do you know?"

"Arsham received a message—an ominous proverb—written in Old Persian around the same time Severin was spotted roaming around London. It seems more than a mere coincidence."

"That old proverb was sent to Arsham by Rahim."

"Who is Rahim?"

"Arsham's half-brother. He's also Severin's sire."

"Arsham's half-brother?" I repeated in surprise.

"Rahim was the son of a royal concubine."

My brow creased as I tried to solve a puzzle. "Arsham told me a slave had turned him into a vampire...Could it have been Rahim?"

"He hated Arsham. Rahim cursed his half-brother with immortality, then traveled east to amass great power and wealth. Severin sought me out when he heard that Arsham had turned me into a vampire."

"Why would he do that?"

"Who better to defeat the great Arsham than a Sauvage with supernatural powers?" Damien chuckled, but there was no mirth in the sound. "I will start by killing Arsham's beloved children."

"No..."

"Everyone that Arsham holds dear will be taken away one by one. He will suffer, he will mourn, and when he weakens, we'll strike."

I was horrified to hear this. "You underestimate Arsham."

"Are you actually defending him?"

"This is madness. Blood will be shed—and for what? Rahim's ambition?"

"I could care less about Rahim's ambition. My goal is to continue the Sauvage legacy."

"No, Damien. Your goal is revenge."

He continued as if I hadn't spoken. "I've been keeping tabs on Micah, Valerio, Omar, Deirdre and Ciara, for a long time."

I stared at him in disbelief. "I love my brothers."

"So does Arsham."

"How can you make others pay for what Arsham has done? My brothers are innocent. Besides, revenge doesn't change anything." I paused, smiling tentatively. "I've found you, Damien. We're together again. And we'll be together forever now that you're an immortal like me.

"What if I refuse to see things your way? Will you go back to London and warn your sire?"

I remained silent as I got out of bed and dressed slowly. My heart was burdened with a heaviness unlike anything I'd ever known. Damien approached me, his eyes ablaze with fury.

"I knew it!" he hissed, baring his fangs.

I instinctively crouched, ready to defend myself. "Have you gone mad?"

He placed his head in his hands and heaved a shuddering breath. "I'm sorry. Please don't leave me…"

"Shhh," I said, taking him into my arms.

His arms went around my waist and I found myself within a vice-like grip. I panicked momentarily out of fear that his madness would return, but it didn't. Eventually, he eased back onto the bed, thus forcing me to lay with him.

"The sun will be up soon, Damien. We need to take cover," I whispered in his ear.

"Wait here."

He got up and went to a panel on the wall. After pushing a few buttons, metal blinds automatically came down to cover every window in the apartment. He then bolted the metal door with a massive lock. Sunlight would never penetrate these rooms.

"Let's not talk about this anymore today," he said from the doorway. "Let's enjoy each other right now."

"We have to deal with this eventually."

Damien came back to bed and pulled me into his arms. "Not now. Make love to me again, Angelique."

My body happily obliged, but my mind remained troubled.

***

Marseilles was a romantic city, but I longed to see the calanques and coaxed my vampire lover into going there with me. We went to Sugiton and descended the steep rocky trail to the crystalline water below. The moonlight on the water resembled thousands of tiny shards of mirrored glass.

"What are you doing?" Damien asked when I began stripping off my clothing.

"Going for a swim, of course."

"I can't join you."

"Why?"

"I don't know how to swim." I laughed aloud and he frowned at me. "What's so funny?"

"You owned a barge."

He smiled. "I suppose it's ironic, isn't it."

"Very. Come on, the water will feel nice."

"I'm serious when I say I can't swim," he pressed. "I never learned how."

"Of course you can swim! Take off your clothes and jump in. You'll see."

Damien reluctantly stripped and followed me into the dark water. Within a few moments he was keeping pace with me stroke for stroke. We swam around a big jutting rock formation to stare out at the open sea.

"How did you know?" he asked, floating effortlessly in the water.

"We're predators. We can naturally run at superhuman speed, jump from great heights, fly into the night, and swim for long distances. We're even faster than sharks."

He grinned and splashed me. "I still have much to learn, don't I?"

"I'm afraid so. Arsham changed you and failed to instruct you in our ways, didn't he?"

"He made me what I am then left me to rot," he said bitterly.

"I'm here now," I assured him.

He pointed to the coast. "Gilles's estate is located a few miles in that direction, on the outskirts of the city by the sea."

"Why not live there instead of the city?"

"Loneliness."

"Well, those days are over."

CHAPTER 14

"It is easier to forgive an enemy than to forgive a friend."
(William Blake)

"I said no, Damien," I said quietly but firmly.

It was the tenth time in the span of a week that Damien had tried to recruit my help in killing my siblings. We were in his ancestral home, trying to make up for lost time, but his obsession with revenge kept ruining my mood. The Sauvage chateau, although old and decrepit, still managed to maintain its elegance; high, frescoed ceilings, finely carved marble mantles, and artistic mosaic floors. I walked onto the balcony overlooking the water. The full moon shone brightly and the sound of waves crashing on the shore soothed my nerves.

"Why not?" he demanded.

For the tenth time I replied, "Because it's wrong to punish the innocent."

"So, you're against me," he accused resentfully.

I turned away from the lovely view to face him. "I'm not against you, my love."

Bitterness and vampirism had made him harsh. How I longed for the young human I fell in love with a decade ago!

"Maybe you're right," he admitted. "Why waste my time on them? I should aim my revenge at the one who deserves to be punished. I'll join forces with Rahim and aid him in overthrowing Arsham. Then, I'll kill our sire."

I was beside him instantly. "Never say such a thing again—don't even think it."

"Why do you insist on protecting Arsham?!"

"I'm not protecting him," I contradicted in the calmest tone I could muster. "I'm protecting us."

"Give me one good reason why I should listen to you."

"Arsham is old, very old, and that means he's powerful."

"Rahim is older."

"Oh, Damien, please! I just found you and I don't want to lose you. I don't want Arsham to hurt us. Let's go far away and live our lives in peace."

He folded me in his arms and kissed the top of my head. "I want to avenge what he did to us."

I pulled away to look up at his face. It was hard, determined. "There's no talking you out of this madness, is there?"

"I've conceded to your wishes regarding your brethren, but I won't back down when it comes to Arsham."

Sooty clouds gathered in night the sky, obliterating the moon and its silvery light. The deep blackness outside matched my mood. I hid my face from Damien as I thought of Arsham. I was angry at him for keeping me locked up for ten years, but I was also grateful he didn't kill me. Even though we were not on the best of terms at the moment—and that was putting it mildly—I certainly didn't want my sire dead. My heart softened as I recalled the golden days of my vampire youth and the love I once bore for my creator. I remembered standing on the Great Wall of China as he confessed his deepest secrets to me. I'd spent so many years at his side…

"Angelique?" he prompted after several minutes of silence.

I couldn't imagine a world without Arsham.

Smiling at Damien, I said, "I'll help Rahim."

His face lit up with relief. "I knew you'd come around. Can you get us into the London lair?"

"Yes."

Severin came to Damien's apartment a few days later. Upon entering, he stopped short and stared at me. "You are the duchess," he said warily. "Arsham's seventh child."

"I am," I said.

Damien stood by my side and placed his arm around me. "Angelique has agreed to help us."

Severin's eyes swept over me coldly. "You know the London lair."

"Every inch," I assured him.

Severin frowned. "As much as we could use your help, I'm

hesitant to accept it. You betrayed your coven by sleeping with an enemy."

"This is bullshit, Severin. She said she'd help us."

Severin narrowed his eyes at me. "Why?"

I held his gaze. "Revenge. Why else?"

Severin said, "Then we leave immediately."

"What? Right now?" Damien demanded.

"The time has come for us to strike. Rahim has ordered me to bring you back to our lair." He looked at me and added, "He will be pleased when I return with two instead of one."

"Where are we going?" I asked.

"Moscow," he replied.

My stomach clenched with anxiety as we left Marseilles and headed northwest.

***

One cannot help but marvel at the sixteenth century cathedral dedicated to St. Basil. At night, the historical monument exploded with color and light. My companions and I cut through the throng of tourists taking photos, then paused to admire the architectural wonder.

"This is impressive," Damien commented.

Although I nodded in agreement, my mind weighed heavily. Was Rahim as ruthless as Arsham? Would he be grateful for my aid or would he view me as a traitor? Although I was willing to help him, certain stipulations needed to be met beforehand. Another thought struck me: was there any chance I could talk him out of this deadly mission?

We continued walking and eventually arrived at a massive metal gate.

Severin said, "Here we are."

A high, white wall stretched to the left and to the right. Barbed wire ran along the top of the wall, much like a prison. A panel by the metal door lit up to reveal a screen. Severin spoke in Russian to the person inside the control room, and the door clicked open.

"Wow," Damien whispered as we both stared at the large expanse of manicured lawn and the building beyond.

Wow, indeed.

Unlike Arsham who resided underground, Rahim owned an enormous mansion nestled inside a secure compound. The edifice was a modern ode to the city's great cathedral, full of towers and whimsical onion domes. Lights poured from the French windows and spilled onto spacious balconies. A few well-dressed vampires came out and looked down on us.

Severin led us into a lavishly decorated space where females flaunted haute-couture gowns and males wore stylish tuxedos. Diamonds and other precious gemstones glittered in the light of the impressive Swarovski crystal chandeliers. The frescoed ceiling depicted Venus emerging from the sea on a giant half shell. Nymphs and satyrs eyed the scene from a turquoise shore.

"Is there a party going on?" I asked.

Severin chuckled. "You could say that. Come, this way. Rahim is upstairs in the ballroom."

We ascended the stairs and traversed a hallway of white marble. The walls were adorned with beautiful oil paintings that any art major could easily identify. Two armed guards in black military uniforms stood watch in front of a set of mahogany double doors. When they were opened, I caught a vast expanse of shiny parquet floor in herringbone design. Gilded mirrors graced the area above the mantles.

A honey-skinned man wearing a sleek tuxedo sat upon a gold and red velvet throne fashioned in the Tudor style. Several armed security guards stood watch as elegant vampires sipped blood wine from delicate crystal goblets. Music played in the background. People automatically moved aside to let Severin pass and regarded Damien and I with open curiosity. I was terribly underdressed in my black tights, boots, and parka.

I immediately noticed the resemblance between Rahim and Arsham: dark eyes, thick brows, and a handsome face that could be sexy or cruel depending on the mood. Rahim wore his black hair cut very short, and his mouth was a bit wider than that of his half-brother. Severin bowed low before making an official introduction. Rahim stood from his throne to face me squarely. I noticed the familiarly arrogant tilt of his chin.

"Ah, the duchess. My lady, your lovely presence graces my home. I bid both of you welcome," Rahim said, turning his head and finally looking at Damien.

"Thank you," I said.

"You know Arsham well."

"I do, my lord," I replied, affording him respect even though he was not my sire.

He tucked my hand into the crook of his elbow. "We have much to talk about. Walk with me, Angelique."

Damien made to follow us, but Rahim held up his hand to stop him. Damien frowned and Severin shook his head in warning. My lover reluctantly backed off. The crowd parted like the Red Sea for Rahim, and I felt the weight of several stares. I allowed him to lead me onto one of the many balconies. He motioned for the others to continue their merrymaking before closing the doors.

"You already know who I am, don't you?" he asked the moment we were alone.

"I was recently informed that you're Arsham's half-brother; the slave who saved his life after he attempted to kill himself."

Rahim frowned in displeasure. "I haven't been a slave since I left Persia. I should never have been subjected to such a lowly fate. I am the son of a king."

"I'm merely repeating the story as Arsham told it, my lord. Forgive me if I offended you."

Eyeing me steadily, he inquired, "What else did your sire tell you?"

"That you disappeared and left him alone to figure things out for himself." I paused. "It was cruel of your father not to acknowledge you as his son."

"Very cruel," he agreed.

"Does Arsham know about you? I mean, does he know that you're his half-brother?"

Rahim's mouth twisted. "The queen and the princes lived apart from the concubines and their children. She resented the king's bastards and never allowed the princes to play with us. In order to not displease the queen, the king pretended we didn't

203

exist. We lived comfortably behind high walls in order not to be seen or heard by the royal family. Bastards were trained as palace servants and given the best jobs, but we were still considered slaves. As I grew older, I was allowed greater freedom to roam within the palace, but never near the royal chambers."

"Forgive my impertinence, my lord, but why didn't you reveal to Arsham that you both share the same paternal bloodline?"

Rahim averted his gaze. "Arsham had sought release from his pain by attempting suicide, but I wanted him to suffer."

"You can't blame him for not knowing about your existence," I said in an attempt to reason with him. "Remember that he, too, lived under rules imposed by his parents."

"I can excuse his ignorance during childhood, but as he grew older he must have known about the concubines. Surely, he suspected that his father had sired children with royal mistresses. Despite this, he never once inquired about us. Never sought us out. We lived under the same roof, yet I may as well have been a ghost."

So Rahim's desire for war was due to Arsham's unperceived slight. How could I possibly aid in mending the rift between these two proud males? "That was a long time ago," I reminded him. "I would think Arsham would be pleased to learn that he has a half-brother."

"You dare speak for your sire?"

"No, my lord. I speak only as a vampire. We are a lonely species." When Rahim's face remained stoic, I said, "You sent that proverb years ago, the one written in Old Persian."

"I did."

"Arsham took the message as a threat."

"I sent it as a threat." He paused. "Tell me about Arsham. I want to know everything about him."

There, under the silvery moonlight, I told Rahim what I knew of my sire. I did my best to portray Arsham in a positive light in the hope that Rahim would reconsider attacking the London lair.

"You forgot to mention that you were his lover," Rahim said after I had finished speaking.

How did he know? "I was one among many."

"I can see why he chose you," Rahim said, his gaze lingering at the base of my throat. "You are exquisite, and your eyes sparkle like midnight sapphires."

I gave him a wry smile. "That's exactly the same term he used to describe my eyes on the night he created me. 'Midnight sapphires.' Perhaps you two have more in common than you realize."

"Perhaps...You wish to betray your sire. Why? Is it because of the male who came with you?"

"I fell in love with a human. I suffered a harsh punishment for my crime and Damien was turned against his will."

"Turned against his will," he repeated. "Loving a man or a woman is not a crime as long as he or she willingly accepts the gift of immortality." Rahim narrowed his eyes. "Damien was quite different from other human males, however."

"Yes," I admitted.

"I wonder how his ancestors would react if they were alive today." He turned to glance through the glass at Damien, who stood watching us from within.

"You know who Damien is?"

"Vampires make it their business to know the identity of every slayer."

"Yet you have no problem accepting him into your lair."

Rahim's lips curved. "Damien would not be standing there unmolested if he posed a threat to me or my coven."

"Damien has no quarrel with you, my lord. He only seeks revenge for the injustice imposed upon him."

His eyes sought mine. "And you do not seek the same?"

"I would prefer to live my life in peace."

"A part of you still loves your sire." It was not a question. "It's obvious that Arsham has lost a precious member of his coven. Hopefully, his loss will be my gain. You're more than welcome to stay here, if you wish. Damien, too."

"I appreciate your generosity, my lord." I hesitated for a

moment. "May I ask you a personal question?"

"Yes."

"Your mansion is grandiose and you have a fine coven of vampires. You seem to enjoy a wonderful lifestyle here in Moscow." I waited until he nodded in agreement before I proceeded. "Why do you wish to overtake Arsham's lair? Why not remain here in Russia and be happy?"

"Because it's in my blood to conquer," Rahim replied. "As I've told you before, I am the son of a king. Although I was not personally groomed to rule, I paid close attention to the upbringing of my two half-brothers. I listened to the king's words when he taught his sons how to fight, how to strategize, and how to seize power." He offered me his hand. "Let's go inside now."

The moment I was back at Damien's side, he placed a possessive arm around me.

"I want you to enjoy yourselves this evening," Rahim said, catching Severin's eye and motioning for him to come over to us. "Severin will show you to a guestroom where you both can bathe and change into fresh clothing before rejoining our party."

"You are most gracious, my lord," Damien said.

"Tomorrow, we'll meet with my elders and military personnel."

"Military personnel?" I repeated, surprised.

Rahim nodded. "I have an impressive army of highly trained vampires. The majority were former soldiers and KGB spies."

Damien and I exchanged glances; I had underestimated Rahim.

"I'll see you both in a bit," Rahim said before turning his back on us and reclaiming his throne.

Severin led us down a maze of marble corridors that ended at a finely decorated bedroom. The cream and gold striped wallpaper complimented the gilded chairs. The king sized bed flaunted a gold and white patterned bedspread, and several Rococo style oil paintings graced the walls.

"See you back in the ballroom," Severin said, closing the

bedroom door and leaving us alone.

We stripped off our travel clothes and walked into the huge bathroom. Two stainless steel showerheads poked out of the wall within the oversized shower stall. While Damien and I showered together, I told him what Rahim and I had talked about on the balcony.

"It amazes me that he wants to leave Russia at all," I said. "I mean, look at this place!"

"Dripping with luxury," he said, turning off the faucet.

"Marble everywhere, gilded antiques, original artwork—this place must have cost a fortune." I stepped out of the stall. "Rahim has obviously done very well for himself."

"Obviously."

"Not to change the subject, but have I told you how much I like your tattoos?"

Damien grinned. "Actually, no. I was wondering when you were going to mention them."

I traced the dragon on his back with my fingertips. "Exquisite."

"Glad you approve. I had the ink done in Japan."

Damien's hands slid down my back to my buttocks. With a hard tug, he pulled my body against his erection. I stepped away from him and shook my head. Smiling coyly, I sank to my knees. His husky chuckle brimmed with anticipated pleasure.

"Don't tease me, Angelique," he warned.

I licked his cock slowly before taking him fully into my mouth. He groaned in pleasure while grabbing a fistful of my hair. When he was fully engorged and throbbing for relief, I stopped. Pulling me up to my feet, he growled with need as he turned me around and bent me over the bathroom sink. Biting my neck, his hands came around to caress my breasts as he slid into my wetness. When his thrusts became urgent, he seized my hips. The deep penetration drove me over the brink and I cried out in ecstasy before he reached his climax. He emptied himself inside of me with a shuddering breath.

"You'll be the death of me yet," he whispered hoarsely.

I peeked at him over my shoulder. "You're already dead,

sweetheart."

Vampirism had changed Damien. His human lovemaking had been tender. Now, it verged on aggressive. I reminded myself that he was still a young vampire, and he would eventually learn to control his base instincts. For now, I needed to be patient and enjoy the thrill and eroticism of what my lover had to offer. "Vampire Damien" added a new dimension to our relationship that I found exciting.

We exited the bathroom to find a black tuxedo and a beautiful cream silk gown carefully laid out on the bed.

"Do you think whoever came in here heard us in the bathroom?" I asked.

Damien shrugged. "If they did, they'll have no doubts about us being a couple."

I put on the stylish gown and admired my reflection in the mirror. Something caught my eye from across the room. A black velvet box and a note from Rahim sat atop the dresser. Scribbled on the note were the words: To match your eyes.

Damien snatched the note out of my hand. "What's this?"

"A gift from Rahim," I replied, opening the box. Nestled inside was a giant sapphire teardrop pendant hanging from a gold chain. "How thoughtful."

Damien grunted. "I'll have to keep my eye on him."

"Stop," I chided. "Here, help me."

His hands were surprisingly agile as he maneuvered the delicate gold clasp on the necklace. I took a step back to admire the dazzling blue flame that shot out of the stone whenever it caught the light.

"He has good taste," Damien admitted.

We found our way back to the ballroom and joined the rest of the vampires. The lights were now dimmed considerably and the classical music had been replaced by dance music. Some vampires were moving to the enticing beat, while others kissed and bit each other in dark corners. Blood wine flowed freely.

Rahim came to me at once. His fingertips reached out to brush against the stone and lingered on my skin. Damien almost snarled in outrage. "Simply gorgeous."

"It's beautiful. Thank you."

"You do it justice, my dear." Rahim tossed an oily smile at Damien. "Please, enjoy yourselves. Plenty of time for serious talk tomorrow."

We spotted Severin across the room chatting to a female. He had changed into a formal tuxedo and now lifted his glass to us.

We accepted glasses of blood wine from a servant and smiled at the vampires who came over to greet us. They were a friendly bunch and Rahim certainly knew how to throw a party.

When Severin joined us, I asked, "What's the occasion, anyway?"

"We're celebrating," Severin replied.

"Celebrating what, exactly?" Damien asked.

"The merging of our House with that of London."

Damien and I shared a look before I said, "Premature, no?"

Severin shrugged. "That's not how Rahim sees it. The moment he decided it was time to make a move was the moment he announced his success. He never acts unless he is absolutely sure of the outcome. And he always gets what he wants." He paused and added for effect, "Always."

"Rather impressive track record," I commented before sipping my blood wine. It was delicious and unlike anything I'd ever tasted.

Damien smirked. "What if he fails?"

"He won't," Severin replied curtly.

That put an end to the conversation. I was on my second glass of blood wine and suddenly realized that I was drunk.

Severin laughed when he noticed me frowning into my glass as I swayed. "Not your ordinary blood wine, is it?"

"What's in this stuff?" I asked incredulously. "I thought we were immune to everything."

"There's a rare and costly opiate from China mixed into the wine. It's fatal to humans, but gives us a slight high. Rahim has also added some of his own blood to the batch in order to further increase our pleasure. He's a generous sire."

Damien and I both peered into our glasses with renewed interest. Rahim motioned to Severin, who excused himself to stand by his sire's side. A moment later, Rahim whispered something into Severin's ear that made the big vampire smile in a way that suggested intimacy between the two of them.

"Is Severin the second in command?" I inquired.

Damien watched the two males with interest. "I'm not sure what's going on there, but Rahim definitely trusts him."

We were becoming inebriated on the wonderful blood wine, and having some much needed, well-deserved fun. We laughed and danced and simply enjoyed Rahim's hospitality. I thought of Micah, Omar, and Valerio. Micah would never attend such an event, and Omar was too prim to fully relish what was being offered, but Valerio was altogether different. My lively Sicilian brother would have a blast if he were here. He would have sniffed out the gay males in the room and they would be eating from the palm of his hand. The thought of my three beloved brothers had a sobering effect on me. I didn't want any harm to come to them, and would try to negotiate a deal with Rahim on their behalf.

The faintest light on the horizon signaled the end of the festivities. The music stopped and the vampires slowly left the ballroom in order to seek shelter from the coming dawn. Our room was outfitted with electronic shutters that blocked out the light. We undressed and got into bed.

After several minutes of silence, Damien asked, "You're thinking about the meeting tomorrow."

I turned onto my side and leaned on my elbow to face him. "I'm going to try to negotiate a deal for my three brothers."

"What about the twins?"

I laughed without mirth. "Do you know what they said at my trial? 'Death to the duchess.' As far as I'm concerned, those two bitches can fend for themselves."

"You may be asking a lot from Rahim."

"If he doesn't want to respect my wishes, then I'll find a way to get a message to my brothers."

This made him sit up and look at me. "You'll risk ruining Rahim's plan and incurring his anger in the process. Do you really want to take that chance? Would your brothers take such a risk for you?"

I thought for a moment. "I believe they would, yes."

Damien flung up his hands. "Then go for it, Angelique."

"Why are you angry?"

"Why screw things up by attracting needless danger?"

"Let's not argue," I said as a plan began to take shape inside my head. "I'm sure my meeting with Rahim tomorrow will go smoothly."

"Do what you have to do, but don't screw this up."

***

Severin was at our door the moment the sun had set, then led us to a room almost as big as the ballroom. The entire length of wall to my left was lined with mahogany bookshelves and thousands of volumes. Opposite the door was a huge fireplace. Three plush sofas were arranged before the roaring fire. A long rectangular table and many chairs dominated most of the room. Two rows of seated vampires stared at us as. Rahim sat at the head of the table with his back to the fire. There were two empty seats beside him, and he motioned for Damien and me to occupy them. Severin remained standing by the door.

"Thank you," Rahim said to Severin. "Now if you would please take care of that other matter we discussed earlier…"

"Yes, my lord," Severin replied before leaving the room.

"I hope you two enjoyed your rest," Rahim said to Damien and I.

"We did, thank you," I replied as Damien inclined his head.

Rahim made brief introductions. There were a total of fifteen military trained vampires, three of which were former KGB spies. What impressed me most was that they varied in age and ethnicity, each bringing a unique talent to the table. One was a hi-tech weapons specialist, another a bomb and explosives expert, two were war strategists, and so on.

"Angelique is—*was*—an elder of the London coven," Rahim said. The vampires whispered among themselves and when they settled down, he added, "She seeks atonement for Arsham's injustices."

"Can we trust a traitor?" asked one of the war strategists.

211

The mature male had silver side burns and piercing green eyes. "That's a good question," I said, meeting his gaze. "I would ask the same if I were in your shoes. I am indeed betraying my coven by going against my sire, but I have good reason."

"Do you?" snapped a female with slanted black eyes and hair as black as pitch. "From what I understand, you fell in love with a slayer." Her eyes flickered in Damien's direction. "You're lucky Arsham spared your life—and his, for that matter." Turning to Rahim, she added, "The only injustice I see is her betrayal, my lord."

Rahim nodded. "I know some of you oppose the idea of recruiting outside help, but Angelique came here of her own accord. I've already confirmed that she's telling the truth about being imprisoned and fleeing London against her sire's wishes." He looked at me. "She's now considered an outlaw and cannot go back."

"What if Arsham tracked her here? What if this is a trap?" the Asian female countered.

"There's no trap. Arsham has no idea I'm here," I retorted.

"So, what's the plan?" asked a strapping young male.

Rahim replied, "We travel to London and infiltrate the lair at dawn as they're getting ready to retire. Angelique knows the location of the secret entrances, which is privy information. We'll lie in wait until they're all asleep."

"And assassinate Arsham and his elders."

I winced at the young male's words. To my surprise, Rahim nodded slightly and I could swear I saw a hint of sadness in his eyes. The world of vampirism proved a lonely one. Family meant everything. Could he be having second thoughts after my conversation with him?

"May I ask you a question, my lord?" I whispered. At his nod, I continued, "What if you tried to speak with Arsham? What if you two could work out an agreement?"

"Negotiate with that arrogant, royal snob?" he snapped.

This attack on Arsham was definitely personal. I said tentatively, "There's something I need in return for my help."

212

Rahim's eyes narrowed. "And what would that be?"

"I don't want any harm to come to my brothers—Micah, Valerio, and Omar—and Omar's wife, of course. They're innocent and dear to my heart."

Some of the vampires at the table hissed in protest, but Rahim held up his hand to silence them. "This is a fair request. How do you suppose we spare them? You cannot guarantee that your brothers won't attack us when we strike, which would only provoke a counter attack from my soldiers."

"I could send them a warning..." I trailed off, knowing how stupid it sounded.

Rahim was already shaking his head.

"This is ridiculous," one of the vampires whispered.

Rahim slammed his fist on the table for order and the room went so silent that you could hear a pin drop. He looked to me again and cocked his head to the side. "Well?"

I turned to Damien for help but he only shrugged. After a few seconds I looked back to Rahim. "I don't know, but I'll think of something."

CHAPTER 15

*"He who fights and runs away, may turn to fight another day;
he who is in battle slain, will never rise to fight again."*
(Tacitus)

Rahim's coven numbered almost three thousand. Arsham's coven had a little over two thousand ten years ago. I had no idea how many vampires currently served my sire. The map I had drawn for Rahim clearly outlined the secret passageways known only to the elders. The ambush plan was easy: arrive in London and immediately attack.

Rahim insisted that we remain in Moscow until each vampire knew his or her role. I refrained from trying to reason with him the way I had on the night of my arrival. Besides, he was too blinded by pride and ambition to listen to me. Instead, I came up with my own plan of action. I didn't dare speak of it with Damien, for I knew he wouldn't approve.

We descended upon London cloaked in darkness thanks to the waning moon. Rahim insisted we wear black from head to foot with balaclavas to hide our faces. The army divided into teams, and each one had been carefully instructed to infiltrate a specific secret entrance within the lair. All ears were tuned into Rahim's radioed commands.

Flanked by Rahim and Damien, I crept along the shadows toward my former lair. We came to a stop outside one of the secret exits.

Rahim turned to me and said, "The moment has arrived, my lady. Any deviation from the plan we agreed upon, and your lover will pay the price." When Damien and I expressed surprised at this new twist, he added, "You didn't think I would really trust a traitor, did you?"

Two vampires restrained Damien.

Rahim never broke eye contact with me. "Five minutes. Not

a second more. Understood?"

My jaw clenched involuntarily at the threat. "Yes."

Rahim had allotted me only five minutes to warn my three brothers before all hell broke loose within the lair. If I tried to warn Arsham, Damien would be killed.

Rahim told his soldiers to 'stand down,' then gave me the signal. I shot forward like an arrow and managed to infiltrate the lair without being detected. I slipped into Micah's room and found him reading a book.

He shot out of his chair. "Angelique."

"Oh, Micah," I cried, throwing my arms around his neck.

"Arsham didn't see you, did he?"

"No…I can't explain right now, but you must tell Omar and Valerio to get out of the lair right now."

"Omar is in Paris with his wife," he said, glancing at his expensive wristwatch. "Valerio is probably in some trendy gay bar at this hour. He never returns before three."

A wave of relief washed over me as I grabbed his hand and pulled him toward the door. "We need to leave right now. Come on, let's go."

Micah's eyes narrowed. "Why?"

"An army of vampires from Russia is outside waiting to attack the lair."

Retrieving his hand, he demanded, "Are you behind this?"

"No…but I led them here. I didn't have a choice. It's complicated."

Micah eyed me coldly. "I will stay and fight with my coven."

My heart sank. "Micah…please…"

"Get out, before I tell Arsham you're here."

Defeated, I went to the door. As I closed it behind me, I heard him utter the word "traitor."

Devastated, I made it back to Damien before my five minutes expired. Rahim cocked a brow at me when I returned alone. "Valerio and Omar are not inside," I explained.

"And Micah?" Damien asked.

"He chose to stay and fight."

Rahim's face became a mask of fury as he balled his fists.

215

"He's already sounded the alarm!" Pushing the button on his sophisticated radio, he commanded, "We attack at once!"

Soldiers invaded Arsham's lair. Rahim, Damien, Severin, and I waited until the teams were inside before following their trail with weapons drawn. Rahim's army had the advantage of a surprise attack. By the time we entered the lair, there were already a few decapitated bodies on the floor.

Crippled by guilt, I did my best to remain invisible. I didn't want to kill my brethren. Damien, on the other hand, took great pleasure in slaughtering Arsham's vampires. When our eyes met, he indicated with a toss of his head that I should leave the lair for my own good. I shook my head at his suggestion and hid in a dark corridor, instead.

Rahim went from room to room in search of his half-brother. Suddenly, a hand clamped down on my mouth and my back slammed up against a wall of muscle. I tensed, recognizing the familiar feel of the body behind my own.

Placing his forearm tightly against my throat and pinning my arms behind my back with his other hand, Arsham hissed in my ear, "You dare to raise your hand against me? I should rip your head right off of your neck."

"And I will blow your head off if you do."

Damien stood in my peripheral vision, aiming a gun at Arsham's head with one hand while holding his menacing katana with the other.

"Guns don't work on vampires, fool," Arsham snapped.

"Guns loaded with silver bullets do," Damien retorted. "Let go of her, asshole, or it will be your head that rolls."

I could sense that Arsham was smiling when he said, "That's not the proper way for a child to address his sire."

Damien spat in Arsham's direction. "Fuck you."

Arsham's forearm tightened around my neck and I tried in vain to free myself. "I love it when you rub your body against mine, Angelique," he whispered huskily in my ear.

My lover growled in outrage at our sire's provocation and raised the katana.

"No!" I cried. "Don't do it!"

216

Damien's eyes flashed. "There you go again! Sticking up for this piece of shit! I swear you're in love with him!"

Upon hearing the last sentence, Arsham relaxed his grip on me. I felt the familiar muscles of his body uncoil as he subtly pressed against me.

"Damien...he is your sire," I reasoned. "He bestowed the gift of eternal life upon you. Upon us."

"Against my will," Damien hissed, placing the wicked blade to Arsham's neck.

"I know," I conceded. "But think—the physical aches and pains, the ugliness of old age—these human burdens will never touch us. We'll never become sick or decrepit...we'll never die. Don't you see, Damien? Arsham has given us Eternity."

Rahim walked in at that moment and quickly assessed the situation. The two alpha males stared at one another for several seconds. After barring the door to prevent anyone else from entering, he said, "Arsham, I am Rahim."

"I remember your face," Arsham snapped.

"As you should," Rahim said. "I am your sire and you should bow down to me."

"Bow down to you?" Arsham seethed. "You abandoned me!"

Rahim crossed his arms, flaunting impressive biceps. "You deserved to suffer, Arsham."

"I did suffer," Arsham retorted. "I was suffering when you found me. You should have walked away and left me to die."

Rahim averted his gaze. "Surrender to me now and your coven will be spared."

"What about those whom you have already slain?" Arsham countered. "Innocent vampires who had no quarrel with you."

"Casualties of war," Rahim replied.

"Yet you demand my surrender. Are you are so powerful that you can resuscitate my dead vampires?"

"No," Rahim replied, frowning in confusion. "No vampire can do that."

"Then why should I concede to you?" Arsham retorted haughtily. "You're not more powerful than me! Besides, I don't take orders from a slave."

Rahim's expression turned cold. "I may be a slave, but the same blood courses through our veins." When Arsham remained silent, he added, "We share the same father."

"Impossible," Arsham retorted.

"My mother was a royal concubine. The king's favorite, in fact," Rahim explained. "My blood is as regal as yours."

"Just because you have been nurturing this fantasy for centuries doesn't make it true."

"He speaks the truth," I managed to say despite my sire's forearm pressing against my windpipe. "Rahim is really your half-brother."

Damien kept the katana at Arsham's neck, ready to send my sire's head flying.

Rahim said, "I think you need a lesson in humility before I kill you and make slaves of your vampires."

"No, Rahim!" I cried. "Don't do it. You share the same father—the same blood."

"Why didn't you seek me out sooner, Rahim?" Arsham demanded. "Why wait until now to tell me of your existence? And in such a violent manner?"

"You've never been as powerful as you are now," Rahim replied. "A bit too powerful."

"So what? I've never provoked you," Arsham shot back.

"Arsham is right, my lord," I said to Rahim. "You are both the sons of a mighty king. Don't you see? You two could unite the covens and co-rule the largest vampire army on the planet." As Rahim and Arsham stared at one another in stony silence, I added, "Both of you went in different directions in life and became powerful rulers. I can only imagine what you two have seen and experienced throughout the centuries. Your combined knowledge must be incredible! Why not use it to your mutual advantages, my lords?"

"Angelique." Damien uttered my name in a tone of disbelief. "What the hell are you doing?"

"Trying to negotiate a deal to save her life," Arsham replied on my behalf.

"Rahim, think about it," I urged, ignoring my lover and my sire. "You and Arsham can call a truce right now and negotiate terms that would benefit you both. You can put an end to the senseless bloodbath going on outside that door."

Damien had not moved a muscle but the murderous intent was still in his eyes. "This was not the plan."

"Lower your weapons, Damien," I said.

"No!"

Arsham chuckled and said, "Pity you're so stubborn, slayer. You would have made a fine addition to my coven."

"Damien, killing Arsham isn't going to make you mortal again," I reasoned.

"Spoken like an ambassador," Rahim noted.

"I believe a truce would work in everyone's benefit," I said. "There's been enough blood spilled today. Please, my lords, show everyone that you are great rulers by putting a stop to this madness. You would garner much more respect by displaying wisdom instead of violence."

Rahim met my eyes. "You make a valid point."

"You still love Arsham," Damien accused, staring at me with a mixture of hurt and disbelief.

Arsham's grip relaxed to the point that I could easily have escaped. When I didn't try to free myself, he let go of my hands and discreetly caressed the base of my spine.

I lowered my head. "He is my sire, Damien."

My tone had betrayed me. I didn't have to see Arsham's face to know it reflected triumph. Damien lowered his weapons and looked to Rahim, who stood studying me intently.

Turning my head to address Arsham, I said, "Sire, please think of my brethren."

"The way you thought of them when you decided to join forces with my enemy?" Arsham countered.

I shook my head. "I never saw Rahim as your enemy. The moment I found out he was your half-brother, I knew I had to convince him. He planned to attack the London lair regardless of my cooperation. I believed that if I went along with his plan, I could get you both to negotiate terms for peace."

Damien shot me a hateful look. "You betrayed me," he said before unbarring the door and storming out of the room.

"She betrayed me, too," Rahim muttered.

I looked at Rahim. "I never meant to betray anyone. Life for our kind is not easy. We already have enough enemies on the outside wanting to cause us harm, we don't need to be fighting each other. It makes no sense."

"A wise elder," Rahim commented.

"The best," Arsham assured him. Placing his lips to my ear, he added, "Leave us."

I left the two alpha vampires facing each other as I ran off in search of Damien. I noticed Rahim's army retreating. No doubt the radioed command to "cease fire" had reached their ears. My brethren must have received the same command because they, too, stopped fighting.

I finally found Damien standing over the decapitated bodies of Deirdre and Ciara. I'm ashamed to admit that I experienced no emotion when I saw their corpses—no sorrow, no remorse. The jealous and envious twins had hated me for two centuries and now they were gone from my life.

Micah came upon the scene and recoiled at the sight of the headless bodies. I noticed that he was unarmed, so I stepped in front of my brother before Damien could do any harm.

"Stop!" I cried.

"Get out of the way, traitor," Damien said as he lifted the katana.

I stood my ground and shook my head. "No, Damien. I love Micah. I won't let you hurt him."

"Damn you, Angelique! How can you take their side after what they've done to you? To me? To us?"

"Micah has never done anything to you. You need to stop this stupid vendetta and embrace your immortality. I know you didn't ask for it, but what's done cannot be undone."

Micah met my gaze and his eyes softened. Our relationship had suffered greatly in the past, but it wasn't totally doomed.

Damien shook his head in defeat.

I stepped to the side. "That's better. I don't think you two require an introduction."

Micah glanced at Damien, then asked, "Is our sire...?"

"Arsham and Rahim are hopefully negotiating a truce in there," I replied, indicating the room I had vacated only moments earlier.

Micah placed a hand on my shoulder. "Forgive me for what I said earlier. You're not a traitor."

"I am. I betrayed Rahim and Damien," I said.

Damien shook his head and said to Micah, "She only did it because she wanted peace."

I tossed a grateful look at Damien for finally understanding.

"Like it or not, you are now one of us," Micah said to Damien. "My sire may not let you reside here—"

"I wouldn't want to!" Damien snapped.

"I don't blame you, but that doesn't change the fact that Arsham made you directly and therefore you are my brother."

I held my breath as Micah put out his hand. Damien stared at it for a few seconds before shaking it. The gesture filled me with joy. If a Sauvage could accept a vampire as his brother, anything was possible.

Arsham and Rahim eventually emerged from the room. The vampires of both covens stared at each other in confusion as the two sires stood side by side.

"Rahim and I are in the process of negotiating terms," Arsham bellowed.

"We have much to discuss in the coming weeks," Rahim added. "We have agreed to a truce—for the time being."

"What now?" Damien demanded in my ear.

"Now, we wait."

"You said that I would rule by your side, Rahim!"

All eyes turned to Severin, who stood on the opposite side of the room glaring at Arsham.

Severin continued, "We need to stick to the plan. Arsham should die."

Arsham growled at the insolent vampire but Rahim restrained him with a hand to the shoulder. To Severin, he said, "I have made my decision and you will abide by it."

221

"We've been planning this attack for months," Severin countered passionately.

"The plans have changed."

Severin's eyes filled with angry tears. "You promised me."

That's when I realized that Severin and Rahim were lovers.

Rahim went to stand before Severin and took his hand. Arsham's eyes slid to where I stood and I gave my sire a pointed look, prompting him to arrive at the same conclusion as me.

Rahim quietly said, "Must I continually remind you that I am your sire, Severin? I have made a decision. There's nothing more to discuss."

Severin pouted. "It's not fair."

"It is what it is," Rahim affirmed.

Severin seemed momentarily confused before his face contorted with fury. Suddenly, the big blond vampire lunged at Arsham. A blur and a whooshing sound made everyone gasp in shock. Damien stood in the center of the room with a bloody katana. Severin's head lay at his feet.

That Damien would intervene on Arsham's behalf shocked us all. I knew he had done it for me.

"Sorry, Rahim, I was only trying to prevent a bloodbath," Damien explained.

Rahim's mouth formed a harsh line, but he inclined his head. "You did the correct thing. Severin's foolish and disobedient outburst has cost him his life."

Rahim's composure and respect for the fragile truce impressed Arsham, who placed a hand on his half-brother's shoulder. I wondered if that simple gesture could be the beginning of a fraternal alliance.

I stood before my sire and stared into his eyes until he held out his hand. There was no need for words between us at this point. I dropped to one knee and kissed the blood ruby.

Arsham placed his hand upon my head and loudly declared for the benefit of the coven, "Angelique has returned and I have decided to extend mercy." He looked down at me and added quietly, "Welcome home."

"Thank you, sire." I paused. "What about Damien?"

Arsham's eyes were hard as they slid to where my lover stood. "The slayer cannot go unpunished for his role in this attack." Before I could protest, he held up his hand "I will spare his life for saving mine, but he cannot remain here in London."

I stood. "Then you condemn us both into exile."

Arsham held my gaze for several seconds and I thought I saw regret in his eyes. "I want you to stay, Angelique."

"If I stay, Damien stays."

"No."

"Goodbye, Arsham."

He said nothing in response. I met Rahim's stare briefly before inclining my head at him, then without another word, I walked to where Damien stood.

Micah ran up to me and pulled me into an embrace. "Our paths will cross again," he whispered. "Take care of yourself."

Damien's jaw clenched as I led him to the exit. Our progress was followed by hundreds of stares. I peeked over my shoulder before opening the door and met Arsham's level gaze. He didn't flinch as I stepped outside into the night.

Damien and I walked several paces in silence before he said, "I can't believe I saved that asshole's life."

"Neither can I, but it was the right thing to do."

He nodded in agreement. "I've been intent on revenge for so long...I don't know what to do now."

I faced him. "Here's an idea: let's live our lives."

"Where?"

I spread my arms wide. "Anywhere! Don't you get it, yet? Arsham set us free. We can go to Brazil or South Africa or the Maldives. We can spend as much time in as many places as we choose. That's the beauty of immortality. We have the luxury of time."

My passionate words must have moved him because he finally nodded. Pulling me into his arms, he kissed the top of my head. "You're absolutely right."

CHAPTER 16
GRAND CAYMAN ISLAND
1 YEAR LATER

"There is no passion to be found playing small—in settling for a life that is less than the one you are capable of living."
(Nelson Mandela)

Seven Mile Beach was deserted at this late hour. The sugar-sand beach resembled an endless white ribbon beneath the full moon. Small waves gently lapped against the smooth shoreline. We admired the moon's reflection shimmering on the crystal clear water as the tropical evening breeze caressed our skin.

"Tomorrow will mark our third month on the island," Damien commented.

"Ready to go somewhere else?"

"Hmm…not yet. I like it here."

Damien—*my Damien*—had finally returned. The night we were exiled, we crossed the English Channel and spent a week in Paris before deciding on the Caribbean. A year of island hopping had done wonders for his spirit and our relationship. We needed some tropical fun and warm waters to forget our troubles.

Every evening after the sun had set, we enjoyed the twilight sky and all the pleasures the island had to offer. We dove, swam, ran, and frolicked to our hearts' content. Of course, there was fine dining on wealthy tourists and first class entertainment to be enjoyed within the five star resorts.

"Do you want to swim with the sea turtles tonight?" I inquired.

"Sounds great."

Two figures emerged on the beach and headed toward us. I recognized them immediately and gripped Damien's arm. His

224

night?"

"Are you hungry?"

"I'm feeling a bit peckish."

"There was a bar back that way," I said, pointing toward a cluster of colorful lights.

"Let's do it."

We wandered to the festive beach bar in search of drunk people, preferably couples. We struck up a conversation with an attractive pair of hearty Americans on their honeymoon. After hearing about life on a Midwestern farm through slurred sentences, we offered to buy a round of drinks, then another. And then one more.

The wife said, "I'm toooooootally shiffaced."

Damien and I played along, slurring our sentences and laughing. The husband stumbled as he got off the barstool and helped his wife, who staggered comically.

"Where are you staying?" I asked. "We can share a taxi."

The husband held up a finger and grinned. "Great idea."

Damien laid several bills on the bar. The bartender noticed we hadn't touched our drinks, but made no comment. Maybe the enormous tip prompted the young man's silence. We led our prey outside and steered them toward the empty beach.

"I think a swim is in order," Damien declared.

The woman was already stripping off her sundress. "Yeah!"

"You can't swim, honey," the man pointed out as she ran toward the shore in pink panties and matching bra.

Damien and I exchanged glances. Sometimes I took the woman, sometimes he did. For us, as long as the humans were appealing, gender didn't matter. Damien ran after the woman and I remained with the man. Blue eyed and built like a bull, he could barely stand. I linked my arm in his and urged him toward a cluster of tall hibiscus trees.

"I shouldn't say this, but…you sure are pretty," he said.

"Oh, dear, your wife wouldn't like that at all."

"Aw, she ain't jealous. Been together five years now."

In my most sultry voice, I purred, "Well, in that case…"

I had barely slid my arms around his neck when his greedy

hands were all over me. *Perfect*. I glanced over my shoulder at Damien, who was already feeding from the limp woman in his arms. I sunk my razor sharp teeth into his skin and he groaned in pleasure as I fed.

"Sweet Jesus," he exclaimed when I pulled away. "I've never had anyone do that to me. Must be a European thing."

"Must be," I agreed, licking my lips in satisfaction.

I heard the woman giggling as she and Damien headed our way. I stepped away from the man and smiled at them. "Did you have a nice swim?"

"Oh, yeah," she replied, walking straight to her husband and throwing her arms around his neck.

"Maybe it's time to leave these two lovebirds alone," Damien suggested, taking my hand.

The newlyweds were kissing passionately by the time we bade them farewell. This is why we chose couples. We never killed our prey, but rather, provided them with immense pleasure. Our bite served them better than a porn film.

Damien said, "Why can't all vampires feed the way we do?"

I laughed. "Are you kidding? Our bite makes humans so horny, they would overpopulate the earth!"

"Speaking of horny," he said before nuzzling my neck.

"Mmm…feisty. I like that."

"Let's go for a swim."

We stripped and entered the Caribbean water, which felt deliciously warm on our naked skin.

"Feels good," he said.

"You know what feels better," I purred before taking his earlobe between my teeth.

"Vixen," he whispered.

Damien splashed me playfully and I splashed back. He suddenly grabbed me and I melted against him.

"I love you," he said before plundering my mouth.

As we made love beneath the glorious moon, I became filled with joy and gratitude. Damien and I had been given the gift of immortality, and forever stretched out before us offering countless possibilities.

The rooms of the luxurious hotel penthouse were unlit, and his muscular body stood silhouetted in black against the moonlit glass of the sliding doors. His jaw clenched as he witnessed their lovemaking; their sublime happiness...*their bliss*. He recalled the taste and scent of the duchess's skin, the sweetness of her mouth, but most of all, he recalled the love she once felt for him.

"You belong to me, Angelique," Arsham whispered into the darkness.

Did you enjoy this novel? The author would appreciate your review on Amazon. Thank you.

Turn the page to sample THE WATCHERS, an exciting, "otherworldly" novel by C. De Melo:

THE WATCHERS

A STORY OF UNDYING LOVE

C. DE MELO

230

PART I

THE ICON

After Dark Times the Icon shall come.
She will walk the Earth as a Sage, but will only provoke rage.
Our Mark she will bear on the Tenth and Twentieth year.

—First Prophecy of the Sacred Oracle

Prologue
Present Day
Lisbon, Portugal

Sooty clouds conceal the moon in a starless sky as a white vein of lightning illuminates an anchored caravela. The fast and mighty sea vessel bobs like a child's toy upon the angry waves of the Tagus River. The sight fills me with dread.

My beloved stands tall and proud, the fierce wind tugging at the strands of his dark hair. Deafening thunder fills our ears only moments before icy water spills from the heavens. We are surrounded by imminent danger. My tears mingle with rain as I desperately plead with him. The thought of losing this man forever pierces my heart with excruciating pain...

I cannot bear it.

I awoke with my own sharp intake of breath and, as the cobwebs of sleep dissipated, the fragile echo of a memory slipped—yet again—from my grasp.

The gloomy light of dawn filled the bedroom. My gaze is drawn to the packed suitcases by the door. Thousands of miles away, a new life awaited...

Could it save me from this madness?

Chapter 1
Lisbon, Portugal
November 1, 1510

"The church bells are ringing in honor of my birthday!"

"As they do every year," my mother reminded me with an indulgent smile. "Now go out and fetch some chestnuts."

I snatched a basket and ran outside with eager steps. All Saint's Day was a holy day of celebration in our kingdom. My mother had already promised to bake apple tarts, so the roasted chestnuts would be an extra treat. Unable to resist their sweet flesh, I usually ate them the moment they were extracted from the fire, inevitably burning my tongue. My mother often scolded me for my lack of patience, but today I would surprise her by waiting for them to cool. After all, as a ten-year-old, I should start displaying a certain measure of maturity.

I followed the footpath through our vegetable garden and slipped through a cluster of trees. The sun-kissed leaves were as translucent as the stained glass windows of the great cathedral. Sunbeams seeped through the branches to create a mosaic of light and shadow on the soft grass beneath my feet.

We lived on a hill just outside of Lisbon, and I could clearly see the fortress of the Castelo de São Jorge. Soldiers moved to and fro along the battlements like industrious ants. Hugging the narrow trunk of a sapling, I admired the sparkling water of the Tagus River and glimpsed the faint silhouette of a merchant spice ship heading out to sea.

A butterfly landed on a nearby branch and I became instantly lost in the intricate maze of its wings. When it flew away, I continued toward the clearing where the chestnut trees grew. I sank to the ground and began collecting the prettiest chestnuts.

The sun warmed my back, making me drowsy, so I stretched out on the grass. The sunlight's pressure against my closed

233

eyelids evoked a riot of colors in the blackness—tiny explosions of bluish red and greenish gold in fantastic patterns. As the lazy drone of bees filled my ears, I imagined my body liquefying and seeping into the earth. I remained in this trance-like state for a long time.

I wasn't sure when the birds stopped singing, but I could no longer hear the insects or the wind. Opening my eyes, I sat up and shivered in the unnatural, disquieting silence. Clouds had gathered in the sky above, blocking the sun.

"Veronica."

Startled, I looked around.

"Veronica..."

This time, I heard my name uttered softly in my ear, causing the tiny hairs on the back of my neck to stand on end. I peeked over my shoulder and saw him standing on the opposite side of the clearing. His serene face reminded me of the Christ figure adorning the altar of our parish church. A long cloak partially hid his powerful body and his shoulder-length hair and goatee were black as pitch.

How did I hear his whisper from so far away?

I was too stunned to move or speak as he held my gaze within the leafy shadows, his yellow eyes glowing in the dimness. Suddenly, the inside of my right wrist burned as a cluster of tiny dots in the shape of a spiral broke through the delicate skin.

"Mama!" I cried.

A moment later, my mother called out, "Veronica, where are you?"

"In the clearing!"

My mother ran toward me. At the sight of my pale face, she demanded, "What is it, child? What do you see?"

"A man is hiding in the trees over there."

Yanking me to my feet, she stood in front of me. "Hello? Is there anyone there?"

Silence.

Gripping my shoulders, she shook me slightly. "Did he speak to you? Did you speak to him? What did he look like?"

I showed her the inside of my wrist. "He had eyes like a wolf, and he did *this* to me."

She recoiled at the sight of my strange mark and shoved me toward home. I bent to retrieve the basket of chestnuts, but she hastily pushed me forward, causing me to stumble through the grass. She locked the door as soon we entered the cottage and led me to our icon of the Virgin Mary.

"Kneel, child," she said, sinking to her knees and forcing me down, too. "Hail Mary, full of grace. The Lord is with thee…"

I lost count of how many times we repeated the prayer. My mouth became dry but I didn't dare risk my mother's anger by asking for water.

She stood abruptly. "Did the man speak to you?"

I nodded. "He said my name twice."

My mother paced the room and eventually paused before the Virgin Mary. As she stared at the statue, her expression went from fear to worry to anger. "Three decades of faith and devotion—I've been nothing but loyal, yet you turn your back on me!" She fixed me with a strange look, making me squirm in my seat. "Veronica comes from the Latin *Vera Iconica*, meaning True Icon. I endowed you with this holy name hoping that it would protect you from harm."

My name held special powers?

My mother's eyes slid to the Virgin Mary's sweet face and she frowned. "Why didn't you spare my precious child?"

As the ensuing silence grew, so did the tension within our cottage. The bland gaze of the Virgin Mary combined with her mocking silence caused my mother to unravel. My father had carved the wooden icon shortly before he died—it was the most treasured material possession in our home. I cried out in shock when my mother violently struck the statue and sent it flying across the room. The figure splintered against a storage chest containing our winter supply of salted cod, and we gasped in unison as its head snapped off. It rolled along the floor and came to a stop at my feet, face up. Mary's eyes glared accusingly, as though blaming me for her current predicament. Impulsively, I kicked the head into the flames. My mother screamed in protest but it was too late. Mary's serene face became blackened and distorted as the fire greedily consumed the wood and melted the paint.

My mother turned away from the hearth to collect the headless figure from the floor. She gazed at the broken neck for a moment, caressing the cerulean robe with touching gentleness before tossing what remained of our icon into the flames.

Stunned, I cried, "Mama!"

She shrugged, mumbling something about her prayers not being heard.

**

My mother remained sullen and preoccupied throughout the day. Although she baked the apple tarts as promised, I didn't feel consoled by them. I thanked her for the treats but I could only manage a few nibbles. The tart tasted like dirt to me, and bile rose in my throat every time I attempted to swallow it down. I knew that something important had happened earlier today, but I didn't know what it was, and not knowing frightened me.

Later that night I watched my mother kneel before the hearth in order to retrieve the burnt remains of the Virgin Mary. Taking a piece of charred wood from the ashes, she etched a cross over her heart. I stared at the smudged black lines upon her skin as penitent tears rolled down her cheeks. She came to me and drew a black cross on my forehead, too. Together, we begged God's forgiveness for our heinous sins.

Chapter 2
Boston, MA
November 1, Present Day

The United States of America...the *New World*.

The plane began its initial descent, so I leaned against the window to take in the view. I could see the Boston skyline clearly despite the cloudy New England day. Seventeen boats glided upon the surface of the liquid lead bay.

My college buddy, Josh, sent me an email offering to pick me up at the airport. We reconnected last year through Facebook after he had casually mentioned that one of his clients served as the Department Chair of Portuguese Studies at Brown University. He also informed me that a few of my art history articles had been featured in the Portuguese newspapers of New England, capturing the attention of some influential academicians. When I told Josh that the private school I worked for in Lisbon had run out of funding, he wasted no time pulling strings. Emails were exchanged, proposals were made, and I scored a research fellowship.

My breath fogged up the window, thus obscuring the view of the bay. Hopefully, this new position at Brown offered a bit more stability than my last job. At least it would look good on my CV. I was pushing thirty and didn't have time to mess around—professionally speaking.

As bravely as I tried to look ahead to the future, I knew I'd pine miserably for my European lifestyle. How could I not? Being surrounded on a daily basis by fine art and architecture, history, culture, excellent food and wine—I was spoiled.

"*Pah-dun* me," said the corpulent man beside me in a thick Bostonian accent.

It was the hundredth time he had bumped my arm during the transatlantic flight.

"No worries," I replied, inching away from his large bulk.

"Miss, please return your seat to the upright position," the flight attendant said while pacing down the narrow aisle.

I obediently complied before stuffing the latest issue of an underground graffiti magazine into the black laptop case resting across my knees. Despite my seemingly intellectual persona and academic prowess—AKA: nerd vibe—there were three secrets about me that challenged the stereotype often attributed to art historians.

My area of expertise focused on sixteenth century Western Europe, but that didn't stop me from nurturing a passion for gritty street art with social or political undercurrents—the more radical, the better.

I wasn't so vocal about my second secret since it could potentially harm both my professional and personal reputations. Not only was I completely fascinated by U.S. government conspiracies involving U.F.O. aircraft and extraterrestrials, I was an Ancient Alien Theorist. I certainly wasn't alone in my belief that aliens came to Earth thousands of years ago to share their technology with humans. Many fellow theorists were accomplished and well-respected historians who kept a low profile, while others foolishly showed their faces in dubious conferences—or even worse—the History Channel.

"Ladies and gentlemen, please make sure that your seatbelts are securely fastened. We'll be landing shortly. Thank you."

I checked my seat belt and gazed thoughtfully at the laptop case. Stored within the laptop, carefully protected with impenetrable security passcodes, existed the third and most dangerous secret in my life: my manifesto. I've been working on it for almost a decade, and harbored no regrets over the illegal means used in obtaining much of the damning evidence. Exposing the deliberate censorship of scientific data seriously endangering the public could easily destroy elitists around the globe—the type of people who would probably seek revenge. Regardless of the threat, I believed humanity had a right to know the truth.

"Sorry," said the big man beside me as he bumped me again

238

with his fleshy arm.

One hundred and one.

"It's okay," I assured him as Logan's tarmac loomed into view in the window.

I peeked into the cockpit to thank the pilots before deplaning, and immediately noticed that the air seemed modern, hollow. After a ten-minute wait at baggage claim, I pulled my luggage off the conveyor belt and headed for the exit. My eyes instantly picked out Josh in the crowd. A good-looking guy, despite the extra pounds and bald spot, he offered me a dazzling smile. Irish freckles and bright blue eyes only added to his charm. Josh never had a problem attracting girls in college, but he was the type who enjoyed chasing the ones who weren't interested.

"Welcome home, Veronica," he cried in a Massachusetts accent. "Oh my God, you look even better in person than on Facebook!" He crushed me to his chest in a bear hug. "It's been a while, huh?"

"Seven years…thanks for picking me up at the airport."

"Maybe I should be thanking you. It's not every day I get to leave work early to meet a beautiful woman in Boston."

"Where's Cindy?" I asked, hoping the mention of his current girlfriend would discourage any attempt at flirtation.

"Working. She couldn't get the night off. Oh—happy birthday, by the way. You look exactly the same as you did when we were in college." Lowering his voice and cocking his brow theatrically, he asked, "Did you make some kind of shady deal with the Devil?"

"Maybe," I replied, keeping my expression serious.

He chuckled. "Here, let me help you with your luggage. Hold on. That's it? Two bags?" When I nodded, he added, "You're the dream woman."

"Well, I gave a lot of stuff away to charity and shipped my books to my new address."

"That reminds me," he said while extracting a metallic green shamrock keychain from his pocket. "I picked up your keys from the landlord."

I dropped the keys in my purse. "That was nice of you."

The moment we stepped outside, I shivered. I'd forgotten how bitterly cold autumn could be in New England.

"You missed a kick-ass Halloween party last night," Josh said as he led me toward a glossy, new silver BMW sports car. "Everyone wore awesome costumes."

"Really? I love Halloween. Nice car, by the way."

"Glad you like it. I got promoted at the law firm recently, so I gave myself a little reward." He put my suitcases and laptop bag in the trunk, and we entered the vehicle. "I'm really happy you're back. You may not believe it, but I've thought of you so many times throughout the years."

Uh oh, Veronica...

I ignored his sappy comment by pretending to be keenly interested in the scenery outside the car window. "What was that, sorry?"

"Nothing," he mumbled irritably as he maneuvered the car onto the highway.

Feeling bad, I cheerfully inquired, "Hey, have you been hitting the gym? You look pretty fit."

His face lit up. "Actually, I started lifting weights a few months ago. Check it out." He removed his right hand from the steering wheel in order to flex his bicep.

Ah, male vanity. I dutifully poked his arm. "Wow."

He dove into his entire lifting regime, complete with recipes for the perfect protein shake to enhance muscle performance. Thankfully, we arrived at the pub in a short amount of time.

Josh glanced at his flashy Rolex. "Are you tired?"

"Nope. Took a nice long nap on the plane."

"Well, there it is—O'Malley's Pub. We sure had some fun times here," he said, cutting the engine after parking the car. "Ah, the awesome years at UMASS Boston."

"Juggling work and school, pulling all-nighters to cram for exams...I was tired most of the time, but I can't complain. I had lots of fun." As he opened his car door, I said, "Wait a sec— would you turn on the light, please? I'd like to freshen up a bit."

"You're gorgeous enough already."

I rolled my eyes at him as he turned on the light. I quickly applied a coat of black mascara to my lashes and some lip gloss to my lips. I finished off with a spritz of perfume.

"Such a diva," he teased.

"Let's not exaggerate."

"Okay, you revel in your femininity—is that better?"

"Actually, yes," I replied primly, tucking the makeup bag into my purse.

He pointed to the little swirl of birthmarks on the inside of my right wrist. "I see you still haven't gotten rid of the tat."

"How many times do I have to tell you? It's not a tattoo."

"It looks too contrived to be a random design of nature."

I traced the spiral of countless dots with my left fingertip before letting it rest on the tiny star in the hollow center. "I was born with this so I'm used to it."

We both got out of the car. The muffled sounds of a bass guitar and drums filtered through the rusty brick walls as we approached the pub's entrance. The poster on the door depicted a medieval Virgin Mary statue with golden eyes and the words "ICON: Live Tonight."

Seized by a powerful déjà-vu, I began to tremble.

Josh paused mid-step. "Hey, are you okay?"

I touched the poster. "This image..."

"Icon is the latest music sensation from Providence." Josh explained as he opened the door and urged me through it. "Come on, it's freezing out here."

The band was in the middle of a song as we headed for the bar. The music had a driving beat and the sound of the lead singer's voice brought to mind supple velvet and rich dark chocolate—all things decadent. I shook my head slightly to clear it of these bizarre thoughts.

The moment the stage came into full view, I couldn't tear my eyes from the lead singer's face. *Drop-dead gorgeous.* Tall and fit with short black hair and chiseled features, he stood out in stark contrast from the other men inside the pub.

Wow. Get a grip, Veronica.

I mentally chastised myself as I scanned the bar to see if

there was anyone I recognized. The sexy musician's presence could not be ignored, however, and he soon had my full attention once again. I wasn't the type to easily fall for a guy, so this inexplicable attraction made me feel a bit unsettled. I couldn't help admiring his sensuous mouth and the strong, elegant curve of his jaw. How would those lips feel against my skin? A sudden, powerful yearning stirred deep within me and my breath caught in my throat.

I really needed to get laid. *Soon*.

His unique golden eyes slid my way as I passed in front of him, making my heartbeat accelerate. Very cool contact lenses—did he wear other funky colors, too?

CHAPTER 3
LISBON, PORTUGAL
OCTOBER 31, 1520

I stretched lazily before getting out of bed and throwing open the shutters. The pre-dawn sky flaunted the most delicate shades of violet and rose.

My mother stirred. "Veronica?"

I detected pain in her voice. "It's early yet, Mother."

She mumbled incoherently and went back to snoring. I prepared a draught to ease her discomfort. Her health had gone from bad to worse in a matter of months.

She won't be baking any birthday treats for you tomorrow...

Every year, I relived the bizarre events that had happened on the day I became physically and mentally branded. The mysterious golden-eyed stranger never visited me again, and I often wondered why he came in the first place.

My mother had eventually fashioned a bracelet by weaving leather straps together to form a thick band. Fastening it around my right wrist, she had admonished in a severe tone, "Never remove your bracelet or reveal your mark to anyone for it would be dangerous. You bear the kiss of Satan, the mark of a witch."

My mother sat up in bed. "Veronica, you're up early."

Her ashy pallor alarmed me. "It's a fine morning," I said with forced cheerfulness. "Would you like to sit in the sunshine for a bit? I could move your chair—"

"No," she cut me off, rubbing her legs while wincing.

"I have prepared a draught for you."

"I need my ointment. Would you go into the city and fetch me some?"

"Of course." I poured the hot draught into a cup and handed it to my mother. "Here, drink this. It will ease your pain."

I donned a wool cloak, placed a few coins into the pouch at

243

my waist, and walked down the hill. I passed the city gates and meandered through narrow streets, pausing briefly to admire the public statues on my way to the apothecary shop. After purchasing the ointment, I went to the market where vendors shouted to potential customers. The heady aromas of cloves, black pepper, and incense blended with pungent aged cheese, salted cod, blood sausages, and overly ripe fruits and vegetables. Dogs, cats, rats, and pigeons foraged for scraps between the crowded market stalls. Traders from the East displayed exotic silks dyed in shades of lilac and amber. One merchant offered silver bud vases etched with Arab curlicues.

Our widowed neighbor called out to me from a nearby donkey cart. "Veronica!"

"Good morning, Dona Maria," I said, shading my eyes from the brilliant morning sunshine.

"We're off to see the tower, my dear. Come with us."

"The Torre de Belem?" I inquired.

When she nodded, I climbed onto the cart and nodded at the familiar man holding the reins.

"You know my nephew, Norberto," Dona Maria said. "His wife is heavy with child and craves blood sausages. Pregnant women should not be deprived, is that not so?"

Norberto nodded. "Happy wife, happy life."

The Torre de Belem, strategically positioned at the mouth of the Tagus River, stood like a proud beacon to incoming ships. Constructed of pristine white stone, it glistened like dew in the sunlight. Inspired by various Portuguese colonies, the exotic design boasted stylistic elements from India and China, including an African rhinoceros.

Dona Maria crossed herself. "What an age we live in—God be praised! What say you, Veronica?"

I shook my head in awe. "It's magnificent."

Norberto eventually turned the cart around to head back.

My mother came outside to greet us. Leaning heavily on her walking stick, she said, "I wondered what was keeping you."

"It's our fault she's late," Dona Maria explained. "We took Veronica to see the new tower."

My mother invited everyone inside for a bit of refreshing ale. As soon as Norberto and Dona Maria took their leave, she regaled me with questions. I described the Torre de Belem as vividly as I could, knowing in my heart that she would not see it anytime soon.

"I think it quite fitting," my mother commented. "Your twentieth birthday is tomorrow and the splendid tower commemorates your second decade of life."

I chuckled at her grandiose thinking. She bent over in pain and I became alarmed. "Mother, are you all right?"

"A cramp, nothing more. Time to put your old mother to bed. Did you get the ointment?"

"Yes," I said, snatching it from the basket.

"You need to marry," she declared, settling into bed. I ignored her comment as I quietly applied the odiferous, greasy concoction to her legs. "I'm *serious*, Veronica."

I inquired sweetly, "Can I make you some dandelion tea to ease your stomach pains?"

"Do not ignore me!"

I set down the ointment, placed my hands on my hips, and sighed tiredly. "Are we having this conversation again?"

"You should spend more time searching for potential spouses and less time with those books of yours."

"So this week you're blaming the books. What will you come up with next week?"

"Mind your tongue, girl. You need to start behaving like the other young women in our parish. You never see them with their noses in books."

"Would you prefer an empty-headed ninny for a daughter instead of one that is dutiful, responsible, and possesses a bit of curious intellect?"

"That's not what I meant and you know it. What good is intelligence if you can't use it to find a husband?"

I sat down. "Whom would you have me marry?"

"There are plenty of eligible young men—like Tiago."

I crossed my arms. "The big buffoon with the axe?"

"He's a lumberjack. That's almost as good as a carpenter."

"Father was a carpenter," I corrected.

"Tiago could build you a house."

I imagined a lopsided house with sloping floors and shook my head. "He's far too oafish for my taste. Besides, I cannot tolerate his meddlesome sister."

"Sara can be difficult," she reluctantly agreed.

I scoffed at her. "Difficult? You're being too kind. Who else is on your marriage list?"

"Francisco."

I raised an eyebrow. "The little man who had me carry a basket of vegetables uphill to his mother's house because it was too heavy for him to do it himself? *That* Francisco?"

"He makes a decent living as an accountant in the city center." She paused with a twinkle in her eye and added matter-of-factly, "He knows how to read and write."

"I know how to read and write *and* I'm capable of physical labor. I won't marry a weakling who can be easily bullied; I would be tempted to boss him around. Next?"

"Well, I suppose that leaves Diego."

I placed my head in my hands. "He's deaf and mute."

"You are far too picky, Veronica. You do realize that you're on the brink of being called an old maid." I shrugged indifferently, which only served to further irritate my mother. "Every girl of marriageable age in our parish is already wed—except you."

"None of them seem to be living blissfully."

"Marriage is not easy, I'll give you that, but it's a blessing."

I went to the table and began chopping carrots. "Are there any turnips left? Perhaps I should gather some kale to make us a nice soup."

"This conversation is not over!" I stared at my mother as her eyes glistened with unshed tears. "Oh, Veronica, I won't be here much longer."

"You *will* get better," I said, trying to sound convincing.

"I desperately wanted to see you married and settled before..." She stopped abruptly, her face red with discomfort and—*something else*.

I became instantly suspicious when she refused to meet my eyes. "Before...?"

"Dear God, it's inevitable." I stared at her expectantly until she finally confessed, "He'll for you come tomorrow."

The golden-eyed stranger.

My heart raced uncontrollably. "How do you know? Did you have another dream?" She nodded, which made me angry. "Why didn't you tell me? Why all this ridiculous secrecy?"

"I believed if you got married and started a family he would leave you alone. Perhaps find someone else to curse. Too late for that now. He'll mark you again." My mother heaved a shuddering sigh, then sobbed. "In the dream, he warned me not to impede you from your destiny."

I paced around the room. "This explains so much. I feel as if I'm meant for something important in life; something more than being a wife and mother."

Eying me warily, she said, "You openly reject your God-given duty to wed and procreate?"

"I'm not afraid of my destiny. Actually, I must confess that I've been eagerly awaiting his return."

"What?!"

"I want to know why he came to me ten years ago." Holding up my wrist, I added, "Why do I bear this mark? What does it mean? I need answers."

"Are you mad? He's not human—he's an evil abomination of nature."

"Not being human doesn't make him evil," I reasoned. "Angels aren't human."

My mother banged her fist against the wall in frustration. "This creature is no angel. This is why I was against your father teaching you to read. It's made you a daft spinster."

"I'm sorry for being such a disappointment to you."

Despite the regret in her eyes, she remained silent.

I continued, "When he comes tomorrow, I'll face him as bravely as I can to find answers to my questions."

"You stupid, stubborn girl! He may be the Devil himself, for all we know."

"But we don't know. Who is he? What is he? How will we know if we're too afraid to ask?"

"No sane, God-fearing person speaks to a demon."

"What if he's not a demon but something else? Something beyond our limited understanding?" I paused, recalling my father's words before he died. "Remember: we are Portuguese. Father used to say that the world's greatest explorers were spawned from our bloodlines. Insatiably curious men who possess no fear are bravely sailing to places that our ancestors only dreamed of seeing. Surely, these noble traits—so common in men—can be present in women? Even in myself, perhaps?"

"Your words are clever, daughter, but extremely foolish. You're dealing with a being who is possibly far more powerful than all of our great men combined."

"Which is exactly why I wish to learn the purpose of his existence, and why he has chosen me."

My mother's lips clamped down to form a hard line and she shook her head in staunch disapproval.

The silence stretched between us until I picked up an empty basket and went to the door. "I'm going out into the garden. I'll be back shortly."

"We need more firewood," she said, not meeting my eyes.

CHAPTER 4
BOSTON, MA
NOVEMBER 1, PRESENT DAY

"Happy birthday, dear Veronica, happy birthday to you!"

My former classmates applauded, cueing me to blow out the twenty-seven candles glowing atop a chocolate cake. A wise-ass in the crowd called out for a fire extinguisher. *Masshole.*

Slices of cake were passed around while I tried to reconnect with my former classmates. Most of the women were stay-at-home moms, and it soon became painfully evident that we had little in common. The pub became stuffy as more Icon fans arrived. I wriggled my arm out of one coat sleeve before Josh helped me with the other.

"Wow." He looked me up and down. "Nice outfit."

"Thanks."

The wine red mini sheath complimented my black tights and Italian leather boots.

"You're looking pretty hot. I may have to fight somebody."

I took my seat. "Very funny."

He winked at me then turned around to talk to someone. I enjoyed my drink while listening to the conversations taking place around me. As the alcohol blurred the edges of my mind, I recalled my last psychotherapy session with Dr. Sousa. The intense memories, powerful déjà-vu, and recurring dreams that I had been experiencing on a regular basis began exactly one year ago today. Despite my psychologist's expertise and high credentials, I still had no idea what had triggered these manifestations, let alone their meaning.

"Another drink?" Josh asked, breaking my reverie.

He rested against the bar, placing his face close to mine. Icon finished their last set and, the minute the band vacated the stage, pre-recorded music poured from the speakers.

"Bartender, can we get another gin and tonic here?" Josh shouted over the noise. "Hey, are you having fun?" I nodded as he handed me the drink. "Better go easy on those, hon, you might take advantage of me when you're drunk."

The girl sitting beside me overheard his comment and rolled her eyes. Seeing this, Josh said something cocky to her and I'm pretty sure she retorted in like manner, but I only half-listened. The lead singer of Icon sauntered toward me with a feline stealth that made me squirm in my seat—in a good way. I was astonished by my sexual response to him. Wearing a snug black T-shirt and slim black pants that highlighted every asset of his magnificent body, he stopped directly in front of me. I noticed that his left bicep sported an intricate black ink tattoo. The medieval coat of arms flaunted the letter "V" surrounded by traditional Manuelino embellishments—nautical ropes, shells, and even a tiny armillary sphere. I almost gasped aloud in pure art historian delight.

It suddenly dawned on me that everyone around the bar had grown silent and still, especially the women. Without breaking eye contact, he reached for my right hand and turned it over. A tiny smile touched his lips when he caught sight of my strange birthmark. He ran his thumb gently over the delicate skin of my inner wrist, causing the mark to tingle. The simple, yet incredibly intimate, act sent a jolt of electricity throughout my entire body. Meeting my eyes once more, he turned my hand over and brought my knuckles to his lips. The gallant gesture took me off guard because it felt both natural and familiar.

"Happy birthday, Veronica," he said softly.

The way his tongue lingered on my name both thrilled and disturbed me. His strange accent triggered déjà-vu. He knew me—I was sure of it—but I had no recollection of him. My brain quickly went through a mental file. Had we shared a college class together? Did we meet at a party?

A giggling couple leaned against the bar to order drinks, thus placing their bodies between me and the golden-eyed Adonis. Before I had the chance to ask him anything, the ever-growing crowd of people swallowed him up.

"Well, *that* was weird," Josh said in a surly tone dripping with male envy. "Who does that? Walk up to a girl and kiss her hand like he's a knight in some medieval role-playing game. And what's with those strange yellow contacts? He may be a talented musician but he's a total freak."

"You're just jealous," said the girl who had had gotten sassy with Josh a few minutes earlier.

The two began to argue again so I slid off the stool. "I need to use the ladies room. Josh, would you please hold my seat and watch my drink?"

"Sure, the bathroom is—"

"I remember," I said over my shoulder.

I practically ran to the ladies room, scanning the crowd in search of my mystery man but he was nowhere in sight. I pulled out my phone and began dialing Dr. Sousa's number. "Yeah, right," I said aloud, hanging up immediately.

I couldn't tell him of yet another strange déjà-vu episode that led nowhere. Besides, Dr. Sousa had already washed his hands of me, so to speak. He had put me in contact with one of the best Past Life Regression therapists in New England and had already set up the first appointment for me.

I went into the ladies room and splashed some cold water on my cheeks. The mirror above the sink reflected an unusual brightness in my mossy green eyes and my fair skin flaunted a pink flush. Who wouldn't be in a state of heightened awareness after such a sexy encounter? I ran a hand through my long hair and took a deep breath before grabbing a paper towel to dry my hands. A blonde woman almost plowed into me as I exited the ladies room.

"Sorry," she offered. "Hey Ronnie!"

"It's Veronica," I corrected as politely as I could.

"Oops, I forgot." She cocked her head to the side. "Don't you remember me?"

I took in the fake blue contacts, overly bleached hair, heavy makeup, breast implants, and micro-mini denim skirt. How did I know this blonde bombshell? Then it hit me—the sorority girl who sat beside me in English Literature during my junior year of college. Cool girl, but not the brightest crayon in the box.

I smiled. "Long time no see, Stephanie."

"I knew you'd remember me. Go UMASS Alumni," she shrieked like a cheerleader. "Welcome home and happy birthday. How was Portugal?"

"Great."

"Did you live in *Lisboa*?" she asked, making an attempt to pronounce the city correctly.

"Yes, and nice pronunciation."

"Cool. I would love to visit Europe someday. I hear the guys are really cute. Is that true?"

I smiled at Josh when I saw him waving at me from the bar. Stephanie followed my gaze and smiled, too. "A lot of European men sport trendy haircuts and dress to impress," I replied with a shrug.

"Oh, I know. They're so ahead in fashion over there. Speaking of which, you look great." She took in my outfit with the appraising eye of a shopaholic. "I like your hair, too. It brings out your eye color. Is that reddish brown natural or from a box?"

"Thanks—oh, it's natural. You look good, too." I refrained from commenting on her overly processed hair. "Hey, I need to get back to Josh and my drink. Great seeing you."

"You, too!"

I took my seat at the bar and Josh said, "I saw you chatting with Slutty Steph. What words of wisdom did she impart?"

"She wished me a happy birthday. Why do you call her 'Slutty Steph'?"

Josh answered my question with a long look and a raised eyebrow. He took a sip of his beer and said, "She lives in Providence, you know."

"Maybe I'll see her around." I followed his example and took a sip of my watered-down gin and tonic. "Hey, after this drink I think I should call it a night. Would you give me a ride home? I know it's a long drive from Boston to Providence, but I'll pay for the gas and you can crash on the couch. The apartment did come furnished as advertised, right?"

"Yes, but there's no need for me to crash on your couch. I'm in Providence now."

This news surprised me. "You don't live in Boston anymore?"

"Nope. My firm opened an office in Providence for the convenience of our clients who live there, and that new branch is being headed by yours truly. They offered me the transfer as a promotion and it came with a decent raise. As much as I love my new car, commuting is a pain in the ass."

"I don't blame you. Boston traffic is atrocious."

"Anyway, I was saving the best surprise for last."

"What surprise?"

"We're neighbors!" Seeing my blank expression, he added, "My office is in College Hill. Your new apartment is upstairs from mine. Why do you think the people at Brown suggested that specific place to you?" When I shrugged, he said, "Because I suggested it to them, silly rabbit!"

"Oh."

"Seriously, it's the perfect location."

Being so close to Josh on a daily basis could lead to problems. I liked him a lot, but his constant flirting and attempts to date me in college grew so tiresome that we stopped hanging out for a few months until he agreed to knock it off. Maybe things would be different now that he had Cindy in his life.

He looked smug. "You're going to fall in love with the apartment, I just know it."

"I'm sure I will," I replied with forced enthusiasm.

Do you want to keep reading? THE WATCHERS is available on Amazon.

Made in the USA
Lexington, KY
01 February 2019